BECOMING CREATURE

JENNIFER L. MOORE

Print Edition ISBN: 978 1 952640 00 1

Ebook Edition ISBN: 978 1 952640 01 8

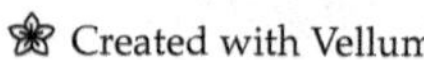 Created with Vellum

For my creatures,
may your lives never be without stories

"Maybe you're a vampire?" Umiko blurted out as she pushed the wet dog tongue from her face. The golden retriever it was attached to leaned against her and caused Umiko to topple over. She landed on her butt on the warm concrete sidewalk. "Gypsy, calm down." Umiko said between giggles as she tried to protect her face.

Lyn stretched out her hand to help Umiko stand. "Gypsy. Romani. Nein." The dogs stopped accosting Umiko with their friendly wet dog kisses and sat facing Lyn with their tongues hanging from their mouths, waiting for their next command.

Lyn looked at the dogs. "Where's your mom? Did you two get out of the fence again?" Lyn pulled out her cell phone and texted her neighbor, Mrs. Henesey, the dogs' owner.

A response returned immediately. "She'll be here soon." Lyn said to Umiko and the dogs.

Lyn put her hand in Romani's neck scruff and scratched. The dog pushed into her hand, eager for the attention.

Gypsy whined, but stayed sitting as Umiko walked over and scratched behind her ear. The dog swung her head around to lick Umiko's face, but the girl neatly dodged the slobbery kiss this time.

A few moments and neck scratched later, an SUV pulled up and an older woman jumped out of the driver's side. "Come on, girls." She said to the dogs before turning to Lyn. "Thanks. They got past me when I was putting out the trash bins." She smiled and turned back to the dogs. "Enough exploring. Time for breakfast." Mrs. Henesey opened the rear passenger door and clicked to the dogs. Gypsy trotted to the car and jumped up. "You too, Romani, let's go."

Romani cocked her head at Lyn.

"Go on, girl, I'll come by to walk you after school." Lyn pat the dog on her head and pointed to the open car door.

Romani licked Lyn's hand before joining her sister.

Mrs. Henesey closed the door behind the second retriever. "Thanks for letting me know where they were, Lyn. Sorry if we made you late for school." Mrs. Henesey walked back around to the driver's side.

"It's okay, Mrs. Henesey." Umiko called out and waved.

"Let me know if you need anything. A meal, a ride to the store. Anything." Mrs. Henesey stood for a moment watching Lyn.

"Thank you." Lyn had to steady her breath before responding. She had to fight back tears often over the past few weeks. It was becoming second nature.

Mrs. Henesey drove off, leaving Lyn and Umiko on the neighborhood sidewalk.

Umiko checked her watch. "We shouldn't be late, if we get moving."

"A vampire?" Lyn looked at her best friend, one hand on her hip. "Really?"

Umiko was hung up on figuring out Lyn's creature type. Lyn, however, still didn't think she was anything other than human, except... *No, mom would have told me.*

It was the middle of the second week of their sophomore year of high school. The pair met up on the corner to walk together to school just like they had done all of last year. Ever since Lyn's mom had demanded, in her own loving way, that Lyn make at least one friend.

Umiko had been the one to approach Lyn and Lyn had accepted the overture and fulfilled her promise to her mom the very first day of ninth grade. Umiko's force of will had done the rest.

This morning they stuck to the shadows and avoided the direct rays of the sun as much as possible. Lyn's weather app had said it was eighty degrees, but on track to be another hundred degree day. She did not look forward to walking home this afternoon. The Texas heat could be brutal, especially if there were no clouds.

Umiko shrugged. "I said maybe."

"Seriously?" Lyn said, exasperated. Her best friend had been trying to figure out what type of creature Lyn was since Lyn let it slip that she had never been sick. Umiko thought that sixteen years without a sniffle was proof of Lyn's creature-ness, even if Lyn did not.

Lyn stared at her friend. Umiko's wardrobe epitomized cuteness. Umiko had paired a pale green boatneck top with a white ruffled skirt. A headband balanced two fuzzy white balls, one on each side of the girl's red hair. It was hard to look at her and not smile.

Umiko stopped mid stride. She let her foot fall, but turned to face Lyn. "Why are you looking at me like that?"

Lyn's appearance was more haphazard. No one would say cute. Most people ignored her and she was fine with that arrangement. Lyn sported a pair of jeans with holes. Not the fashionable ones put there by a machine to charge twice as much. Hers were worn through by wear and actual tears. Her shirt was a size too big and made her body look square instead of showing off the curves underneath. Her mouse brown hair was curly, but not the cute solid ringlets most girls primped to have. Instead, clumps of hair rolled together then fractured into frizz. No matter how much Lyn tried, the frizz and the mutinous curls made her hair a nest of vipers that could defeat any brush.

Lyn continued to look at Umiko and pointed at the sun shining from its perch over Umiko's shoulder. She waited for Umiko to acknowledge her pointing before she continued walking.

To be honest, she was looking for any excuse to delay school this morning. She had promised her mom she would go, but they never expressly said she had to be there right when school started. Just that she had to attend school every day. Even if she didn't feel like it.

Her mother wouldn't be holding her accountable anymore, but Lyn had never broken a promise to her mom and she wouldn't start now. She took a slow step forward, then another. She would make good on her promise.

"The whole sun thing, is just a myth. Sasha says that she's never burst into flames and she loves to go to the beach. The sun doesn't bother her at all. Most of the old stories were meant to scare humans. Now that creatures are part of society, there's a lot of misconceptions coming to light. Did you know that werewolves don't only turn on full moons?" Umiko started walking again.

Lyn felt a twinge of jealousy. Umiko was friends with just about everyone. "Sasha is a vampire?"

"Seriously, Lyn. Have you been living under a rock?"

"No." Lyn tried to hide her hurt feelings. "I guess Sasha is pretty pale. Paler than you and me. And we're pale enough as it is."

Lyn felt Umiko's eyes drilling into her, waiting for her to agree.

"Fine, but they still drink blood right?" Lyn looked at Umiko. "You know I like my meat fully cooked, and I have never been compelled to drink blood." Lyn caught up to Umiko. "Or eat people." Lyn added because she knew her friend.

"I guess we can rule out zombies then." Umiko said.

Lyn smiled. She liked having a friend and she was glad her mother had insisted. Prior to Umiko, Lyn had stuck to the fringes of the school social structure. She frequented back rows and avoided eye contact whenever possible. Lyn had been trained to be a fringe member since the first grade. The other kids stayed away from her and she did her best to blend in and not be noticed.

Umiko was the opposite. Her cheerful disposition acted like a magnet as far as friends went. She could easily flit from one social group to another.

"I am definitely not a zombie." Lyn suspected that Umiko had a mental list of creature types and was testing her way down it by trial and error mixed with observation. Lyn felt like a wild monkey in a behavioral study.

Lyn turned her foot in and took a step to mock the ambling gait of a horror movie zombie. "Brains. Where can I get brains?" She made a big deal of turning away from Umiko. "Braaaaains." Lyn felt a friendly slap on her arm and she turned back.

"Don't be rude. They can't help the way they're made. You know they aren't dumb like those old TV shows and movies."

She smiled at her friend and said, "Fair enough, but I am NOT a vampire, OR a zombie. Let's just go ahead and rule out everything dead or undead. Okay?"

Umiko nodded, the short fuzz from the headband flowing with the motion.

The girls walked another block in silence.

Lyn smelled the roses planted beside Mr. Franklin's driveway and ran her hand through the rosemary bush along the fence two houses down. A tear gathered and fell. Her mother had loved the bright color of roses and the fresh scent of rosemary.

"So, how are you?" Umiko asked, less animatedly.

Lyn brushed the tear from her cheek and bristled at the question. It was a stupid question. One she had been asked every day for the past two weeks. Starting an hour after her mom had died from a stupid accident.

They said she fell. That there was nothing anyone could do. One horrible, stupid accident and Lyn was alone in the world.

Lyn took a breath. Umiko meant well. Lyn knew the girl was at a loss for how to comfort her, and Lyn couldn't blame her. "I woke up this morning and expected to smell breakfast cooking downstairs. The house is too quiet. My cereal tasted like wet cardboard. The grocery subscription arrived and now we...I have too much oatmeal." Lyn took another breath. She could continue to list all the ways her life was worse now, but dwelling in the details would not make it any different. "It's not fair." It sounded trite even to Lyn's ears. She knew that life and fairness weren't dependent on each other.

"I know." Umiko put her arm around her friend's shoulder and gave a quick squeeze before letting go. "I'm so sorry. I wish I could do something to make it better. But I know there's nothing." Umiko swung her shoulder bag around and pulled out a granola bar. "Except breakfast, want a sweet and salty rectangle of cardboard?" Umiko asked and in a singsong voice added, "I have two."

Lyn smiled and took the bar. "Thanks." She opened the proffered package and took a bite. The sweet chocolate layer melted on her tongue and contrasted the salty almond crunch. It was nothing like cardboard. Lyn took another bite and looked down at her feet while she walked.

"Want to come home with me after school? I'll try to distract you. We can swim and eat junk food."

Umiko might not have been great at figuring out a way to console Lyn, but she was the best at distractions.

"Sure." Lyn faked a smile for her friend. She'd figure out a suitable excuse to bail later. Lyn just wanted to go home after school and take a nap. Just like yesterday and the day before.

"Great. I have something to tell you and there hasn't been a good time. I'm not sure there will be a good time for a while, but I really want to share." Umiko's words fell out all at once through a full smile.

Lyn's fake smile became a real one. She loved Umiko's enthusiasm for everything. Her best friend could get equally excited about a rainbow, or a lone snail trailing goo across a sidewalk. A perfect score on a test sent her into orbit. Lyn needed that energy right now. She had none of her own. She had a feeling that a perfect score on anything would just make her cry because she couldn't share it with the one person in the world she wanted. Lyn shook off her grief for a moment and allowed herself to be swept up in Umiko's excitement. "What's the news?"

Umiko shook her head. "Nope. You'll just have to wait. If I tell you now, you'll have no reason to come over later," Umiko teased.

Lyn felt a twinge in her chest about ditching her friend repeatedly over the past week, but she hadn't felt like being around people. She just now realized how Umiko must have felt, watching her friend mourn and not being able to help.

"I'll come. I promise." Lyn smiled at Umiko and watched her friend's eyes nearly glow with joy. "We'll swim, and you'll spill."

"Deal!" Umiko said as she grabbed Lyn's hand.

Lyn felt a jolt of static electricity jump between their palms.

"Ouch!" both girls said in unison and burst into giggles as they stepped onto school property.

CHAPTER TWO

edar Oaks Creature Inclusive High School.

'Creature' stood out against the aged stone sign in front of the school. A new sign was planned, but had yet to be delivered, so students took the matters into their own hands with a can of black spray paint.

Every weekday morning, the school opened the cafeteria doors at 8:00am to students arriving early. Some hung around outside, under the drop-off lane awning and the few short oak trees in the courtyard, but most went inside to avoid the heat. During lunches, the large room held a third of the student body comfortably. In the mornings, it was overcrowded.

Lyn and Umiko stepped through tight groupings of students and into the high school cafeteria just before the bell rang and the herd was released to roam the halls.

With the loud buzz of what passed for the school bell, the student body streamed out into the main hallway through the two sets of double doors. The students in front continued on to lockers and classrooms, oblivious to the crowd of people behind them. The bottleneck at the cafeteria doors and the press of people all trying to get through kept

Lyn and Umiko pinned together and moving with the crowd.

"Coming through." Lyn heard a voice to her left and was pushed toward her right as a football player rushed past smelling of cedar, with his backpack flung over one shoulder. "Ladies." He said as he shimmied between them with a little less force.

The student body had ten minutes to get to lockers, bathrooms, change for PE or Athletics (if that was how the day started for them), and get to class. No one was allowed in the halls after the bell rang, for safety reasons.

"The nation's eyes are on us," the principal said at the beginning of the year assembly.

Lyn wondered what that meant, exactly. To her it was as it had always been. Nation's eyes or no, it was the same school setting she'd been in since kindergarten. Social butterflies, mean kids, the outcasts, they were all the same. Even if the world was slowly changing.

Cedar Oaks was a progressive city, but creatures had only just started to come out. They followed in the footsteps of other marginalized groups. Most of the nation had finally come to terms with non-gender bathrooms, but creatures were still judged and feared.

While most of the world's creatures waited to see what would happen in politics, those in Cedar Oaks had stepped into the light en masse. Various creature councils had enacted rules for their kind to keep them out of trouble, not so much because they themselves would cause the trouble, but to be beyond reproach. Creatures with a predatory mythology, the big three, had the toughest struggle.

Lyn now knew one vampire, Sasha. Lyn looked around the crowded cafeteria to catch a glimpse of the girl in the crowd. As if summoned, Sasha passed her on the right and Lyn got a whiff of dirt and peat and a light scent of rose.

Lyn knew exactly zero witches. They were still reluctant to

be open about their otherness. No wonder, with a history as fiery as theirs.

But, she knew a lot of werewolves, or shifters, as they preferred. A large portion of the sports teams were made up of shifters. Football, cross-country, probably basketball too, but Lyn was uninterested in the details.

Lyn knew that this crowd she was trapped in was made up of more creatures than she was aware of. But it was considered rude to ask and those in this school were good at passing for human and preferred to do so, at least for now.

Statistics said that creatures outnumbered humans in Cedar Oaks High, 5 to 1.

That might account for Lyn feeling like prey most of the time, her kind was scarce. Lyn's skin prickled and her heart skipped a beat. She preferred the times when she just felt invisible.

She chanced a glance around her. Umiko was on her immediate right, slightly ahead. She stepped closer to her friend and wished the crowd would clear the doors.

Lyn felt something push against her foot and she lost her balance. The sting of her tail bone, as it connected with the tile, tingled up her spine. The press of people to her sides and front continued and the void created when she fell quickly filled with students.

Lyn watched Umiko get swept away from her by the current.

"Oops. Need a hand?" A rich baritone voice offered.

A hand extended into Lyn's view. The forearm attached to it looked muscular. Lyn accepted without looking past the elbow. She didn't have a choice, the ground was no place to be with the rush of the mob around her.

She put her weight into the hand and pulled herself up. Half way to her feet, the hand let go and Lyn fell back onto the floor.

Lyn was surrounded by laughter, but the amusement wore off when Lyn didn't immediately stand up.

The smell of wet dog wafted down to her. She should have recognized that voice.

Killian had been her own personal bully since close to the beginning of her freshman year. The first few weeks, he didn't have favorites. He was equally bullish to everyone smaller than himself. Lyn wasn't sure what made him fixate on her, but she was sure that the rest of his targets were happy he had a new obsession. Lyn envied them, she wished his obsession was someone else too.

Last year, Killian figured out where Lyn's locker was and most of her classes, despite being a sophomore to her freshman. One day, after school, she found him and three of his lackeys standing on the wall opposite her locker. She tried to ignore their eyes drilling into the back of her skull as she stood facing her locker. She struggled to open her lock several times, even though she was 100% confident in her combination. The whole time, the muscles standing on the wall behind her, murmured. She heard them congratulating themselves on changing the lock and realized that she would never get in.

Lyn had two viable options, that day. She could either ask them for help, which she was sure they would deny, or she could go to the office and hope someone was still around who could cut the lock off. Since her phone and house keys were inside her locked locker, her preferred option of walking away wouldn't work. She thought about waiting for them to wander off, but that wouldn't get her locker opened and it would make her late getting home.

She never told her mom about the bullying. Lyn's mom worked long hours at the hospital dealing with other people's problems. Problems that were bigger than a group of emotional bullies. Lyn wanted home to be just about the two of them, not the pettiness of the world outside.

The group of boys laughed as Lyn walked away from her locker toward the front office and help.

She returned fifteen minutes later with a teacher and a custodian carrying bolt cutters. The boys had gone. The teacher made her try her combination one last time. Lyn knew it wouldn't work but did it anyway.

To Lyn's surprise, the lock opened easily. She stood with the open lock in her hand, her head hung to her chest, and received a lecture from the teacher and disparaging looks from the custodian before he walked away, annoyed at the delay in his afternoon.

Lyn Davis hated Killian Jacobs.

The people behind Lyn sighed and pushed with annoyance. Lyn folded in on herself, careful to keep her fingers off the ground, and made a smaller obstacle.

"What the hell, Killian?" A second baritone growled near Lyn's ear as he bent down to help her.

Lyn accepted the lift, but her guard was up. She looked over her shoulder to see who had his hands under her arms.

"Bug off, Gregar, it was an accident. I was trying to help the girl up," Killian said.

"Inept as usual, Jacobs," Greg countered as Lyn found her feet. He smiled at her. Van Gregar, the school knight in shining armor. The bane of bullies and the rescuer of the down trodden. Literally, in this case.

Greg had stood between her and Killian on several occasions the year before. The two boys were in the same grade. Both ahead of Lyn and Umiko. Greg had a reputation of stepping between Killian and many of his targets throughout the school years. Some of the kids he helped had named him Sir Greg, but Lyn never heard them call him that to his face. To his face it was all fist bumps and high fives.

Umiko pointed out her benefactor once, until then Lyn had not paid much attention, preferring to get away from altercations as soon as possible. Now, she paid a little more attention before she fled. But, no matter how cute the boys might be, she still just wanted to run away.

"Thanks," Lyn whispered, her head tucked low. She looked around for Umiko.

She saw her friend trying to walk against the current of students, despite the draw in the opposite direction. One small fish against a school of salmon.

"You're fine. No harm done, right, sweetheart?" Killian's words dripped with saccharine and razor blades.

Lyn didn't look at him, instead she was trying to map her way around the captain of the football team and out the double doors into the hallway. Her main obstacle stood too close and directly in front, trapping her. He would have to move for her to pass, and she didn't think it was likely that Killian Jacobs would move until he was ready.

Greg stepped to Lyn's left and into Killian's personal space. Lyn saw the football players's body turn away from her to address the threat.

"Just leave the girl alone. She's not in your weight class," Greg said.

"And if I don't want to?" Killian asked. He puffed out his chest and glared at Greg.

Lyn felt Umiko's hand on her arm. Her best friend pulled her into the current of students and Lyn and Umiko became one with the salmon run, propelled by the crush of students trying to get to class on time.

Behind them a chant rippled through the crowd of people closest to Killian and Greg. "Fight." The word took on volume and voices as it continued. "Fight." Yet more voices added to the chant as the rush of students out the cafeteria door paused.

Lyn and Umiko's progress stalled.

"Fight."

Lyn wished she were anywhere but here at this moment. The crowd pressed in on her. There was nowhere to run, nowhere to hide. She was at the mercy of classmates that never bothered to learn her name.

Lyn heard the taunts and watched as the press of people divided into avoiders and provokers. This was her opening. She and Umiko threaded and pushed through the people turning around to watch the fight, and walked out the cafeteria door with those who didn't want to get involved.

"What's happening?" Lyn heard a teacher in the hallway ask.

"There's gonna be a fight," a random voice called from inside the cafeteria.

"What? Between whom?" the teacher asked, her voice pitched higher.

None of the exiting students answered. They didn't care, it was just another Thursday in Cedar Oaks High. A shifter throwing his weight around and a… Lyn wasn't sure what Greg was, more than human, probably, or else he had a death wish. You don't mess with the shifters.

Lyn was surprised by the teacher's reaction. It wasn't the first fight Killian had been involved in and it wouldn't be the last. Lyn guessed that she was looking at one of the new teachers, someone who didn't yet know the ways of their creature inclusive high school. She wondered what the small woman thought she could do, stuck outside the room. From this distance, her authority was powerless to stop the inevitable. And Killian Jacobs was inevitable.

"Umiko," the teacher waved to get their attention, "go to the gym and get Coach Davis."

Lyn didn't know how the new face knew Umiko's name, but Umiko, given a task, would fulfill it and Lyn would follow in her wake. Plus, she'd do just about anything to get away from Killian.

Umiko nodded and they set out at a run through the halls. They pushed through the crush of students with their newly found, teacher given, authority. Umiko in the lead, and Lyn following close on her heels.

Lyn ran, happy to be away from both the crowd and Killian. Her legs were good at running. They liked it. Craved it even. The movement used some of the nervous energy that the confrontation with Killian had built up.

Umiko opened the door to the gym and called for Coach Davis. He stepped out of his office holding a deflated basketball and an inflation needle. She told him about the fight in the cafeteria and that he had been requested to help break it up. Lyn stood silently by as the man thrust the ball into her hands, and pocketed the needle.

Lyn looked at the ball she held as the big man hustled out the door and down the hallway.

In a just school, Lyn figured the football coach would punish his team for starting fights. But in Texas, where football is life, she knew the star of the team would get a pass. He always did.

"We should get to first period." Umiko turned to Lyn.

Lyn dropped the ball and it flattened to the gym floor. Lyn sighed at how perfectly a mound of molded plastic could mirror her feelings. She let herself be led to their bank of lockers in the sophomore hall. Umiko's was six down from hers. Close enough to talk over the heads of the students unlucky enough to get bottom lockers.

Umiko closed her locker and grabbed Lyn's hand. "I'll meet you after school. Deal?" She locked eyes with Lyn.

Umiko had a gift for wrangling promises out of Lyn and Umiko was so incredibly trusting that Lyn always felt physically ill if she tried to break them. "Deal."

A tingle spread from the center of the girls' palms. "Oh, wait. I have a swim team meeting after school." Umiko stomped her foot. "Will you wait for me?" she pleaded.

"Sure," Lyn agreed, "I'll go to the auditorium. When is your meeting over?"

"I don't know, but it shouldn't be long, we're not starting practice today. I'll text you, when I know." Umiko hurried down the hall and around the corner to her first class of the day.

Lyn turned and stepped across the hall and through the first door on the left just before the bell rang.

CHAPTER THREE

"Clark, what do you have first period?" Coach Davis asked, a frown permanently etched on his face.

Clark lifted his eyebrows. He was amazed that the man knew his name and chose to use it. "Theater," Clark responded.

"Something frivolous," Coach said. "I thought so."

Clark heard the disdain drip from the man's words. Arts, English, math, science, all were equally frivolous to Coach D. Only gym and athletics held intrinsic value to the head football coach.

"Take Greg to the school nurse. Ask her for a pass to class." Coach dismissed them by turning away.

Clark stood up from the last of the cafeteria tables to be rolled away by the cafeteria staff. Black pants hung loosely from his skinny frame. His belt, black leather, held his pants to his middle, where hips might have been, if not hidden from the world by his untucked shirt. A silver chain hung from his belt buckle and wrapped around to his rear pocket. His shirt advertised some death metal band, long gone from the performing world.

"I'm fine." Greg squeezed his nose between his fingers, to stop the bleeding. He held his head forward, chin to chest.

Killian stood behind the only staff in the room. The rest had gone on to class, leaving the football team to deal with its own. A red splotch bloomed on Killian's forehead where it met Greg's nose minutes before. Killian smiled.

"Do it anyway," Coach demanded.

Clark handed Greg a paper napkin from a dispenser on the table.

Greg took it and placed it to his nose. "Thanks," he said to Clark.

"Pretty boy won't look so pretty with a crooked nose," Killian taunted as Greg and Clark walked to the door.

Greg turned on a dime to face Killian, his hand coming away from the bloody mess in the center of his face. He stared at Killian. "What's your excuse?"

Killian barred his teeth and leapt at Greg, who planted his feet and lowered his center of gravity to stand his ground.

Coach grabbed Killian by his shirt's collar before he could close the distance.

"Clark!" Coach bellowed.

Clark put his hand on Greg's arm and led him into the hall and down to the front offices. "He's an ass," Clark said after the door closed behind them. He walked slow. Not in a hurry to get anywhere or do anything. This was his senior year and he was determined to live it on his own terms, plus the theater teacher liked him. He could come into class half an hour late, with no note, and it wouldn't show up on the attendance roll.

"Coach or Killian?" Greg asked. He refolded the bloody napkin and reapplied it to his nose. He pulled it away to see if there was still fresh blood. There wasn't.

"Your choice." Clark opened the door to the nurse's office and stepped inside.

"Both," Greg said following Clark.

The nurse stood by her desk. She turned her head as the two boys entered.

"There you are. I was wondering if I was going to get anyone in here after all the commotion about a fight." Ms. Banes pulled two latex gloves out of a box on her countertop.

The nurse sat Greg in her swivel chair and looked him over. She asked Clark to hand her gauze from one cabinet and rubbing alcohol from another. She cleaned Greg's face from the outside in.

"Not broken." The nurse declared a few minutes later.

"Really?" Clark asked. He had seen it happen and was surprised that the nose didn't need to be set.

"See for yourself." The nurse gathered the bloody gauze and other trash to throw away.

Clark looked at the junior and his nose. Perfectly straight, as if the loud crack of Killian's forehead striking bone didn't happen at all.

Clark wondered what the boy was. Superman seemed a stretch, but only because of the alien angle.

"Need anything for the pain?" the nurse asked.

Greg shook his head. "Can I wash my hands?" Greg held his hands out, palms up. They were covered in blood, mostly dried.

The nurse apologized for not thinking and pointed him to a small sink in the bathroom cubicle attached to her office.

"How's your mother?" Clark asked the nurse while he waited for Greg to finish with his hands.

Clark sometimes worked in the school nurse's office before school or during his off period. He knew Ms. Banes' mother from his after school job at the nursing home where the older woman lived.

"Not too good." The nurse sighed. "She's not eating. I think it's time." She shook her head and removed her gloves. "She needs to just let go."

Clark nodded. He preferred the family that was accepting

of death, if not welcoming. The ones that kicked and screamed to keep their loved ones in agony made his skin crawl. He'd seen plenty of both.

"I'll try to visit this afternoon." Clark promised.

"You're sweet. She perks up when she sees you." The nurse patted him on the shoulder.

Clark let a hint of a smile play on his lips. He wondered who would come for the older lady. Most of the time relatives came to escort the dying to the next place. Rarely the shrouded figure. Even less likely, the person Clark wanted to talk to.

The one and only time he had met his dad was when the tumor won. It had taken everything from her, but death had returned the love of her life.

Clark remembered his mom and dad, standing together, hand in hand, as the veil between worlds fogged up. The ferryman had finally come for his bride and left his son stuck on this side of the line between life and death without an explanation, only a haunting smile.

Clark grinned at the bittersweet memory. Happiness for his mom warring with the loneliness of his life now. Only, Clark realized, he didn't have to be alone. He pictured Umiko's smiling face and his own smile grew. His mom would have loved her.

The sight faded as Greg stepped out of the bathroom, the blood gone from his hands and face, but not from his shirt collar.

"Do you have a spare shirt?" Nurse Bane asked.

"In my locker," Greg answered.

"Okay, change shirts and get to class." She wrote them both passes and shooed them out of her office. "And stay out of trouble."

"Your nose was broken," Clark whispered when the door closed behind them.

"She said it's fine." Greg stepped away from the nurse's door.

"Oh, it is now, but it wasn't before." Clark walked toward the upper class wing.

"Are you going to ask what I am?" Greg walked beside the older boy.

"Nope. I figured that's a very personal question and one that reciprocates. You can have your secrets so that I can have mine."

Clark had told someone about meeting his dad once a couple of years ago. His friend had been so happy for him that he'd also let it slip to his parents. His friend's dad got a job transfer less than a month later. Clark didn't think it was a coincidence. He started to wonder what Umiko would think when she found out.

Greg's voice snapped him out of the troubled thought. "Fair enough." Greg nodded once.

"Why didn't you fight back?" Clark asked.

"The point at the moment wasn't to beat Killian, although, that does sound satisfying." Greg ran his right index finger down the ridge of his straight nose. "The point was to let the girl get away. Plus, if I had thrown a punch, I would have lost the moral high ground. I'm better than him."

"Easily. That wolf and his pack are a menace."

"They think it's their territory, that they're the law and Coach D. doesn't dissuade them. One day, someone is going to have to teach them otherwise."

Clark stopped at the end of the hall and turned to Greg. "You?"

"If no one else steps up." The boy shrugged. "But he's the star of the team, and that's a much larger fight than one bully." Greg crossed his arms in defiance.

"Not your fight?" Clark asked.

"Not yet." Greg shrugged. "I choose my battles. I try to only start a fight I know I can win."

"And the girl?" Clark asked as the pair moved apart to walk in different directions.

"What about her?" Greg asked.

"You like her," Clark said and a smile crept across his lips. He watched the expressions flit across the younger man's face. He lifted his hands in surrender. "Too personal, I get it." He turned and walked away. "But I saw that look," he called over his shoulder. "There's something there. I'm not sure what, but you think it's worth a bloody nose, maybe more."

"You've never seen her dance." Clark heard Greg say as he walked around the corner.

"Definitely more," Clark murmured to himself.

CHAPTER FOUR

$\mathcal{L}$yn and Umiko shared one class. Algebra II. They found seats in the far back corner, Umiko behind Lyn, just like in their freshman Geometry class.

Both girls excelled at math and found the lessons to be boring, monotonous, and other words meaning the worst thing ever. Umiko usually doodled in her notebook, while Lyn stared out the window and tapped silent rhythms with the pads of her fingers on her desk. To be fair, Lyn stared out the window in most of her classes.

Once, last year, Lyn had fallen asleep while Umiko brushed her hair. The teacher was furious, but since they had the two highest scores in the class, and constantly ruined the curve for others, they had come to an arrangement. Umiko and Lyn would sit in the back, and not interrupt or otherwise distract the class in any way, and the teacher would ignore them. It was a great year, as far as math was concerned.

Lyn and Umiko hoped the teachers talked amongst themselves and the same accommodation would work this year.

Lyn rolled her eyes at the notes on the board. The first few weeks of school were always frustrating. Nothing new was taught. Instead, classes reviewed last years' closing lessons to make sure no one forgot anything over the summer. Lyn didn't know anyone that enjoyed the recap. She sure didn't.

Lyn smelled the scent of wet peat and turned to see Sasha sitting in the opposite back row corner filing her nails. Why would a vampire even go to school? She wondered how many times Sasha found herself sitting through the same lectures lifetimes apart.

Sasha turned and waved her red manicured nails in Lyn's direction.

Lyn looked away as a smile bloomed on the girl's face.

Umiko ran her fingers through Lyn's hair, while Lyn stared out the window at nothing in particular.

Lyn's mind paced, as if in a cage, wanting to escape. To run, or walk, or just move. Anything but sit in this hard plastic chair and learn about points, lines, and rays.

A piece of paper fell from Lyn's shoulder and tumbled down her chest. She picked it up from her lap and unfolded, making sure to keep it out of sight of the teacher and any nosy students.

Your hair is redder today! Umiko's crisp handwriting read.

Lyn separated some of her hair from the side of her head and examined it. She pulled some around from the other side. The light streamed in from the window in such a way that her hair did look more red, almost the same shade as Umiko's. Lyn didn't know what to think.

"Anything to share with the class, Ms..." The teacher looked from the girls in the back corner to the class roster on a podium in the front of the room.

"Davis. And no, I just thought I saw some split ends. I'll need to make an appointment." Lyn pushed her hair out of her face and sat up straighter.

Sasha tittered from her corner.

"On my own time, of course." She gave the teacher her full attention.

"Lyn," the teacher said. "Right. And you must be Umiko Clare." The teacher glanced in Umiko's direction. She did not look like she bought Lyn's explanation, but she turned away.

Lyn swore she saw the teacher roll her own eyes before she picked up where she left off talking about the difference between lines and rays.

Lyn leaned back in her chair. Math teachers did share notes. Lyn stared out the window and imagined the ninth and tenth grade teachers in an empty classroom discussing their problem students. The ninth grade teachers would be happy to be rid of them. The tenth grade teachers would be convinced that they would fare better. The ninth knew they wouldn't. Lyn stifled a laugh.

A tap tap tap came from the classroom's closed door. When it opened, a dark haired student peeked his head in. "Ms. Maloney, you're needed in the front office."

The teacher took a moment to write down some busy work on the white board and told the class it would be graded. A collective groan escaped the students. Ms. Maloney ignored their complaints and walked out of the class room, leaving the door open behind her.

The students were quiet until the click of heels disappeared down the hallway, then desks were turned and gossip began with a few whispered words. The boys talked about the earlier fight. They discussed tactics and what they thought Greg or Killian should have done different. The girls were more concerned about making plans for after school. A few students tried to hush the many, as they scribbled down the assignment in their notebooks, but they were ignored.

Lyn turned around in her seat to face Umiko.

"Weird right?" Umiko asked and leaned in to hold a section of her hair next to a section of Lyn's. "It's even straight. Well, the red anyway. The brown parts are still curly."

The color, Lyn could have prescribed to the light filtering

in through the window, but the lack of curl was not as easily explained away. She looked at the length of hair Umiko stretched between her hands. Lyn couldn't tell which of the straight strands were hers and which belonged to her best friend.

Lyn turned back to the window and ran her fingers through her hair, curly and straight. Her fingers stalled in tangled brown sections, while the red flowed freely past. What would make part of her hair go flat without an iron? She had showered this morning, but that usually caused the curls to be more fluffy, not straighten them.

The bell rang twenty minutes later. When the classroom emptied, Umiko and Lyn were the last ones out.

"Are you really going to make me wait to hear your news?" Lyn asked as they stepped into the hall.

"Yes, I am."

Lyn noticed a glint in the girl's eye. "You are such a tease."

"What are friends for?" Umiko giggled. She waved at someone over Lyn's shoulder before she turned to go to her next class. She left Lyn standing by the doorway.

Lyn turned and stepped into a solid mass. For a split second she thought it might be Killian, and her body shrank in on itself. Her shoulders curled and her head bowed to her chest.

"Whoa." The voice was not abrasive. It was smooth and gentle. Plus, there was no lingering smell of damp canine. Instead, it smelled of fresh grass and open spaces.

"Sorry." She looked up in the face of the guy she ran into.

Greg smiled back at her. "In a hurry to get to your next class?"

Lyn gave a little snort, and quickly regretted the sound. She found her words and tried to cover it up. "Yes. Coach Davis. History."

Greg nodded. "Oh, I remember him. He likes to yell. The

year I had him, he threw a stapler at a kid in my class. That kid never snored in Coach's class again." Greg laughed.

"Yeah, so…um…I should go." Lyn moved to step around Greg, but stopped. "Thanks, for earlier, btw."

Greg smiled again. "Oh, it was nothing. That's what friends are for."

Lyn cocked her head. "O-kay," she drew out the word longer than the two syllables deserved. Lyn didn't think she and Greg were friends. She didn't really have friends besides Umiko. Was he making fun of her? No, that seemed out of character from what she knew of him. She wondered how long he had been listening to her and Umiko's conversation.

Greg looked at his watch, "You better get going. I don't want you to get a stapler thrown at you because I made you late." He stepped to the side to let Lyn pass.

"Right." She stepped past him. "Thanks again!" she called behind her.

"No problem," Greg replied.

Lyn walked to her next class as fast as she could without getting yelled at to stop running in the halls. She looked back briefly and saw Greg smiling at her. She turned and fled before her skin changed from pale to pink.

CHAPTER FIVE

*U*miko pushed open the faded wood gate to her back yard and led Lyn in. "Come on, there are suits and towels in the bathhouse."

Lyn followed, but her mind was elsewhere.

Today was the first time Lyn and Killian had crossed paths since school ended in May. She knew he lived in the neighborhood because she'd sometimes see his Jeep drive down her street, but she managed to avoid being a target all summer.

Even the first week of school went by without incident and she foolishly let herself imagine that she would be free of him this year. That he found a new target. She enjoyed the bully free summer and wasn't looking forward to another whole year of abuse, especially since not only did she feel alone and abandoned, she actually was alone and abandoned. Sixteen was too young to be on her own. If her mother hadn't died, she might not have moved out for five or six more years.

Lyn brushed a small tear from her eye.

Lyn and her mom had discussed a nursing program instead of a four year college. Lyn could stay at home and commute to a local community college to get her nursing degree. She could get a job at the hospital where her mom worked and maybe never leave home. She guessed she could still do those things, follow through on a future she had shared with her mom, but 'without her mom' sounded horrible.

Lyn stepped through the gate and under a drape of greenery. The magic of Umiko's backyard landscaping drew her attention away from her thoughts. Lyn took a deliberate step into the storybook and made an effort to leave her current and future worries on the other side of the wooden gate as she closed it behind her.

Umiko's backyard looked like a slice of Japanese garden. A strange sight in central Texas. It was a shallow rectangle with tall vegetation on the three sides not overlooked by the house. A long, thin pool was positioned in the middle. It wasn't the artificial blue of a chlorinated pool. It was more of a pond green and fit seamlessly in with the landscaping. Branches hung over the edges of the pool casting gentle shadows on the surface of the water.

The pool was flanked on one side by a stone bench. Literally, a stone, sitting on top of two smaller stones in such a way that Lyn's feet would hang down and skim the water of the pool. On the other side was a small wooden cabana, with towels hung on hooks on the back wall.

Umiko dropped her few school items on the patio table, removed her black flats with a flick of her toes, and walked between the house and the pool on rough hewn stepping stones. She lifted the lid on a brown plastic wicker laundry basket. "Want a suit?" Umiko lifted out two one-piece swim team suits. One black, one red. Their school colors.

Lyn shook her head. She added her bags to Umiko's on the table and slipped off her tennis shoes. "I'm not feeling up to a swim, but I'll put my feet in while you do."

Umiko nodded and let both suits fall back into the basket.

Lyn stepped over on the stepping stones and walked to the edge of the pond. She sat on a smooth stone with her back to Umiko and her legs in the water up to her knees. She paddled her feet and felt the water swish between her legs. She watched the ripples spread out from her legs to the edges of the pool.

A dry towel landed on the ground beside Lyn. Umiko stepped up and laced her hands in the air above her head.

Lyn saw Umiko's toned form out of the corner of her eye. Her friend folded at her middle and dove into the water hands first.

Umiko wasn't afraid of anyone seeing her naked. The landscaping prevented snooping eyes. Only Lyn's window could see into the yard, and even that was mostly obstructed by overhanging branches.

The water enveloped Umiko with a tiny splash. She was born for the water. Even with her two legs she was graceful and her strokes were perfection. Umiko had won several medals while on the swim team, but Lyn still thought her friend held back her potential. There was no way human swimmers could compete with a selkie.

Lyn learned what a selkie was three months after she and Umiko decided to be best friends for life. It was an unusually warm November day and Umiko had brought her here to her backyard pool, and pushed her in, clothes and all, before she jumped in herself.

Umiko's pool did not have the traditional gradual decline from shallow end to deep end. It was all deep end. Deep meaning deep enough to dive into and not worry about concussions.

Lyn's head had gone immediately underwater. Her mother had taught her to swim as a baby. Presumably, Lyn could do it, but she was so thrown off by her BFF tossing her in, that she panicked and lost her bearings when the bottom of the pool had not been where she had expected it to be. Umiko had to rescue her and hold her head above water until Lyn calmed enough to tread water, with Umiko's direction. Lyn had never been that angry with her friend. Before or since.

She found out two things that day. Her best friend was not only from a Japanese and Irish background, which you could easily see in her features, Umiko was also the Irish equivalent of a mermaid, less fish more seal, and she, Lyn, was not.

Lyn imagined that's when Umiko's mental checklist of creatures that Lyn was not had started.

Lyn watched as her friend finished a butterfly lap and came up next to Lyn's legs.

"How long can you stay under?" Lyn asked.

"I don't know." Umiko shrugged her shoulders.

"Come on, you've never once tried?"

"Once," Umiko confessed. "I was seven. I don't know how long I was down, but my mom was really angry. She had been calling for me and I didn't hear her from under the water." Umiko sighed. "I don't know why she was mad. She knows what I am, what my dad was."

"Maybe she was afraid you'd drown?" Lyn splashed water in her friend's face.

Umiko laughed and wiped her face. "I don't think that's possible, not unless I hit my head or something."

"So, you don't know for sure?"

Umiko shook her head and floated away, flicking her seal tail.

"So, your mom must be gone this afternoon?" Lyn asked.

"Yeah. She's tutoring at the library. She should be home around five o'clock."

Lyn nodded. That explained Umiko's partial transformation. When her mother was around, Umiko didn't indulge in her selkie abilities. Lyn imagined it was so her mom wouldn't think too much about being abandoned by her older son and husband. But she thought it was sad that her friend held something of herself back around someone who loved her so much.

"Do you miss your dad?"

Umiko shrugged. "I've only met him twice. He only comes to find us once every seven years. I think that's a selkie thing, but my research is limited since we've never talked about it and my mom isn't sure. Anyway, the first time, I was six, I thought it was pretty cool. We went to the beach and swam and it was like having a whole family. That was when I learned what we were. My dad taught me how to change. What caused it, how to control it. The sort of things my mom couldn't. But he left after a week and my mom got sad and struggled to cheer up my brother and I." Umiko settled her arms on the edge of the pool near Lyn's legs and let her stubby tail float out on the surface of the water. "She was the one that hammered in the fact that creatures might exist, but not all of us would be accepted and we should be selective about who we told. She said it was better to blend in as a human than to stand out as an other."

"Was she right?" Lyn asked.

"I hope not," Umiko replied. "Then creatures started coming out. My mom hasn't quite gotten used to the idea, but she's getting better."

Lyn let the politics of being different slide. "The next time you saw your dad was when your brother chose him over you and your mom."

"Yeah, exactly seven years later. My dad spent less time with me, and more time with Ian. I felt left out, but I was old enough that I could tell my mom was anxious. I tried to be happy and cheerful for her and not fight with Ian to spend more time with dad. Ian, of course, was over the moon to get to spend so much time with him. He didn't notice how sad mom was feeling." Umiko laid her head on her arms. "When Ian left, she broke."

"She misses him."

"She misses them both a lot. She really loves my dad. She just wishes he would stay longer. Choose her for a while." Umiko flicked her smooth tail on the surface of the water. "What about your dad? Will he be the one to take care of you now?"

"Father," Lyn corrected her. She felt like the word choice was important. "I don't remember ever meeting him. I'm not sure I could find him if I had to."

"Well, you might have to test that theory. I mean, you can stay here, as long as you need, obviously. My mom wouldn't kick you out and I like having a sister, but having a dad, or father…" Umiko shrugged and Lyn noticed a flash of sadness cross her friend's face. "It might be nice."

Lyn was not persuaded. She picked up a stray leaf and ripped it, piece by piece, with her fingers.

"We don't know what happened between him and your mom. Maybe he doesn't know you exist. That happens." Umiko looked hopeful. "And even if we find him, you can still be my sister."

"What if we find him and he wants me to move?"

Umiko opened her mouth to speak and closed it again.

Lyn regretted her question. It was too close to what would happen with Umiko's father When he came back next, Umiko would have to choose between him and her mom.

"Umiko? Lyn?" a voice called from the house.

"Oh, no, she's home early." Umiko pulled her tail down underneath her, sank her bare shoulders into the water and rested close to the edge of the pool. "Yes, mama, we're out here." Umiko called and smiled sweetly as her mother came out of the house.

"That lady from CPS is coming by to talk to Lyn in about fifteen minutes. Please get dried off and come inside."

"Yes, ma'am," Umiko said, but didn't move from her spot on the edge of the pool.

"Well, come on." Umiko's mom stood on the patio near the back door and watched the two girls.

Lyn pulled her legs out of the water and stood up. She needed to buy her friend a little time to change. "I'm a little hungry, do you mind if I have a snack while we wait? Fruit, maybe?" Lyn also knew that Umiko's mom would not refuse to feed anyone, much less her daughter's best friend and Lyn was hungry. She was constantly hungry.

"Of course, come on." Mrs. Clare invited Lyn into the kitchen and turned her back on the pool and her daughter.

Umiko came in a few moments later, dressed in her school clothes, with a towel wrapped around her head.

Mrs. Clare placed a bowl of grapes on the kitchen bar.

Lyn popped a grape into her mouth. The sweet yet sour juice spilled over her tongue as she bit it in half.

The doorbell rang.

"Oh." Umiko's mom put down the basket of fruit the she was washing. "She's early. I'm not ready." Mrs. Clare wiped her wet hands on her apron and hurried to open the door.

Umiko and Lyn stood in the space between the kitchen and living room. Lyn's eyes glued to the door.

The initials CPS were imposing, the woman wielding them matched. She stood a head taller than Umiko's mom, who was Lyn's exact height the last time they measured. The government official wore a black pencil skirt, with a solid pale blue button up blouse. Her hair was pulled back in a tight bun that Lyn thought was also pulling her face taut.

"Thank you for inviting me to your home, Mrs. Clare. I'm Rebecca Sanchez, with CPS. We spoke on the phone earlier." The lady held out her hand.

Umiko's mom took it and bowed slightly. Her Japanese manners surfacing.

"I would have been happy to meet with Lyn at her own

house," the lady continued, "but she hasn't returned my phone calls." The CPS woman turned to face Lyn.

"Sorry," Lyn faked an apology, "I unplugged the house phone because I couldn't take another condolence call."

The woman softened. "Of course, I would have done something similar. Luckily, I had Mrs. Clare's name and phone number from our first meeting. How are you…" She looked at Lyn and broke off her question. "Stupid question. Anyway, may we sit?" she asked Umiko's mom who gave a slight nod.

"We will be in the kitchen. Come, Umiko." Mrs. Clare reached for her daughter's arm and pulled her away.

"But…" Umiko protested.

"Please help with dinner. Lyn said she was hungry."

Umiko acquiesced, but made eye contact with Lyn that said they'd be doing a LOT of talking tonight. Lyn hoped it would be less about her and more about the news that Umiko had yet to share with her.

"My name is Ms. Sanchez, in case you forgot. I know you've had a lot of stuff going on and my name was probably not high on your list of important things at the time."

Lyn sat silently and watched the woman's lips move.

"We need to discuss guardianship." She held up a hand to Lyn's objection. "I know. You're sixteen and you are fully capable of doing everything yourself, but this is the way it has to be. I need to do my best to make sure you are taken care of until you are eighteen, and God willing, beyond. It's what your mother would have wanted."

Lyn crossed her arms and sulked. She hated it when people spoke for her mom. Especially people who thought they had Lyn's best interest in mind, like Ms. Evans from across the street. She did the same thing, but at least Ms. Evans knew her mom. This woman didn't and she didn't know Lyn either. She did not know what was best for Lyn or what her mother would have wanted. Lyn was better informed on that count by far. This woman probably didn't even have children.

"Let's just rip the bandage off. Do you know if your mother had a will? Did she ever tell you what she wanted for you in the event of her…" The woman stopped.

"Death," Lyn finished for her. "It's a word you can say. My mother is dead and since I'm underage, you don't want me to live at home, or on the street, or whatever."

"Yes, well," the woman paled, "it's not just me. I'm sure a lot of people care very much about your well being, I'm just the face of the tragedy." She folded one hand into the other in her lap and regained her poise. "Now, Ms. Alice Evans says she's trying to find a document that your mother gave her for safe keeping. She claims it says that your mom wanted Ms. Evans to be your legal guardian."

"What?" Lyn sat up straight and uncrossed her arms. "That can't be right."

"If the paper is real and there is no other blood relations, it would be fine for a family friend to have guardianship. You're human, right? You don't have a creature clan to claim you? The rules are a little more complicated with a creature affiliation."

Lyn ignored the creature question. "What if that's not what I want?" Lyn demanded.

"We will try to take your wants into consideration, within reason. Of course, a father, uncle, aunt, even a grandparent would be better equipped to request guardianship on your behalf. If they are willing, but unable to care for you full time, there are boarding schools. Saint Michael's awards several hard-ship scholarships every year, even mid-term. I can leave you a brochure, as well as a few others, just in case."

"But I don't know any of those relatives." Lyn's shoulders sank, she blinked and forced the tears away. Boarding school went in one ear and out the other.

"Your mom might have left something. A will for

example," Rebecca prompted. "That could tell us exactly what she wanted for you."

"Except I don't know where to find it, if she did have one." Lyn didn't know anything about a will. She and her mom talked about a lot of things, what would happen in the event of her death was not one Lyn ever wanted to consider. When her mother tried, Lyn always descended into a panic attack and the conversation never got started.

"She seemed like a pretty on top of it woman from what I can gather. She'll have made one. I'm almost positive."

"How long do I have to look for it?"

"Ms. Evans has to produce her paper for verification. We can't just hand children over to anyone who says they will take you, even creature clans have to prove they have your best interest in mind. There are some cross checking and forms that need to be filled out. I can give you some time to contact relatives. You can even call me." She reached in her briefcase for a card and handed it to Lyn, along with 2 brochures. The top of which had a picture of a brick and columned building and a crest of some sort. "I can make those phone calls for you, if it's too hard. I want this to be as easy a transition as I can make it."

Lyn took the card and stood up. "Anything else?" She brushed off any further discussion and began walking to the door as the CPS woman stood and gathered her things.

"I have a meeting with Ms. Evans tomorrow at three o'clock. I assume you get out of school around four? I can stop by your house after and give you an update."

Lyn nodded and opened the door.

"This too shall pass," the woman said as she stepped across the threshold.

Lyn closed the door with more force than was necessary. "This too shall pass," Lyn mocked with a sneer as the glass pane in the center of the door rattled. She shoved the card and brochures in her back pocket.

Umiko came out of the kitchen. "Ms. Evans? The so and so who lives across the street?"

"Yeah," Lyn said with the beginning of a growl. She normally giggled at the way Umiko cursed without cursing. A trait Lyn did not make use of. "Damn it." Lyn hit the flat of her hand on the wall by the door.

"Language." Umiko's mom called from the kitchen.

"Sorry, mama," Umiko apologized for Lyn, who would have done it herself, had she the brain capacity to remember her manners.

"Why would your mom give her guardianship?" Umiko asked.

"Why wouldn't she have told me?" Lyn added. She sat back on the sofa and clutched a throw pillow to her chest, the tears flowed free.

Umiko handed Lyn a box of tissues and waited.

"Ms. Evans was my nurse," Lyn answered after a few deep breaths when she had the waterworks controlled.

"Nurse?"

"It's a long story and I'm not in the best of moods at the moment. Can we eat and maybe talk about your news instead?"

"Yeah, but I also think we need to revisit finding your dad, unless you don't mind living with Ms. Evans."

"That is not going to happen." Lyn's words were forceful, but her voice betrayed her worry. "I don't think my mom trusted that woman in the end, even if the paper is real, it's probably old and I don't think it was what my mom would have wanted now."

"Then I really think we need to figure out who your dad is."

"Like he'd be any better." Lyn rubbed her head. It was filled with a mash of new and old information and twice as much worry.

"He might." Umiko shrugged. "But food first." She led her

best friend into the kitchen for a bowl of teriyaki. "Have you gotten any better with chopsticks?"

"I still feed most of my rice to the floor," Lyn admitted and wiped her eyes.

Umiko smirked. "I'll get you a fork."

CHAPTER SIX

"Okay, spill it," Umiko demanded as she closed the door to her bedroom. "You have a nurse? I thought you said you never get sick?" Umiko sat on her bed and stared at Lyn.

"I don't get sick. It's no big deal." Lyn sat in the chair at Umiko's desk and swiveled away from her friend's gaze.

"Maybe not before, but I think it is now. She wants to be your guardian." Umiko sounded worried.

Lyn swiveled toward Umiko. "It really is no big deal. I've been anemic my entire life. My body doesn't like to absorb iron." Lyn turned away when Umiko made eye contact. She faced the mirror over the desk that doubled as a vanity. She picked up a bottle of frosted pink nail polish and held it next to her pale fingers.

"So what? Anemia is a normal thing. You can take supplements. It doesn't need a personal nurse," Umiko said.

"The supplements make me sick." Lyn opened the bottle and applied the polish to her left thumb. "I think I'm allergic to something in them. I don't remember. Anyway, Ms. Evans and my mom knew each other from the hospital, I guess." Lyn screwed the lid back on the bottle and blew her freshly painted nail. "When she moved in down the street, it made sense to my mom to just have her monitor my levels instead of going through clinics and insurance companies."

"What do you mean by monitor?" Umiko asked, her eyes narrowed more than normal.

Lyn sighed. "Once a month or so, Ms. Evans came over and drew blood. Just a little at first. I hated it as a kid, and I think she pitied me enough to only take the minimum she needed for testing."

"And now?" Umiko grabbed one of the many pillows on her bed to hold.

"Well, the last time she came over, she drew 4 vials." Lyn looked at herself in the mirror. "That was at least a month before my mom's accident." Lyn turned her focus on the reflection of Umiko. "I think my mom was getting frustrated with her. All I know is that she took blood for tests and gave me drops to take every morning."

"What were the drops for?" Umiko's reflection asked.

"Some sort of herbal remedy that I used to take every morning before school. An iron supplement I didn't react negatively to, I guess." Lyn shrugged and tapped her freshly painted thumb nail with the index finger on her other hand.

"What did the tests show?"

Lyn swiveled around and faced the real Umiko. "I don't know. I never saw them, I overheard Ms. Evans and my mom talking once. Ms. Evans made it sound bad, she wanted to start running a different test, with more blood, but when my mom asked for copies of the latest test results, Ms. Evans said she didn't keep them at home for privacy reasons, and would need to get them from a secure location." Lyn held her hand out for Umiko. "Yes or no?"

Umiko sat up and looked at Lyn's hand. "It's a good color for you. So, does Ms. Evans work at the hospital?"

"I don't know. I thought she was retired. I know she's not old enough, but I supposed she could be independently wealthy. She's always outside watering her yard and snooping on the neighbors. I've never seen or heard of her having a husband." Lyn spun back to the mirror and opened the nail polish bottle.

"Have you talked to Ms. Evans since your mom died?" Umiko asked.

Lyn appreciated that she didn't sugar coat, or choke on the word. "No, and I haven't taken the herbs either. They tasted awful anyway." Lyn stuck out her tongue in the mirror.

Umiko nodded. "How do yo feel without them?"

"Fine, I guess." Lyn brushed the pinkie on her left hand and placed the nail polish brush back into the bottle. She blew on her fingernails.

"Your skin is a little paler, could that be something."

"Maybe." Lyn compared her skin color to Umiko's reflection. They were close to the same shade, but Umiko's looked darker because of her freckles. "Wow, I didn't think I could be paler than you." Lyn stared closer at the reflection of her friend. "That's weird."

Umiko threw her pillow at Lyn who used the wheels on the chair to dodge and bumped into the desk. She deflected the projectile with her unpolished hand before it could spill the still open nail polish bottle.

"Why didn't you tell me? We tell each other everything." Umiko pouted

"It was just that one thing. I promise. I didn't want you to think of me as less than I am." But her last statement felt wrong, hollow somehow. Lyn felt bad that she had disappointed her best friend by keeping the anemia to herself. It wasn't even supposed to be a secret. Lyn wondered why she hadn't said anything before.

"I wouldn't have." Umiko sounded hurt.

"I know, I'm sorry." Lyn threw the pillow back at Umiko. "Still friends?" she asked.

The pillow bounced off the wall behind the bed and landed on Umiko's chest. She grabbed it and nodded.

"Good. Now you spill. I have waited all day and you've just made me talk about myself." Lyn turned back to the vanity and started to paint the nails on her dominant hand.

Umiko smiled and picked up a second pillow. Her bed was covered in them. Heart shaped ones, furry ones, ones with flowered covers. She made a space for Lyn in the pillow pile. "Let me do that hand."

Lyn brought the half opened bottle and plopped down beside Umiko.

Umiko took the bottle and started on Lyn's right thumb nail.

"Well," Umiko began, "I have a date tomorrow night," she whispered, even though her door was closed.

"Wow, really? Wait, how does your mom feel about that? You did tell her right?" Lyn asked. She felt a sadness start in her chest and build. She tried to keep it from her features. Blinking back the tears that threatened to fall. She wouldn't get to tell her mom about any dates, but she didn't want to take away Umiko's happiness. She watched the blood flush to Umiko's face. Lyn wondered if her own blush would be that noticeable now that her skin wasn't pinking up with the herbs.

"Of course, I did. I asked her if I could go, and she looked sad and happy at the same time." Umiko placed the brush in the bottle and ran her own nail around the one she had just painted on Lyn's hand before moving on. "She was quiet for a moment, but she asked for more details, like where and when and what his name was. She finally said I could. I was afraid she would say I was too young."

"But you're sixteen, surely..." Lyn lifted her hand to her face and blew the wet polish.

Umiko secured the lid to the bottle and placed it on her

bedside table. "I know, I was ready for that argument. But I didn't have to use it."

"So," Lyn dragged out the word. "Who's the boy? Where are you going? When? What?" Lyn teased.

"Clark. He's a senior."

"Really?"

"I kind of didn't tell my mom that part, yet."

"You don't think she'd approve."

Umiko shrugged. "He's a really nice guy. He's on the swim team and in theater. He volunteers at the Senior Living Center on Broadside and he has a part-time job."

Lyn took another breath to blow her nails and nodded for Umiko to continue.

"We're going to meet at the skate park at 5. My mom and I nearly fought over that. She wanted him to come to the door, knock, and meet her like it's the 1950s or something. But I dodged that by saying it was going to be a small group. That settled her down a bit, but she made me promise to bring him by to meet her soon." Umiko sank back into her pillows and leaned on the headboard.

"Will there be a small group?" Lyn asked.

Umiko shook her head. "Not unless the other people at the skate park count."

"You lied to your mom?"

Umiko grimaced. "A little one."

Lyn couldn't imagine lying to her own mom and didn't think Umiko would have in a million years either. "Clark? The name sounds familiar. Do I know him?"

"I don't think so." Umiko paused and then perked up. "Wait. You might. He worked at the hospital over the summer."

"How did you meet him?"

Umiko and Lyn spent the next couple of hours talking about Clark and picking out clothes for Umiko's date.

When Umiko's mom called up for lights out, the girls had

crossed nearly every item of Umiko's closet off the list. She said it was all too bright and cheery. She wanted something darker.

"You can borrow something of mine," Lyn offered.

Umiko and Lyn bounded out of the room and begged her mom to let them run to get a few things from Lyn's house. "We forgot to get Lyn clothes for tomorrow." Umiko gave her a half truth and her mom gave in.

"Hurry back," Mrs. Clare called after them as they ran out the back door.

Last year, after a storm had come through the area with wind that had knocked down many of the fences in the neighborhood, including the one between Lyn's and Umiko's houses, the girls convinced their moms to install a gate between the two yards.

The girls ran out the back door of Umiko's house, around the pool on stepping stones and ducked under an overgrown honeysuckle vine. The smell drifted into Lyn's nose and she took a deeper breath. Honeysuckle, salty air, and a hint of sunshine even though it was after dark.

They opened the gate into Lyn's yard. From fairy tale forrest, to overgrown weed field.

Lyn took a step into the yard and waved her hands above her head. A flood light came on and the girls ran across the yard, avoiding anything that looked more weed than grass. Lyn opened the door to her kitchen with a hidden key and the girls bolted up to her room.

Where Umiko's closet was filled with colors and patterns, Lyn's closet was not. Umiko thumbed through the few clothes still on hangers while Lyn searched for a few necessary items scattered around her messy room.

Umiko pulled off her shirt and tried on a plain navy T-shirt, with criss-crossed straps in the back and a scoop necked collar.

"This with jeans?"

Lyn smiled and nodded. She thought that shirt never would have looked as good on her as it did on Umiko. Lyn wasn't one to spend a lot of time on clothing but Umiko could make a burlap sack look nice, given enough time.

Lyn grabbed a change of clothes from a pile under the window and threw it and a few bathroom items into a drawstring bag from the closet floor.

"Got everything?" Umiko asked.

Lyn nodded and led Umiko out of the room and down the stairs.

The girls locked the house and closed the gate. Lyn almost lost her balance on the stones around the pool but, thanks to her dancer's reflexes and a well timed leap, she landed on less wobbly ground.

"Good night, mama." Umiko kissed her mom on their way back upstairs.

"Lights out and don't stay up too late talking."

"We know," Umiko called back.

"Yes, ma'am," Lyn added.

CHAPTER SEVEN

*B*ack upstairs, Umiko draped the shirt across the chair back and picked her hairbrush up from her vanity. She turned the lights off while Lyn flipped on the bedside lamp and hung a thin red cloth over the shade.

Umiko sat on her bed and brushed and braided her hair in the low light. "We need to make a plan to find your dad."

"Are you shifting missions without figuring out my creature type?" Lyn teased as she smoothed out her wrinkled sleeping bag.

Umiko shrugged. "Without more to go on..." She perked up and twisted the last loop of ponytail holder around the end of her braid. "Wait, do we have more to go on? Because finding your creature type could also be a solution of your guardianship problem."

Lyn saw a spark in her friend's eye, even in the red light. Umiko would jump at the chance to delve more fully into Lyn's creature type. Lyn wasn't sure why Umiko cared so much. Why it was hard for her to accept that Lyn was just a run of the mill human.

Lyn shook her head and watched as the spark faded, and Umiko's shoulders slumped.

"Well, I'm not giving up my mission. Not really. Realistically, it will be better to find your dad anyway. And he'll be able to tell us your creature type. Both missions accomplished!" Umiko admitted.

"If he even cares," Lyn said to herself. She was already curled up in her sleeping bag on the floor.

"Besides, I don't think Ms. Evans is a good option," Umiko continued uninterrupted. "There's something off about the whole anemia thing and if she does have a piece of paper that says she's your official guardian, we need to solve that problem first. " Umiko said.

"You're right. We can start tomorrow after school. Until you have to leave for your date, I mean."

"Do you know anything about your father?" Umiko asked.

"No." Lyn shook her head. Her father was a complete mystery to her.

Lyn heard plastic tap wood as Umiko placed the brush on her side table. Umiko leaned off the edge of her bed closest to Lyn's spot on the floor.

"Do you know where your mom kept important papers? Like your birth certificate?" Umiko asked.

"Her office?" Lyn answered, watching the fan spin. "I'm not sure, but I know there are a lot of files in there. The CPS lady thought she must have a will. They are probably together in one of those files, don't you think?" Lyn looked at her friend.

Umiko nodded. "What about a photo album? Any pictures of your dad? I wonder what he looks like? I always thought you looked like your mom. Like almost a perfect mini-me type of match," Umiko trailed off.

Lyn was at a loss. "I don't know. I've never seen any."

"Hmm. Tomorrow then." Umiko rolled away from the edge.

Lyn closed her eyes and turned on her side.

"Maybe the paper will be a fake, or she won't be able to find it. We wouldn't have to worry about finding my father then. Your mom could say she'd foster me, make it official." Lyn clung to a sliver of hope as she looked into the darkness under Umiko's bed.

"I don't think it'll be that easy, and my mom would want you to try to find your dad too. Family is important to her," Umiko said before a yawn. "My mom keeps a box in her closet with my brother's old baby stuff in it. Maybe your mom has one too."

"Maybe," Lyn said. She rolled over to her other side and flattened out a wrinkle beneath her in the sleeping bag.

Lyn stared out the window, well after her friend had fallen asleep. She did not like the idea of looking for a man who, for all she knew, chose to never know her. But her current alternative, to live with a woman her mother didn't trust anymore and that Lyn had never liked, was no more appealing.

"Rock, meet hard place," Lyn whispered to the sliver of a moon and closed her eyes. Tears began to puddle in the corners of her eyes.

CHAPTER EIGHT

The next day at school, more teachers patrolled the edges of the large cafeteria because of the fight. The crowd of students was quieter underneath the gaze of authority, but only slightly. The voices of hundreds of students all chatting at once still sounded like constant rolling thunder.

The bell rang to get to class, splitting the thunder like lightning strikes. The teachers stayed behind the press of students instead of being the first ones through the room like normal.

Lyn and Umiko moved with the current, keeping to the middle of the pack.

"How is our little orphan today? Have any weekend plans?" Killian came up behind them as they filtered through the doors into the hallway.

Lyn ignored her bully and concentrated on keeping her feet underneath her and her butt off of the floor. She made sure to keep Umiko beside her, which was hard when Umiko stopped walking with the crowd.

"Leave her alone." Umiko faced him. She was at least a foot shorter and fifty pounds lighter than Killian.

He turned his focus to her and laughed. "What's that, Ginger?"

"Coach, is going to have a heart attack if we're not dressed out by the bell. Come on," the boy that smelled like cedar said.

"Killian, Scout, get to class." Coach Davis roared from the cafeteria side of the doorway.

"Speak of the Devil," Scout winked at Lyn and Umiko and slapped Killian on the shoulder.

Killian smiled at Umiko and Lyn and walked through the doors.

As Killian passed, Coach slapped the back of Killian's head.

Killian's smile tuned into a glare as he turned toward the Junior's wing of lockers under Coach Davis' watchful stare.

Umiko and Lyn exchanged eye rolls and walked to the Sophomore wing.

Umiko twisted the dial on her combination lock and changed out a few items before closing the door back. Lyn stood silently by. She didn't use her locker anymore. There was no point. He could get in and she couldn't. She carried everything she needed with her. Her school laptop bag with a notebook and pencil case tucked inside, her water bottle, and her purse.

"See you in Algebra." Umiko waved at Lyn and walked toward her first period class.

Lyn stepped across the hall into hers. Her desk was in the back. She preferred it that way. She chose the farthest seat from the teacher and the door in every class. A seat that no one could sneak up on her in, and that she could either use to hide or to blend into the background.

Lyn groaned to herself. She didn't think she could sit for an hour, her body already ached to move. She settled into her seat as the teacher came in. Lyn spent the next forty-five minutes trying to get comfortable in the plastic seat while Mr. Ripley said something about science that Lyn ignored.

It must have worked, because her head jerked up from her desk top as the bell rang. She rubbed the cheek that had been stuck to the desk, gathered her stuff and noticed the teacher looking at her with pity. "Sorry," Lyn mouthed as she hurried off to her next class.

Only, she didn't make it there. She dreaded the idea of sitting still in another class and when she found herself outside the auditorium doors, she decided to take a mental health break. Who would the school call about her skipping class anyway? A phone that would never be answered? Lyn looked left and right down the hallway and slipped through a side door while no one was watching.

~

The auditorium was pitch black, like all the stars had been plucked from the night sky. Lyn stood just inside the door while her eyes adjusted to the darkness.

After a moment, she could make out the silhouette of seat backs and she felt her way down the side aisle and up the stage steps.

A few moments later and she could see more than silhouettes.

The heavy red curtains, black in the darkness, were open. Lyn smiled to herself. Usually Lyn came after school when the curtains were closed. Now, the whole stage beckoned her forward.

Lyn didn't need a huge space to dance. A small empty classroom would have been sufficient for her, but they were all in use during school hours and the dance studio would include a dance teacher who would inevitably tell her to get back to class, especially since Lyn wasn't even enrolled in any dance classes. Here, in the dark, she would be unnoticed. Free.

She placed her bags on the corner of the stage by the steps she had just climbed and grabbed her phone and earbuds out of her purse. She connected them, pressed play on her playlist and slid her phone into the back pocket of her jeans.

A slow pull on a stringed instrument met her ears. Her head filled with the sounds that Lindsey Sterling coaxed out of her violin and Lyn let everything else fade away. She made her way to the back of the stage stretching her arms, legs, and back in exaggerated movements to warm up her body as if she were the violin coming to life. When the first song faded into the second, Lyn's muscles were warm and her body took over while her mind fell into the music.

Lyn used a set play list. She had several that varied in length, and she always chose based on how much time she had. Today, she chose a forty-five minute set. It would be over in plenty of time to get to her next class. She didn't want anyone finding her in here or they'd know where to look for her the next time she cut class, and there would always be a next time. Going to school did not necessarily mean going to class.

School rules and parental deals faded as the music freed her from her worry and stress. The melody carried her away from this space and time as the strong beats gave her muscles a reason to exist, her brain a reason to chill, and her soul a reason to dance.

When the third song started, Lyn closed her eyes and checked out of reality altogether. She wasn't a body dancing on a stage. She was the music itself. No concentration, no counting to 4 or to 8, just Lyn, moving the way the music demanded.

Most of Lyn's playlists began with a warm up and ended with a cool down. Matching songs. Ending with the same song she started with helped ground Lyn and bring her focus back to the world around her. Lyn wasn't sure she'd stop unless the music did. Not until her legs gave way to jelly. Between the two bookend songs was a mix of genres. Instrumental and not, fast and slow, sometimes just a drum beat.

When the last song came on, the beat slowed her movements and Lyn opened her eyes. She allowed her muscles to cool and relax. She wouldn't stop until the last beats of the song died in her ears.

To Lyn, all music was a pulse to connect with. Even the rhythm of spoken words could lull Lyn into a meditative state. Maybe that's why she fell asleep in Science earlier. Mr. Ripley could easily be a professional reader if he ever tired of the drama of high school teaching.

As much as she hated the idea of it, Lyn felt that she was better able to sit in hard plastic chairs and listen to boring lectures now. Even though, that was the last thing she wanted to do. A promise was a promise.

When the song was over she removed her earbuds, stuck them in the front pocket of her jeans and gathered her things. She had to be out of the auditorium doors before the halls filled with students who could see where she had been.

When her foot touched the bottom of the stage steps, she heard a door close on the balcony. Her head flicked up, but there were no lights to tell her where the noise had come from.

Lyn ran up the side of the aisle and slid out of the door she had entered. Her heart pounded. Had someone been watching her? Who?

She stood in the hallway and looked at her phone. Five minutes until the bell rang. She decided to wait for the bell in the bathroom. She could easily explain her location away if she had to. But she hoped that who ever had closed that door wouldn't give her secret away.

CHAPTER NINE

reg was supposed to be in class, but when he saw Lyn sneak into the auditorium, he decided to take a detour to the balcony.

He sprinted around a different corner from Lyn and up the steps to the second level of the auditorium. He opened the door just enough to slip through and stood in complete darkness. Closing the door quietly behind him.

Dark vision was not a creature trait he possessed. Greg tried to remember the lay out of the space in front of him. He might heal quickly, but a fall over the balcony rail would likely still kill him, and any noise he made would definitely scare Lyn away.

If he remembered right. The door led to an aisle that divided the balcony into two sections. There should be steps and rows of seats in front of him. But he couldn't remember if there were two or three rows to the railing.

He inched a single foot away from the door and held out his hands to find the nearest seat back. Once he had that, he used his hands and feet to guide him down the short set of stairs to the front row of seats. *Three rows, then railing.* He made a mental note in case he ever needed to know again.

With his hand on the railing, he slowly and quietly opened up the chair nearest him and sat, just as a dim glow started from the stage.

He couldn't make out more than a faded twinkle of starlight in the darkness, but the grace of that starlight captivated him.

The music he couldn't hear came alive to his eyes in the way Lyn's light played across the stage.

When the music faded and Lyn's light twinkled out, Greg was thrust back into the darkness as if dropped down a deep dark well with a tight fitting lid.

He checked his watch. Greg hid the glow of his watch face in cupped hands below the level of the railing. "Shit," he whispered.

He reached his hand out for the stair rails and made his way back toward the door as quickly as he could. The door opened and closed louder than he would have liked, but he'd just lost 45 minutes and someone was going to notice.

CHAPTER TEN

*L*yn sat through the rest of her classes that day in a fugue. Umiko silently brushed Lyn's hair with her fingers during math. Lyn felt the tug of the tangles even if her mind wouldn't focus on the sensation or her friend.

Umiko had tried to talk to her at lunch. Lyn had listened and nodded appropriately, but part of her mind played through slightly different versions of her meeting with Ms. Sanchez later in the afternoon. The other part kept a steady beat for her pulse to follow. Umiko couldn't cut through either for very long.

~

*W*hen the last bell of the day rang, Lyn's nerves were tight strings ready to be plucked or more likely snapped. She waited for Umiko at her locker, oblivious to the push of students trying to get to their own lockers and off of school property.

"Go. You need to decompress," Umiko said when she

finally arrived. "I'll see you in about an hour. I have a swim team meeting."

Lyn thanked her friend and ran.

Dancing was better, but running was the next best thing.

Lyn dodged the lingering students in the hallway and jogged until she got to the school's fence line and out of range of teachers who would tell her to walk.

That fence was her cue. Lyn ran the rest of the way home.

She ran home and unlocked the door of her house. She wasn't ready to stop, instead she dropped her bags in the foyer before locking the door back. She avoided looking across the street to Ms. Evans house and took off for a quick loop around the neighborhood.

She ran down her street, around a corner and up Umiko's. Greg waved at her from his driveway as she passed his house on the way to the front of the skate park before she turned around to run her path in reverse.

When she got back to her house, she was barely straining her breath. She checked her watch. She considered doing the lap again, but she didn't have a lot of time left, Ms. CPS had a habit of being early.

She looked across the street at Ms. Evans yard. The nosy woman was nowhere in sight. Lyn let out a breath she didn't know she had been holding.

~

*L*yn finished the little homework she had just before the doorbell rang. She closed her laptop, kissed two of her finger tips and placed them on a picture of her mom that hung on the bulletin board above her desk. She stepped over piles of discarded clothes and other careless messes and raced down the stairs.

"Umiko!" Lyn opened the door to let her friend in, but it

was Ms. Sanchez, the CPS lady. "Sorry, I was expecting someone else."

"I did say I'd drop by. Is this a good time?" Ms. Sanchez asked and waited for Lyn to open the door wider.

"Sure, come in." Lyn stepped aside to allow Ms. Sanchez in and scanned the street for Umiko. She had hoped her friend would be here by now. It had been over an hour since Lyn had left her at school but there was no sign of her. As Lyn closed the front door, she noticed Ms. Evans standing across the street watering her bushes, again.

Those bushes should be water logged as often and they get drowned with that hose. Lyn thought to herself.

The so and so, as Umiko would say, smiled a crooked smile and Lyn closed the door without acknowledging it.

Lyn wished Umiko would hurry up. She looked past the CPS lady toward the backyard.

"Alright, I'll get right to it. I don't want to keep you from your evening plans. I remember how busy I was at sixteen," Ms. Sanchez said. She pulled a plastic protective report cover out of her brief case and handed it to Lyn. "Ms. Evans gave me this."

Lyn looked at the paper inside the protective sheet. Her knees threatened to buckle and she walked over to sit on the couch.

"Is that your mother's signature?" Ms. Sanchez took a seat in an arm chair near the couch.

Lyn moved her eyes to the only handwritten ink on the page. She traced the curly lines with her eyes as they filled with water. The peaks of the M, and light suggestion of a dot over the i. The large belly of the D, and the flourish at the end of the s. Lyn had seen her mom's signature many times before. She might not be a handwriting expert but she knew this was indeed her mother's signature. "She never told me." Lyn tried to read the letter through the tears building in her eyes.

It was dated March 10, two years ago.

Lyn thought back and remembered that her mother had had a lump removed from her breast around that time that she didn't tell Lyn about until after the results came back benign. Lyn remembered being angry that her mom didn't tell her, but secretly relived that she had missed the weeks of worry.

Lyn held the paper between her hands and thought her mother must have written this letter to soothe her own worries about what would happen if it was cancer.

She traced the signature with her eyes and realized her mother must not have thought her father would step up either.

Lyn tried to keep her tears to a trickle.

Instead of relying on her father, her mother had asked a stranger. Only, Lyn tried to be objective, Ms. Evans wasn't a stranger, and Maria Davis had trusted the nurse enough at the time to give her daughter's care over to her if she couldn't.

Tears flowed freely and Lyn closed her eyes as she tried and failed to stop them.

Ms. Sanchez handed Lyn a tissue and took the plastic sleeve. "I will take that as a yes. It looked legitimate to me as well." She said.

Lyn recognized the pity on the woman's face.

Lyn sniffed and wiped her eyes with the tissue. "It's two years old." Her voice sounded like a toddler on the verge of pitching a tantrum. She took a breath and tried to let go of the petulance. "I realize it's what my mom might have wanted at the time, but a lot changed in those two years. I don't think it's what my mom would have wanted now."

"That's fair," Ms. Sanchez said.

Lyn bristled at the soft words mixed with pity meant to placate her.

Ms. Sanchez continued, "If you can find instructions more recent, a will, even a hand written note, notarized and dated."

"That one isn't notarized." Lyn pointed out.

"True, it's not ideal, but it's what I have at the moment."

"So it'll stand unless I produce something better," Lyn countered. She heard the petulance in her voice and didn't care.

Ms. Sanchez nodded. "Or a blood relative. Did you contact your father yet?"

Lyn shook her head. "My best friend and I were going to do that today. I thought the doorbell was her."

Ms. Sanchez nodded. "Since you are staying with Ms. Clare for the time being and since it's almost quitting time on a Friday. I can give you 48 hours." She smiled. "I try to avoid working on weekends, whenever possible." Ms. Sanchez winked and stood. "But, if you need me, call. Otherwise, I will see you Monday after school."

Lyn stood and walked Ms. Sanchez to the door. "Thank you," Lyn said.

"You're welcome, Lyn. I hope you find what you are looking for."

Lyn opened the door wide and stood behind it to avoid seeing Ms. Evans.

Ms. Sanchez stepped onto the porch. "I'm serious, if you need anything, please call." She offered her hand.

Lyn took it out of reflex. "48 hours," Lyn said.

"48 hours," Ms. Sanchez repeated and let go of Lyn's hand. She stepped from the porch steps onto the sidewalk.

"Lyn!" Umiko called from the back patio door.

Lyn closed and locked the front door. "In here." She called and tried to refresh her damp face with another tissue.

"Did she come yet? I tried to get here sooner, but the meeting ran long. I managed to do my homework while coach talked, but my mom wanted to talk when I got home. She wanted to ask me more questions about Clark and my date. What is he like? Have I met his parents?" Umiko met Lyn in the living room, a bag slung over her shoulder. She put the bag on the couch. "I thought she'd never let me leave."

"The CPS woman just left."

She looked at Lyn. "I'm sorry I wasn't here. What did she say?" Umiko closed the distance and wrapped her friend in a hug.

Lyn cried. She couldn't hold the tears back from her friend this time. Lyn lifted her chin to speak over Umiko's shoulder. "Pretty much that I need to find good old sperm donor dad, or live with the gossipy moth ball lady." Lyn pulled back and wiped her nose with the already wet tissue.

Umiko reached for the tissue box. "Does she really smell like moth balls?" Umiko held the box out for Lyn.

Lyn let out a struggled giggle and grabbed a fresh tissue to wipe her eyes.

"I didn't think she was that old," Umiko continued.

"She's not, but she does smell funny," Lyn shook her head, "and I still don't want her being able to tell me what to do." Lyn made fists and shoved her hands into her pockets as far as they would go, which wasn't far. "She's not my mom."

"I know, both options suck, but let's dwell later. We need to look for clues." Umiko rubbed her hands together like a child choosing candy from a wall of colorful candy bins.

"You'll need to get ready for your date soon," Lyn said.

"Actually," Umiko said drawing out the word. "I asked Clark to meet me here. He's bringing pizza at six."

Lyn cocked her head. "Okay?"

"It's cool, you'll like him."

Lyn smiled at her friend. Umiko was a force when she had a mission, and Lyn's missions always became bigger when Umiko took over. This one was no exception. Especially since it had to do with dads. Umiko's personal obsession. Only second to her obsession over Lyn's creature type.

"Let's get started." Umiko took charge without waiting for a reply.

Lyn's shoulders sagged and she pulled in a deep breath. She grabbed a dry tissue and wiped away the moisture from her face. She took another deep breath and looked at her friend.

"Better than moth balls." Umiko cheered.

Lyn forced a smile and straightened her spine. She stepped toward the office door. "I guess we can start in here." Lyn opened the double doors into her mom's office.

CHAPTER ELEVEN

*L*yn and Umiko stepped into the office. It was situated at the base of the stairs next to the living room. The original floor plan labeled it as a formal dinning room, but you had to walk through the living room to get there from the kitchen.

Lyn and her mom always ate in the kitchen, so they turned this oddly placed formal dining room into an office.

One that looked like a picture in a design magazine. It was pristine, like no one worked here. Ever. Her mother kept the space tidy and it was the one room in the house that Lyn's stuff didn't spill into. Keeping the door closed helped, as did the fact that Lyn had no reason to use it since her mom died, until now.

The desk top, big enough for her and her mom to work facing each other, was clear. The shelves that lined the longest wall were clutter free. The books were lined up along the front edge of the shelf and alphabetized.

"Wow. I forgot how organized your mom was. This should go quickly." Umiko sat at the desk chair on one side of the T shaped desk. Lyn's mother's side.

Lyn watched her friend and wished she was looking at her

mom instead. She sat in her chair and thought about the last time she and her mother had sat in the office.

A month ago, maybe? They had been meal planning. They found a new recipe to try and scheduled it for a Wednesday, her mom's day off. It had gone horribly wrong and they had ended up ordering Chinese from the place across from the park instead.

Umiko started opening drawers, while Lyn sat frozen in memories. This is where Lyn would do her homework while her mom would pay bills and plan meals and shopping trips. This was command central for the life she and her mom managed together.

Lyn brushed away another tear. She would have to manage everything alone now. Or be forced to eat TV dinners and the souls of small children, like Ms. Evans.

"Lyn, are you gonna start looking?" Umiko asked as she flipped through a drawer of green hanging files.

"What?" Lyn shook her head and tried to focus on her task. "Sorry."

"What were you thinking about?" Umiko moved a section of folders so she could look through the ones behind.

"The souls of small children," Lyn answered, straight faced and without thinking.

Umiko froze, her fingers between file folders. She looked at Lyn. Her eyes scrunched up as if she were trying to figure out if Lyn was telling the truth.

Umiko speechless was a rare thing and Lyn took a moment to enjoy it before clarifying. Not wanting soul eating to be on Umiko's list of Lyn's imaginary creature traits.

"Who's going to plan meals and buy groceries?" Lyn amended.

"Ms. Evans if you don't start looking for a will or your birth certificate. You should probably pull out anything that looks important too, insurance papers, bank statements."

Lyn sat back with her hands on either side of her head.

"One problem at a time, please. I know it needs to get done, but..."

"It's overwhelming. I get it," Umiko interrupted. "We can get my mom to help with the money part. Just look for your birth certificate and your mom's will."

Lyn took a deep breath and opened a drawer. Pens, post-its, paper clips. She opened two more drawers with various office supplies before she found one with hanging files. Lyn thumbed through files marked for cable, phone, electricity, bank, insurance, mortgage. Lyn told Umiko and moved to the next drawer when she didn't see anything labeled 'birth certificate' or 'what to do with Lyn when her world falls apart.'

Umiko found old tax returns and investment statements.

Twenty minutes later, they had gone through everything in the office and found out that the life insurance policy was current and that Lyn was probably taken care of for at least a few years but did not find out anything about Lyn's dad or plans for Lyn's guardianship.

"Next." Umiko closed the door on the last cabinet and stood up.

It was Lyn's turn to look at Umiko blankly. There wasn't a next. They had been through all the files, the bookshelves just held books and a few old art projects from Lyn's younger years.

"Where would your mom keep your baby things? Ooh, or a wedding album? He's got to be in there, right?"

"I don't know." Lyn shrugged and shook her head.

"Mine keeps a box for my brother and I in her closet," Umiko said. "Let's try your mom's."

Lyn stood up slowly and followed Umiko out of the room. Lyn took one slow step to Umiko's two excited ones up the stairs. Lyn envied the ease it was for Umiko. To Lyn, this task was daunting and scary. She wouldn't be able to do it, if not for her friend pushing her.

Lyn knew Umiko was on the hunt for Lyn's father because she had no idea how to find her own, or if she would even be able to before this seven year cycle was up. Would Lyn be able to help her friend if their roles were reversed? She hoped so.

When they got upstairs, Umiko stood facing Lyn's mom's closed bedroom door and put her hand around the handle. "This is weird for you, huh?" She asked Lyn.

"Very."

"Have you been in here yet?" Umiko turned the handle.

"Yeah, I slept in here a couple of nights when I wasn't at the hospital. The fold out couches in the hospital are far from comfortable. There was a nurse that worked there that said he'd stay with her while I came home for a shower and a night's rest. I took him up on it only twice, when I knew I didn't smell all that good." Lyn nodded at her to go inside. "I meant to shower and go back to the hospital, but I crashed in her bed instead." Lyn left off the fact that she cried herself to sleep both nights and countless other nights.

Lyn heard a faint buzzing sound.

Umiko pushed open the door. "One second." Umiko pulled her phone out of her pocket and checked the screen. "It's Clark. I should take it."

Lyn waved her off and stepped into her mother's room.

Umiko went into Lyn's room across the hall, with the phone to her ear. "Hi." Lyn heard her say before she turned her focus to her task.

CHAPTER TWELVE

*L*yn stepped away from the door and into her mother's room.

The sheets were still rumpled on her mother's queen sized bed from the last time Lyn slept here. Without her mom.

Lyn walked over and pulled the sheets straight and comforter up. She never made her own bed, even though her mother taught her how. She just never felt like it mattered and having the sheet tucked in when she slept was frustrating.

She and her mom had, on several occasions, fallen asleep watching movies together and Lyn always had to untuck her side of the sheet before she could get comfortable.Lyn picked up her mom's pillow and held it to her nose. She took a deep breath. It smelled better than any of Lyn's own pillows because it smelled like her mother, like love and safety. Popcorn and late night movies. She'd slept in this bed twice since her mom died. Both times she had cried herself to sleep. But it was too big and sleeping there just made her realize what was missing. She took another breath of her mom.

She dreaded the day she would need to wash theses

pillow cases. Lyn tucked the comforter over the now fluffed pillow and wiped her hand under her damp eyes.

Lyn picked up an oversized hoodie that was draped on the bench at the foot of the bed. It smelled the same as the pillows, including the buttery smell of movie theater popcorn. Nothing had been cleaned since their last movie in bed.

Lyn put the hoodie on and wrapped her arms around her chest, pretending that it was her mom's hug. She stood there for a moment, then pulled the fabric to her nose and took a deep breath of safety to use as a shield against her grief.

The few times Lyn had been in her mother's room since her death, she treated it like a sanctuary. Besides the bed and the closet, Lyn had cherished the space and left them as her mother had.

This time, Lyn was coming in to snoop for secrets. A clear desecration of the shrine she had created.

My mom would understand. Lyn thought to herself and allowed the scent of her mom's hoodie to steel her nerves. She repeated the statement two more times until the words sank in and the tension in her neck lessened.

Years ago, when Lyn was much younger and more naive, she wished that her father would reach out to her, but he never did so she stopped wishing. From then on, Lyn told herself that she wasn't going to reach out to a man, who obviously hated her, unless she had to.

Now, she had to. Lyn knew he wasn't the answer that she wanted, but she thought he might be the answer she needed, for now. He was the best person to stand between her and a woman that ate babies slathered in jam and dunked in tea.

Lyn knew she was being dramatic but she didn't care. She wanted another way. A way to get what she needed without involving a man that didn't care about her. For all she knew, the man kicked kittens.

She walked to her mother's closet and opened the door before she chickened out.

The closet was a mess. At odds with the neat habits of Lyn's mother. Clothes once hung on hangers, and now, after Lyn had pillaged a few over the past weeks, they hung at odd angles, if at all. Among the fallen clothes on the floor and above the hangers on a shelf were cardboard boxes, all unlabeled from what Lyn could see.

Lyn picked up a few fallen articles of clothing. She hung a black dress, a pair of black pants, and a few blouses in varying muted colors beside the boring selection of nursing scrubs. When there was no more clothing in the way, she slid out the boxes from the floor.

She opened the first and it burst with sweaters as if they could no longer be contained by a folded over cardboard top. Beneath the freed sweaters were more out of season clothing and shoes. She inspected two more boxes, and found warm hats and hand knit scarves. Clothing that was rarely called for in the warmth of what passed for winter in Texas. She shoved all the inspected boxes back underneath the hanging clothes and made sure the stack looked as neat as her mom had left it.

When she had finished the floor boxes, Lyn reached up and pulled a box down from the shelf. She opened a cardboard boot box just to confirm it was just shoes, she was glad she did. Instead of boots, she found jewelry and letters. She stepped over to the bed, box in hand.

Lyn pulled out a bundle of letters. She unwrapped the rubber band and flipped though them. The whole stack was to and from a J. Davis. They had to be between her mom and her mom's husband. The postmarks ranged from nearly twenty years ago to before she was born.

The next stack was more recent and only contained from J. Davis. *He still wrote her.* Lyn sat beside the box, the letters in her hands. *And she didn't throw them away.*

Lyn examined the tops of the envelopes. Her mother always opened letters from the top, bills too. She had a fancy letter opener on her desk in the corner that she would use to avoid the imminent paper cuts that came with sliding thin finger flesh underneath stiff paper edges. Lyn glanced over at the desk. The letter opener was laying to the side of the desk blotter, exactly where her mom had left it.

Frayed tops denoted a few opened letters among the oldest envelopes in Lyn's hands, while the most recent ones were still sealed. She doubted they held anything she wanted to read right now, but she chose one of the torn envelopes and slid out the pages. She flipped to the end of the last page, ignoring the bulk of the words, and looked for a signature. It was signed with a J. She folded the pages and put the letter back. She retrieved a second. It was also signed with a J.

She needed more than an initial. She tried a third and a fourth. All signed with the same stark J. She let her eyes skim the words of the open letter, but quickly folded the pages before her mind could comprehend anything.

One day, Lyn might be brave enough to read the letters between her parents. To learn a bit about their life together. But today, that rabbit hole gaped at her and it was an unknown that she was not ready to face. She bundled the letters and put them back into the boot box with the various jewelry boxes and bags. She flipped the lid closed and slid the box to the end of the bed.

The next box she pulled down from the shelf was a white bankers box. The lid was labeled on the top with black permanent marker. The faint acrid smell still lingered. 'Baby R.' She creased her brow. *Who is R?*

She took the box to the bed and sat beside it. She lifted off the cardboard lid and pulled out a blue knit blanket. She brought it to her nose and sniffed, then forced it away and held it at arm's length.

It smelled horrible. Like dust and old wool, misery and pain. She took a clean breath, then held it while she folded the cloth and placed in on top of the box lid. The corner was embroidered with a cursive R. Puzzled, she released her breath and continued into the box. The box held boy items. Well kept, baby boy items. A blue rattle. Tiny sneakers wrapped in tissue paper. Socks with dinosaurs on them. She placed each item on top of the blanket belonging to a boy whose named must have started with the letter R. In the bottom of the box was a thin 8x8 scrapbook.

Lyn removed the book and held it in her lap. The cover was a pale blue with a window cut out of it. A black and white picture framed in the center. She could just make out the shape of a baby head in the lines of the sonogram photo.

She opened the cover and peeled apart the first plastic covered pages, sticky with time. She picked up a small piece of yellowed paper folded in thirds. Wrapped inside was a small square sonogram picture with an arrow and a smiling face pointing at what was presumably the boy parts of a fetus. She set it aside and looked at the old paper. She held a letter addressed to 'Richie, my sweet baby boy,' in her mother's handwriting. Lyn's heart sank. A brother?

Lyn's eyes dampened as she read the letter. Her parents had been happily expecting a baby boy three years before she was born. Lyn had an older brother? She folded the letter back into thirds and flipped through the rest of the book. There were no pictures. Except for the sonograms, the book was empty. She looked back over the selection of boy items. The socks were still clipped together with a tiny piece of plastic, meant to keep them as a pair. The sneaker's white soles were pristine. Her older brother, Richie, had never used any of it.

Her mother had never spoken of a previous pregnancy and Lyn wondered why.

But she kept finding things she and her mother never talked about. Her father, a breast cancer scare, and now a miscarriage. Lyn thought they talked about everything, shared all their secrets, but Lyn realized she was the one doing most of the sharing, with her mother's encouragement.

This memory must have been too horrible for her mother to share. A sad memory best left in a box in the closet.

Lyn would respect that. She packed the box back with care, placing each item in the same spot her mother had. Laying the blanket on top. The embroidered 'R' facing up this time.

She closed the box on this painful secret and apologized to her mother and the universe for opening old wounds. She went to put the box back on the shelf, but it didn't slide easily in. Something was blocking the box.

She stood on her toes and reached to the back of the shelf. Her fingers grazed an envelope and she managed to pull it forward with her finger nails after a few moments of scratching.

She tossed the envelope to the bed and replaced Richie's baby box. She grabbed the next box off the shelf. Lyn set an identical bankers box on the bed and noticed that there was a thick black letter L on the top which smelled more strongly that the last. More recent.

Lyn's box held a pink knit blanket with an embroidered 'L.' After the horrid smell of the blue blanket, she took a tentative sniff and quickly turned her head. But it smelled like baby powder. She took a deeper breath of the relic. Baby powder and hope and something else. Something she couldn't place. She folded it and placed it to the side to pull out more items. A pink rattle with a slight crack in the handle. Tiny ballet slippers with stained brown soles. Lyn noted that there was no plastic tab to hold these together. She unpacked the pieces of her babyhood that had meant the most to her mother and reached for the baby book on the bottom of her box.

The thick pink scrapbook had a similar black and white sonogram picture of a baby head in the window of the front cover. It was nearly identical to the one in the blue baby book. She opened the cover and peeled apart the first pages. A piece of lined paper, less yellow than the letter to her brother, lay between the pages.

Lyn read her mother's hopes and fears. A tear fell down Lyn's cheek. A second followed and a torrent was unleashed. A drop fell on her mother's neat handwriting and a bloom of ink unfolded. She blotted the ink splash off on her jeans and put the letter away. Through the ebb and flow of her tears she flipped through the pages of her baby book.

The first picture showed a happy, exhausted mom, and a fresh born baby in need of her first bath. The bathed baby in the second picture was less pink, almost white. Lyn rubbed the baby's flat cheek and wondered how she survived if she looked near death in this photo. How bad was the anemia if the pink had faded within what might have been only minutes? Her finger felt a ridge in the page that didn't fit with the page itself or the next.

Lyn tilted the book up to look at the top edge. The scrapbook paper was sandwiched, two sheets inside of the plastic covering, but something was tucked between the sheets.

Lyn removed a legal sized envelope. It was addressed to her mom at this address from 'The State Department of Health'. She separated the torn top edges and slid the contents of the envelope into her hand.

She unfolded a blue certified copy of her birth certificate and read: Lyn Michelle Davis, Female. She skimmed the page looking for her parents' names. She found them half way down the form. Maria Lee Davis, mother. Jonathan Michael Davis, father.

This was it. This is what Lyn needed to find. Jonathan Michael Davis was the name of her father. She put the paper back in the envelope and slipped it under her thigh. She picked up the baby book and flipped through the rest of the pages.

The mom in the pictures never wavered in her happiness

and the baby looked more healthy in each set of photos. She was born with pale blonde hair, almost white. That darkened over her first year.

The last pages in the book were devoted to Lyn's first birthday. A pale Lyn with cake and icing smeared across her face smiled at the camera. Her eyes were darker than Lyn's eyes now.

Lyn furrowed her brow. She flipped backwards through the pages looking for someone. When she got to the pale white haired baby at the beginning, she realized that there was not a single photo of a man.

"Clark is ordering the pizzas now and will be here in twenty-five minutes." Umiko came into the room. "What did you find?"

Lyn handed Umiko the book. Umiko sat on the other side of the bed and flipped through the pages.

Umiko turned one page and squinted at each photo before moving on to the next.

"I can see the anemia. You were so pale. Almost..." Umiko paused and glanced at Lyn.

"I am not a vampire," Lyn interrupted.

"Half vampire?" Umiko smiled a teasing smile.

"Whatever I am," Lyn paused. When had she started thinking that she was anything besides human? When had Umiko's creature theory taken hold in her own head?

"Yes?" Umiko asked grinning like the cheshire cat pleased with her shenanigans.

Lyn sighed and continued. "If I am something, I think it comes from my dad's side." Lyn nodded at the book.

"Why?" Umiko examined the photos on this page and turned to the next.

"Because he's not in any of the pictures."

"Vampire!" Umiko yelled triumphant.

"I take it back, I'm not a thing. I'm human. I look human, I sound human. I have no reason to think otherwise.

Can you stop with the vampire obsession now?" Lyn begged.

Umiko looked back at the book. She flipped back a few pages, keeping her place with her other hand. She returned to her spot and flipped forward.

"I knew it. We just need to find your dad and we solve two problems at once," Umiko said as if it was going to be the easiest thing in the world to find a man that Lyn had no memories of. "Did you find your birth certificate?"

Lyn handed her the envelope from the Department of Health.

Umiko slid the document out. "BINGO!" she said as she unfolded the paper. "Jonathan Michel Davis. Maybe he's a contact in your mom's phone? Do you know where that is?"

"One of my mom's friends dropped off a box of her things from the hospital. It's in the garage. I haven't gone through it." Lyn still didn't want to go through it. She imagined a list of missed calls from people wandering where her mother was and she dreaded all the people she'd be expected notify. "The battery has to be dead by now."

Umiko slid the paper back into the envelope and picked up the book. "Anything else up here that will help?" She looked at Lyn. "Her laptop? Does she keep a date book?"

"It's all on her laptop." Lyn pointed to a silver rectangle plugged into the charger on her mom's writing desk.

"Down we go then. Want me to help put this stuff back in the closet?" Umiko walked over and unplugged the laptop before adding it to the pile in her hands.

Lyn shook her head.

"Okay, I'll meet you down stairs." Umiko left Lyn with her few baby things and the shadow of her mom and dad.

Lyn packed her baby box back how she had found it, minus the scrapbook. She laid the 'L' blanket on top and closed the lid. She put it back on the shelf along with the boot box filled with letters and the manilla envelope with her mother's name on the front and the letters P. I. I. on top left corner.

"I'll be in the office," Umiko called from below.

She closed the closet door, apologized again to the universe for snooping and closed her mother's bedroom door.

CHAPTER THIRTEEN

"Hey, Greg. Do you have plans for tonight?" Clark asked through his open car window.

Greg wiped his greasy hands on a red shop cloth. "No." He stepped closer to the rusted red and white classic mustang.

"Great." Clark reached into his back pocket and pulled out his wallet. The chain jangled as he opened the folds. He handed Greg two twenty dollar bills. "I need to run an errand. Can you wait for the pizza guy? He should be at my house in about 10 or 15 minutes." He pointed to a house down the street. "1895, with the blue door. What kind of soda do you like?"

"What?" Greg looked at the bills in his hand. He barely knew Clark, but the guy just handed him $40 in cash.

"Root beer, cream soda, other? Nevermind, I'll just get a selection. I don't know what the girls like anyway."

"Girls?" Greg's brow furrowed and he looked at Clark.

Clark smiled.

Greg noted a hint of mischief in the older boy's eyes.

"Umiko and Lyn. We're supposed to be there at six."

Greg stood at the end of his driveway and stared at Clark, speechless.

"It's time to step up, man. Turn your knight in shining armor facade to PI for hire. Well, maybe not 'the hire' part. That wouldn't win over a girl."

"What are you talking about?" Greg asked.

"Later. You wait for the pizza. Maybe change shirts. That one has a…" Clark pointed to a black streak of grease down the side. "I'll be back as fast as I can with sodas."

Greg watched as the car turned off the street. He shoved the money into his front pocket and wondered what Clark was talking about.

~

Ten minutes later, Greg was sitting on the front steps at Clark's house in a clean white T-shirt when the pizza guy drove up.

"Are you Greg?" The pizza guy asked from the front curb.

"Yes," Greg said as he walked to meet the guy on the sidewalk.

"Cool. Here's your order." The guy handed over 3 pizzas from a warming bag.

Greg didn't question the order being in his name. It was already strange that a senior he barely knew had trusted him with a ludicrous task. He just handed over the cash Clark had given him and accepted the warm boxes.

"Thanks for the tip, man!"

"Sure." Greg held the three boxes as he walked back to the porch. "Hey, how did you know I was Greg?"

"Clark told me you'd be waiting for them. If you weren't, I was supposed to go to 1907 to deliver. Says so on the box."

Greg recognized his house number. "That wasn't odd to you?"

"Clark's a regular and it's not like it's out of my way. It's just a few houses down. Plus, he tips well." The guy waved the folded bills in the air.

The pizza guy stepped back into his car as Clark drove up the street.

"Thanks, Billy."

"Night, Clark!" The pizza guy waved out the open window as he drove away.

"You told him I'd be waiting? How did you know I would accept?" Greg asked.

"I said the magic word." Greg noticed the mischief in the boy's face.

"What's that?"

"Lyn."

Greg felt his cheeks flush.

miko sat in Lyn's mother's office chair, the laptop open in front of her. The baby book and the envelope from the Department of Health lay on the desk in front of Lyn's chair.

"Clark should be here soon. He's bringing pizza and sodas. Do you have paper plates? Napkins?" Umiko stepped around Lyn to go into the kitchen.

"Top shelf of the pantry in a plastic box," Lyn said to her back. She stepped to the desk and ran her index finger along the curve of the sonogram baby's head. Lyn heard the sounds of the computer booting up.

"I see it. Do you have a stool?" Umiko called.

Lyn went into the kitchen to help her friend prepare for what suddenly struck Lyn as a third wheel type of situation.

"You can still go on your date, we found his name, we can track him down tomorrow." Lyn tried to get out of the awkward evening Umiko had planned. She got the plastic box down from the shelf by standing on her tip toes. She handed the box to Umiko.

"No way!" Umiko exclaimed. "This is exciting, and we have a deadline. 48 hours, remember?" Umiko opened the bin and pulled out several paper plates before handing the box back. "We shouldn't waste time."

"Technically, since it's Friday night, the 48 hours starts tomorrow. We have extra time. Time you can use for your date." Lyn put the box back on the shelf and closed the pantry door.

Lyn knew her friend wouldn't budge. Events were set in motion and Umiko was the tide pulling Lyn, and anyone else that got close, along with her. But she tried anyway. "It's your first date."

Umiko smiled. "Nice try. Password?" She walked out of the kitchen and Lyn followed.

When they got to the office, Lyn typed in her mother's password and let Umiko sit at the computer.

Lyn wondered away from her best friend's clicking and typing and out of the office.

Lyn was moments away from talking to her father on the phone. Maybe a text would be easier? Email? She needed to sit down. She half sat, half fell onto the couch. She contemplated putting her head between her knees like they tell you to do when you are hyperventilating or, as Lyn mused, in a plane crash. Lyn hoped this wasn't about to be a plane crash. She tilted her head down toward her lap when she heard metal on metal, culminating in a crunch.

She steadied herself with a deep breath and stood back up. She walked to the office door. Umiko, who was focused on the computer screen, didn't seem to notice Lyn or the sound of the car door.

"I think Clark is here." Lyn tried to get Umiko's attention.

"Great," Umiko said but didn't look up from the screen. "Can you let him in?"

"Don't you think you should? It's your date." Lyn put her hand on her hip and cocked her head to the side.

"Thanks!" Umiko said. The click clack of the keyboard continued.

Lyn heard more metal on metal followed by a crunch as a second car door slammed.

Lyn knew Umiko was too focused to hear her words. "I'll just let an axe murderer or two in now, shall I?"

Umiko made a vague noise of agreement. Lyn sighed and turned to walk to the door.

She opened it as two guys climbed the porch steps.

"Hey, Lyn." The lead guy, whom she decided must be Clark, extended his free hand.

Lyn took the offered hand. "Hey. You look familiar. Have we met?" She held his hand a moment, before letting it go. She tried to place his face in her recent memories, to no avail.

Clark looked at her. "We have." He lifted a divided cardboard box of bottled soda.

Lyn took his hint. "Umiko is in the office, but we'll put the food in the kitchen. Can I grab anything?"

"No, we have it covered. You know Greg, right?" Clark stepped past her and the second boy shuffled the pizza boxes to one hand.

Greg waved a quick wave and put his hand back on top of the stack of boxes before they toppled to the porch floor.

"Sure. The school knight." Lyn smiled and watched faint color surface on the boy's cheeks. "Come in. Umiko and the office are on your left. The kitchen is through the living room."

Greg wiped his feet on the mat and stepped into the house. He looked like he wasn't sure he should be here. "Clark said that Umiko said you were looking for your bio dad."

"Of course, she did," Lyn mumbled to herself. She closed and locked the door behind him.

The smell of warm pepperoni and melted cheese made Lyn's mouth water. She led Greg to the kitchen.

Clark set the selection of sodas on the counter and Greg

placed the pizza boxes on the stove top after confirming that the heat was off and there would be no fire.

"Mind if I rummage for glasses and ice?" Clark asked.

"Go for it. Cabinet by the fridge, middle shelf." Lyn pointed. "I'm still trying to figure out where I know you from?" She narrowed her eyes at his face.

"School?" Greg offered. "Clark is a senior. You've probably seen him around." He opened the first pizza lid. "He sometimes volunteers in the nurse's office during his free time."

"That's not it." She shook her head. "I feel like we've talked before."

Clark found the glasses and pulled down four. Lyn picked one up and filled it with ice from the refrigerator door as she examined the older boy. His face was familiar, the cut of his jaw, his pronounced cheekbones. His hair and clothing was not.

Jeans and a navy T-shirt with some logo on the front pocket that Lyn didn't bother reading.

Clark took a moment to pull his straight black hair back into a low pony tail with a black elastic from his wrist. "I worked at the hospital over the summer." He looked at her with his hair back.

"That's it. You were the guy that told me to go home and take a shower," Lyn said. "I knew you looked familiar."

"I hope I said it more tactful than that." Clark smiled.

"Thanks," Lyn said and busied herself filling glasses with ice.

"For being tactful?" Clark asked.

"For never looking at me with pity. For telling me to take care of myself when I was only focused on my mom." Lyn filled the last glass but didn't turn away from the fridge. "For being there so I knew she wasn't alone." She fought off the burn of impending tears.

"You're welcome." Clark took the glass from her. "I liked

her. She talked about you all the time." He chose a soda from a matching pair and poured it into a glass. "I feel like we are already friends."

"He does that a lot," Greg chimed in.

Lyn's cheeks reddened. She watched as the soda bubbles threatened to flow over the rim of the glass, but they burst and settled instead. She counted to four, forcing the tears in her eyes to not overflow and her nerves to settle. *No losing it in front of cute guys.*

"I was overwhelmed my first day at the hospital," Clark continued. "So many people rushing around. They mostly avoided me. Your mom treated me like I was more than just an intern."

"You were a candy striper?" Greg asked.

Lyn wiped her eyes while no one was watching.

"We can't all be Wonder Woman." Clark said, looking at Greg with his eyebrows lifted. "And I rocked that pink and white stripped apron."

He and Greg laughed and Lyn managed to put her sadness in a box for later.

"I didn't know what type of soda everyone liked, so I picked a few. Help yourselves," Clark said.

Lyn picked a cream soda. Greg grabbed a root beer.

"Umiko will want the cherry." Lyn pointed.

"Thanks," Clark said and twisted open the cap. He poured the cherry soda into the glass, adding more when the bubbles died. "Sorry they aren't cold already. Plans changed quickly this afternoon."

"Sorry about that. Umiko didn't tell me she had changed anything until after she had already talked to you. I would have tried to talk her out of it." Lyn struggled to open her bottle. She picked up the hem of her shirt to use to keep her hand from getting cut.

"Let me." Greg held out his hand for her bottle.

She handed it to him and he twisted the lid off with one smooth motion. "Trash can?" He asked.

Lyn pointed to the corner next to the breakfast table and the windows to the back yard. She turned back to Clark. "You two can still go out. My stuff can wait." She made the offer before she realized that if Umiko and Clark left, she would be alone with Greg. She wondered how Umiko had managed to set her up so completely.

"I found him," Umiko said and walked into the room. "We have a name, a phone number, and an address. Oh, hi Greg. I didn't know you were coming."

Lyn noted that she sounded sincere.

"It was a last minute thing. Clark needed someone to hold the pizza apparently."

All eyes turned to Clark. He was sipping from his glass.

"Greg has some special skills I thought might come in handy for a manhunt." Clark handed Umiko a glass and she took a sip.

"Cherry, my favorite. How did you know?" She smiled at the older boy.

"A little bird told me." Clark winked at Lyn. "The pizza smells delicious. I'm starving." Clark grabbed two paper plates from the counter and handed one to Umiko.

Greg handed Lyn a plate and introduced her dinning options. "We have pepperoni, for the purists. Mushrooms and bell pepper for the vegetarians. And, my personal favorite, a meat trio with sausage, bacon, and ham."

Lyn took one of each and sat in her spot at the breakfast table. Umiko took two slices of the vegetable pizza and sat across from her. The boys filled in the other two seats with their plates piled high with pizza. Clark had vegetarian slices. Greg, meat.

They ate while Umiko summed up Lyn's situation. "Long story, short, we need to talk to Lyn's bio dad. This weekend.

It's important." It was, by no accounts, the whole story, but it was enough. "You in?"

Clark and Greg nodded. Lyn shouldn't have been surprised. Umiko was a leader that people jumped to follow, no questions asked.

Lyn was getting more comfortable being the center of attention since the accident but it still felt weird to her. She preferred the fringe. Being just on the edge of life, where the only three people who noticed her were her mom, her best friend, and the school bully. And she would gladly fade away from the bully's attention, given half a chance.

CHAPTER FIFTEEN

After they ate, the group moved to the living room. Umiko and Clark shared the couch, sitting close, but not touching. Lyn and Greg sat across from each other in the chairs. Lyn put her bare feet on the coffee table.

"So, let's call the number," Greg said when everyone was seated. "What's the worst that can happen?"

Lyn blanched, if it was possible to be paler than her normal skin color, she imagined she was. She started a list of worst things in her head. *He could not know who I am. He could know who I am and not care. He could know who I am and tell me he never wanted anything to do with me, ever. He could hang up.* And that was just what he could do. She could also make a list of how she could screw it up. *I could come across as whiney, or needy, or just after his money. I could trip over my words and make him think I'm dumb. I could become mute as soon as he picks up the phone.*

She looked around at the faces staring at her. She wanted to melt into the background and hide, but there was no background in the center of attention.

Lyn squirmed in her seat. She missed the anonymity of the fringe. Umiko looked at Lyn and cocked her head, her eyes prodding Lyn to answer Greg's question. Clark was looking down at his hand on the couch cushion, centimeters from Umiko's.

When she finally turned to Greg, he smiled at her. Lyn's breath caught in her chest.

Greg handed Umiko his phone. "Put the number in. I'll make the call."

Lyn struggled for another breath.

Lyn knew she had never been in control of her life. She had let her mom guide most her decisions. Umiko ran with the rest, and Lyn was happy for both. She found it easier to let other people lead. The back seat was safer than the front.

But these were two new people. She supposed, she has already given Clark unspoken permission to tell her what to do at the hospital. And sure, she let Greg fight her battles for her at school. But why did these two guys even care?

Lyn took a deep breath and tried to settle her mind and the butterflies in her stomach. Even with her reservations about his motives, she was thankful that Greg offered and wondered how much of her nerves he had read in her face. She didn't think she was as open a book as Umiko. But in this instance, she was sure she was wrong. She was certain her anxiety showed like a billboard across her face. This whole finding her bio dad thing was going too fast for her. She didn't like talking on the phone under normal circumstances. Calling to reschedule a dentist appointment made her twitch. A call that would have to begin, 'Hello, I'm the daughter you didn't like enough to stick around,' sounded like psychological torture. She'd rather be bullied.

Lyn shook her head. That was a lie. Making this phone call was not worse than being bullied. Though she felt the same vulnerability and no way out that she faced every day at school. She felt the same compulsion to be small and fade away.

Lyn pulled her feet off the table and planted them on the

floor. She looked around at the people in her living room. This ragtag group of what? Friends? No one was looking at her. They all looked at the phone in Umiko's hand. The phone that Lyn imagined exploding like a bomb in all their faces, while the person on the other end didn't care.

Lyn watched, her eyes stuck to the phone like everyone else's as Umiko dialed the number and handed the device to Greg.

Lyn hummed to herself and pressed her back into the chair to stop the tremble that was building inside her. The rhythm in her head barely calmed the need to run and hide. She slid a hand, palm down, under each of her thighs. Her fingers flexed underneath her, keeping beat in the plush cushions.

Lyn watched Greg's face as he listened to the ring tone. The silence in the room continued. The only noise Lyn heard was the sound of the tone. It filled the space of her ears and grew in pitch, threatening to overwhelm her. She combined it with the rhythm in her head and fingers, and gave it a purpose other than making her nervous. A third trill of signal and she moved her hands to her lap to kept beat on her wrist.

A fourth trill and an automated voice clicked on. "Dead end." Greg cut off the robotic voice mid sentence and placed his phone on the coffee table.

Lyn stared at the unexploded bomb and forced the air from her lungs. She took in a new breath and slowed the rhythm on her wrist and in her head.

"Anyone want anything from the kitchen?" Clark stood next to Lyn.

Lyn pulled her legs up into her seat to let him pass and decided to use them as armor. She pulled her legs closer and wrapped her arms around them.

No answer at all. Lyn tried to think if she had put that in her worst things that could happen list. She didn't think so, and decided it didn't belong there anyway. No answer could mean a lot of things. He's out of the house. He didn't pay his bill. It could have nothing to do with Lyn at all. There's no way her bio dad, a stranger to her, could be screening her calls. It wasn't even her phone number that showed up on the caller ID. It was Greg's.

"Water, please?" Umiko asked. "For Lyn, too."

"Sure." Clark bent down to pick up the girls' empty glasses. "Greg?"

"I'm good." Greg turned to Umiko. "You said you had an address?"

"Yeah. The laptop is in the office. I left the contact open."

"May I?" He looked at Lyn.

She wrapped her arms around her legs more tightly and shifted in her seat. She couldn't form words or thoughts. She wanted to dance, or run, not sit here and be vulnerable.

She looked to Umiko. Umiko nodded and Lyn followed suit.

Greg retrieved the laptop from the office and brought it into the living room. He handed it to Lyn. She unwrapped her arms long enough to type in the short pass phrase. Once the computer logged in, Greg sat back down in his chair with it on his lap.

Lyn counted her inhales and exhales.

Clark laid three glasses of water on the coffee table and went back to the kitchen. He returned with a box of pizza. He had combined the rest of the slices into the one box which he placed in the middle of the coffee table.

Lyn let him pass her again and leaned forward to grab a piece at random. She wasn't hungry for once. Her nerves had seen to that, but pizza didn't disappoint a girl like family could.

Lyn took a bite of her slice and looked over at the computer. She could hear a quick succession of clicks and clacks as Greg typed. He was up to something, but she didn't know what.

"How old is that contact info?" He looked between the girls.

Umiko and Lyn both shrugged.

Greg closed the computer. "It's another dead end. Maps doesn't recognize the address. I searched the internet for Jonathan Michael Davis. I got a bunch of hits, but it would be trial and error without something more to go on. We don't even know if he left the state." He looked from Lyn to Umiko and back again. "Do you have a photo? We could try to narrow it down on social media. I know someone who can do wonders with facial recognition."

Umiko spoke first. "We have a baby book, but there are no pictures of her dad. I can get it." Umiko started to stand.

Color rose in Lyn's cheeks. Her heart raced. Umiko was about to pull a mom and show baby pictures to boyfriends. *Boyfriends?*

Lyn looked over at Greg who smiled at her and looked interested in the photo album idea.

She broke eye contact. "48 hours," she reminded Umiko and made eye contact with her instead.

Umiko settled back down and nodded. "Right."

Lyn was glad she got the hint. Her pulse slowed. Only slightly though. Her thoughts hung up on Clark and Greg. Did Umiko intend for tonight to be a double date?

"Now what?" Umiko asked as she picked up her water and took a sip.

"I can make a call and get a few people on it that owe me favors," Greg said. "Well, not favors exactly. My dad's their boss. They like to impress him by impressing the kid."

Lyn watched color flush his cheeks. Was he just as uncomfortable as her?

"I mean..." Greg stumbled trying to back track. "I've worked with them. They're pretty cool guys. I'm sure they'll help us out."

"You think they can find better info?" Clark put his arm

on the back of the couch behind Umiko so he could turn toward Greg.

"Oh, yeah. There are private security channels that know way more than Google and sometimes more than the government. Plus, there is far less red tape. We can find info without too many people knowing we are looking."

"Make the call," Umiko and Clark said in unison.

Lyn noted the awkward smile they shared and the differences between them. Umiko was light, even dressed in darker colors. Her pale freckled skin and red hair almost glowed. In the sunshine, it did. Clark on the other hand was darkness. His jet black hair was reminiscent of raven wings and his skin reminded her of the color of butterscotch. He was good looking, Lyn admitted, but the pair was a strange combination to her eyes. Strange but well paired. Like the sun and the moon, good and evil, life and death.

"The birth certificate is on the desk in the office. It'll give you a place to start," Umiko said.

Lyn shifted her focus back to Greg as he stood up and walked into the office, his phone at his ear.

"So, you worked at the hospital this summer?" Umiko asked Clark.

"Yeah. I also volunteered in local nursing homes when I could," Clark added.

"Did you like it?" Lyn asked Clark as she watched Greg.

"I did. Older people really just want someone to listen to them. They have pretty great stories if you have the patience to listen. This one old man, Morris, told me all about his wife. I think I sat with him for 3 or 4 hours. He built her a house in the middle of the woods so she could hear the birds and watch wild animals from her porch. They shared two children and two grandchildren. All girls. He would smile from ear to ear when he talked about them. I asked him if he had been disappointed not to have sons. He laughed this huge belly laugh. 'His daughters,' he said, 'could do anything a boy could do, maybe better'." Clark smiled. "His wife had already moved on and his granddaughters were making their own lives. He beamed with pride at what they had become. He was so happy he got to see it all before he died."

Lyn didn't know what to say. Her mother wouldn't get to see what she became. She'd never meet her grandchildren, if Lyn chose to have children. She wouldn't be there for first dates, weddings, the birth of children. She'd miss everything. Lyn covered the emotions warring in her features with a sip of water. She shifted her focus to Greg while Umiko asked Clark about what he did at the hospital.

Greg's wardrobe was usually more army surplus than what he was wearing today. Lyn noted that Greg's jeans fit well, not loose like a lot of guys her age, but not tight either. There was a black smudge on one thigh, almost in the shape of a hand. His plain white T-shirt stretched across his biceps. She was sure he worked out. He turned to face the living room and smiled at Lyn.

She looked away and took another bite of her pizza.

Greg hung up and stepped back to his chair.

"Alright, I've got some people getting us info on our Jonathan Davis." He looked disappointed when he sat down. "I don't think we'll have anything until tomorrow morning though."

Lyn felt like she had been given a short reprieve. She might be able to relax for the rest of the evening. Maybe she could persuade everyone to leave so she could take a long bath and watch stupid movies with the volume way up. Then she realized she only had 48 hours to find this man and convince him to care about her life and they had no current leads.

She looked at Umiko who also looked disappointed for a moment, but Lyn watched as her friend's face moved from disappointed to determined.

"That's that then. We're on hold while we wait for a better

lead. Greg will make the call in the morning and as soon as he gets an address or phone number we'll meet back here and make a game plan."

"Sounds good. I'm sure I'll have something by 10," Greg said. "In the mean time, don't talk to Ms. Evans." He turned his blue eyes toward Lyn. "I'd avoid her altogether."

Lyn nodded and broke eye contact. She didn't want those eyes to see the thinly veiled nervous breakdown that was hiding behind her own.

Lyn picked up her water and took a big sip. She was getting just a touch warm.

"Lyn, where's the remote?" Umiko asked. "We can watch a movie until we have to get home."

Everyone relaxed a little. Umiko leaned awkwardly into the space of Clark's armpit. Greg closed the laptop and placed it underneath the coffee table. He sat back in the plush chair and adjusted to face toward the television. Lyn handed Umiko the remote and mirrored Greg's actions to get comfortable in her own chair.

"What should we watch?" Umiko asked as the TV turned on.

Four very different people discussed the merits of several different movies. They couldn't agree on anything in the meager selection and instead of watching one, they ended up talking about a lot.

After an intense discussion about the Marvel movies compared to the DC movies, Umiko picked up her phone. "Oh no. I was supposed to be home five minutes ago. My mom just texted."

"Will she be mad?" Clark asked. "Should I go apologize?"

"No, I texted her our change in plans. Well, a version of our change in plans." Umiko stood up. "But I need to go and so does Lyn. My mom is a stickler for curfews."

Greg and Clark stood up.

"Sorry, we made you miss curfew." Greg was the first person to the door.

Lyn stood and stretched her back. She was fairly sure she was asleep for some of the movie discussion.

She stepped over to Greg and unlocked the door. "Thank for coming over. It was nice."

"Maybe we can do it again sometime?" Greg asked and stepped outside, keeping his face turned to her.

Lyn nodded, unable to form words. Her mouth had gone dry.

Clark and Umiko hugged at the threshold and everyone said good bye before Lyn shut and locked the door.

Umiko and Lyn decided they would clean up tomorrow and turned off the lights on their way out the backyard and through the shared gate to Umiko's house.

"He's cute right?" Umiko asked leaving Lyn to close the gate.

"Yeah." Lyn wasn't sure which boy Umiko was talking about. But agreement seemed like a valid answer.

"I think he likes you."

Lyn tripped over the first stepping stone but Umiko grabbed her before she could fall into the pond.

CHAPTER SIXTEEN

*L*yn rolled over in the half light. She had spent many nights on Umiko's floor. She had a thin mattress on the ground, a sleeping bag, and as many pillows as she needed. She usually slept fine, but tonight she was having trouble getting more than a few minutes of sleep at a time.

She sat up and fluffed her pillow again. Her eyes sought out the clock on her phone's lock screen. 4:02am.

Umiko was still asleep, at least Lyn assumed she was, it was hard to find her in the nest of pillows and blankets on her bed.

Lyn fell back onto her pillow with a silent groan. She closed her eyes and counted backwards from 100. Between numbers, her mind wandered from Greg's eyes, to the piercing dial tone on the end of the phone call, to her father. Between the phone call and her brain not getting the hint, she lost count three times. At thirty-two she gave up.

Lyn crawled out of her cocoon and walked over to the bedroom door. She picked up a dry erase marker from the ledge of a small board hung by Umiko's door. She erased the board and left a note in big letters for Umiko. She didn't want her friend to worry when she woke up and Lyn was missing.

Going for a run, see you at 10. -L

Lyn crept as quietly as she could, out of the room, down the stairs, and to the back door. She grabbed her shoes from beside the door and stepped into the early morning. She closed the door behind her without making a sound and went the back way home.

Lyn wouldn't be getting any more sleep, she needed to move. She ran up the stairs in her own house trying to decide between dancing or running. The speed at which she took the stairs started a longing in her legs for more. She changed into appropriate running clothes. A sports bra under a white tank top and a pair of navy Gym shorts. She tied her running shoes while sitting on the bottom stair.

She opened the front door after putting in one earbud and a delivery man jumped back.

"Sorry," Lyn said and did her own little jump. She held the second ear bud in her hand.

"No, I'm sorry. I just never expect anyone this early."

"That makes two of us." Lyn smiled.

"Do you want this inside?"

Lyn stepped back. "That would be great. Thanks."

He put a large box just inside the door and walked back to his van. "Have a good day."

"You too."Lyn locked the door behind her and the delivery man.

She'd put groceries away later. Right now, her muscles begged to run. Lyn put in her second earbud and kept the van between her and the house across the street. She felt silly, but it was there and she didn't want to let Ms. Evans see her, in case the older woman was watering her yard. Lyn doubted that even the early hour would dissuade the lady from her poorly veiled snooping. When the van pulled away from the curb, Lyn jogged along with it.

Lyn increased the volume on her running playlist. It began with Frozen Grass by Etherwood. The beats were steady and strong. Easy to hear over her pulse, breath, and the ambient sounds of a neighborhood starting its day. Her shoes hit the pavement as if they were drum beats.

Lyn was only five minutes into her run, when she was set upon by dogs coming from the other direction.

"Come on, girls. I need to get ready for work." The dog's owner tried to pull the two golden retrievers past Lyn.

Lyn removed one ear bud. "Good morning, Mrs. H." Lyn looked down at the dogs each vying for her attention. "Good morning, Gypsy. Good morning, Romani." She pet both of them and they wagged their tails.

"They think they need a longer walk, but I woke up late this morning and can't make the time," Mrs. Henesey said.

"I can take them if you want." Lyn shrugged. "I just started my run. I'd feel safer with these two big guard dogs at my heels anyway." She lowered her face to the dogs and let them lick her cheeks.

"Are you sure?" Mrs. Henesey asked.

"Yeah, I should be back in about 30 minutes. I can let them into the back yard, and you can let them in the house when you're ready for them."

"Lyn, you are a wonderful person."

Lyn's face started to tingle with embarrassment and sadness. "It's no big deal. You'd be doing me a favor."

"You girls be good for Lyn," Mrs. Henesey said to her dogs and handed Lyn the tandem leash.

"They always are," Lyn said. She smiled at Mrs. Henesey and put her ear bud back in place. "I'll have them home in about half an hour." She turned to continue her run.

Five minutes later, Lyn felt a second beat come up behind her. The dogs looked up at Lyn from their position at her side, but kept jogging. Not a threat. She moved to the right to allow the second runner to pass but it changed its pace to match hers. She turned to see who it was and smiled. She slid the earbud closest to the newcomer out of her ear.

"I didn't know you were a runner," Greg said, his breath even.

"Not always, but I needed the movement this morning, and it's not 100 degrees yet," Lyn said. Her breath was only a little strained from her pace.

"I know these dogs," Greg said.

"They're my neighbor's."

"Mrs. H's? Gypsy and Romani?"

At the mention of their names, the dogs moved to sniff Greg. He ran his hand over their necks, one at a time.

"Is it okay if I join you? You can keep your music on." Greg held up his own.

"Sure." She slid the earbud back in and continued her run, the dogs moved slightly ahead and Greg filled in the space beside Lyn.

Fifteen minutes later, the midpoint to her playlist, a drum only beat picked up her pace slightly. This would be her top speed before the beat started its downward slide.

She noticed Greg slow. She pulled her earbud out to tease him about not being able to keep up with her, but her words caught in her throat when she heard a second voice. Her foot faltered and she stumbled over a crack in the street. She hoped Killian didn't notice.

The dogs stopped their forward momentum and came back to her, they nuzzled for pets.

"You've got to pick your feet up higher. Or else the ground will jump up and bite you," Killian said, stepping to her right to run along side.

She was now flanked by two dogs and two guys. Her run had gotten crowded. She should have stayed home and danced in the back yard, even with the calf high weeds.

She made a mental note to mow the yard.

"What do you want?" Greg asked over her head.

Lyn almost answered him, but Killian did instead. Lyn took a moment to look at the dogs. They tilted their heads to look at her, as if to say, what's up? She was surprised that they didn't think Killian was a threat. She sure did.

"I'm just out for a run. It's better with company. Don't you think?" Killian asked Lyn.

"No," Lyn answered. She put her earbud back in and increased the volume. Her feet located the beat and used it to drown out her bully and her knight. She pulled ahead slightly, leaving the pair to squabble behind her. Lyn ran the rest of her route alone with her music, the dogs just ahead of her, while the two guys matched pace two steps behind.

The sidewalk felt small, and she felt trapped, but she was thankful that Killian seemed more interested in goading Greg this morning than messing with her.

She slowed past the music's beat when she turned onto her street. She usually jogged the last part, to allow her pulse to slow, but she planted her foot and came to a full stop when she looked toward her house. The dogs strained on the end of the leash and Lyn's other companions were forced to stop, or run her over.

Ms. Evans stood in her front yard, with a green garden hose snaked around her feet, watering her yard.

Killian stepped onto the grass instead of letting Lyn stop his pace. "I'll see you later, Lyn. Push yourself faster next time, that pace was child's play." The dogs sniffed him as he passed. "I know you can do better." Killian broke into a sprint and moved down the street.

Greg's hand brushed her arm. She took a step and focused on putting one foot in front of the other. She ignored the outside world and found the beat of the music. She heard a rumble from the dogs, and they moved to be between her and the road. The grumble grew as the dogs stayed between Lyn's body and what they considered a threat.

Seriously, girls? Why didn't you growl at Killian? Lyn thought.

Greg matched Lyn's pace as they walked up to Mrs.

Henesey's side gate. While Lyn tugged at the dogs' leash, Greg opened the latch. Lyn maneuvered herself and the dogs inside and Greg closed the gate behind them as Lyn removed one earbud.

"Lyn, is that you?" a voice called from the back of the house.

"Yes, ma'am," Lyn called to the voice and dropped the leash . The dogs ran around the corner of the house for their owner. "I've got to go. See you later."

"Thanks again for running the dogs!" Mrs. Henesey called back.

"Anytime," Lyn replied.

Greg and Lyn left the yard and made sure the gate was secured behind them. At Lyn's front door, she pulled her other earbud out as the last song faded.

"Thanks for the run," Greg said.

"Thanks for the company."

"I'll see you at 10." Greg took a step back and off of the porch.

"Do me a favor?" Lyn asked before he turned away.

"What's that?" Greg stepped forward again.

"Text me when you get here? I like to know who's at the door before I open it."

Greg nodded. "Sure. Give me your phone?" He held his hand out, palm up. She pulled her device out of her pocket and handed it over. He thumbed a few numbers in a text message and hit send. "Digits traded." He handed her phone back. "I'll stand here looking busy until I hear the door lock."

"Thanks." Lyn turned and went inside her house. She locked the door and ran upstairs for a shower.

You're welcome. A text flashed on her phone.

~

lark and I are on the porch. Lyn's notification screen read. It was ten o'clock, exactly. "It's them," Lyn said loud enough that Umiko could hear her from the other room.

Umiko had arrived earlier and the girls were putting away the last of the groceries from the delivery box. Lyn had showered and was dressed in a pair of denim shorts and one of her mom's fitted v-neck T-shirts. The bright green made the new red highlights in Lyn's hair stand out even more.

Umiko, wearing a black scoop neck, ran to open the front door while Lyn put a 4-pack of single serving tomato soups in the cabinet by the stove.

Lyn was thankful her mom insisted on putting Lyn on all the bank and credit accounts the day she turned sixteen. Otherwise, soup would have been much harder to come by.

Lyn remembered her mom had made a big deal out of her last birthday, treating her like a queen. Lyn had refused a party. Instead, they spent the whole day together, just the two of them. Mani-pedis, a trip to the bank to get her own debit card, and curbside take away with movies that night. To Lyn, it was perfection.

A smile bloomed across her face.

Lyn paused. She ran a finger between her eye and her nose. It was dry. She had just thought about a wonderful and happy moment with her mom and she hadn't cried.

"I've got good news and bad news." Greg's voice cut through her thoughts before he rounded the corner behind Umiko.

"We brought breakfast!" Clark held out several small white paper bags with donuts stamped on the side. He walked them over to the table and set them in the middle.

"Is that the good news?" Lyn asked as she pulled out plates and set them on the table as well.

"No," Greg said as he set down a quart of milk and a carry tray with four cups of coffee. "I have an address, which is not paved under a road, but there's no phone number. My guys couldn't find any recent utilities in his name. Phone, or otherwise."

"It looks like we are going on a road trip," Clark said. He grabbed a cup of coffee and took a sip. He emptied a bag of breakfast tacos onto the table. "I got an assortment. You and Umiko can choose first."

"Road trip, as in not around town?" Lyn asked. She read the stickers on the foil and grabbed a bacon and egg taco before she peeked in the other bags. She found a cream cheese danish and a bag of donut holes. She put the danish on her plate and added a few holes before she sat in her usual spot.

"Nope, more like an hour and a half," Greg said.

Umiko sat opposite her, adding a sugar dish and spoon to the assorted goodies on the table. "I'll need to tell my mom," Umiko said. She selected a sausage and egg taco, a chocolate donut and a few donut holes. "I'll be right back." She popped a bit of fried dough into her mouth and left out the back door.

"Her mom is in the backyard?" Clark asked peering through the blinds.

"No," Lyn said. "But it's the most direct way to get to her house."

"By jumping the fence? I know she's a great swimmer, but she climbs fences?" Greg walked to the back door and watched the small girl.

Lyn giggled. "No, there is a gate."

Greg smiled. "How disappointing. Also cool." He stepped back to the table. "And it makes a lot more sense than Umiko leaping fences." He sat down with his black coffee and selected a taco at random. He opened the foil and poured a small container of salsa verde between the folds of the flour tortilla before wrapping it back.

"I need to stop and put gas in the car on the way out. Greg didn't want to be late or I would have done it before we came here." Clark winked at Lyn.

Lyn noticed that Greg shot Clark a dirty look. She averted her eyes and smiled.

Clark took his cup of coffee out back and Greg took a bite of his taco.

"There's a lot of space to dance on your back porch," Greg said after he swallowed his bite.

Lyn froze with the bacon and egg wrap half way to her mouth.

Greg hurried to fill the silence. "I can come mow your yard later, if you want." He shifted in his seat. "I mean I need to do mine too. It wouldn't be any trouble to add a yard."

Lyn remembered the door closing in the auditorium yesterday. "It is a great space, but I don't use it much." Was it him? It must have been. How else would he know? She doesn't dance for anyone, except her mom and Umiko. "Did Umiko tell you I dance?"

Greg took a sip of his coffee. "Um, she might have let it slip. Don't get mad at her though, I'd feel terrible."

Lyn walked into the kitchen for a roll of paper towels. She tore one off and handed it to Greg. She tore a few more off and put the roll back on the raised bar behind the sink.

With her back turned to hide the mischief she knew would show on her face and with a calm in her voice that she didn't feel, she asked, "Did she also tell you I'm a vampire?"

Greg spewed his sip of coffee.

Lyn wrapped her arms around her belly as she doubled over in laughter.

Greg set his cup down and stared at the mess and the girl. He raised his eyebrows and smiled. "You got me, good." He picked up his paper towel and dried his face.

Lyn's laughter doubled, she opened a drawer and pulled out two towels. She dampened one in the sink and tossed it to Greg.

He wiped up coffee from the table while she continued to laugh.

She was wiping tears away from her face when he finished. Lyn looked at her finger tips, wet with laughing tears, not grieving tears.

"You good now?" Greg eyed her.

She turned her face to Greg and a giggle escaped. He was on his hands and knees on the floor with a damp rag. Lyn put her hand on her chest and took a deep breath. "I think so." She calmed herself as he watched her.

"So, you're not a vampire?"

"Not even close," Lyn said with a huge grin. She tucked her lips in to stifle another burst of laughter.

"So, do you want to tell me what you are?"

Lyn sobered. "As far as I know, I'm 100% human. Umiko has this crazy idea that I'm not."

"Why is that?"

"I've never been sick." She watched as Greg cleaned the coffee off of the floor between the kitchen and the breakfast table.

"She could be right." Greg stood and handed her the dirty towels.

Lyn rolled her eyes. "Don't you start." She tossed them into one side of the sink to deal with later.

He shrugged and they both walked back to the table.

"Umiko is pretty sure I'm not just human." Even Lyn was starting to think her friend might be right. After all, her hair was changing in a very non-human way. "I guess we'll find out for sure today."

"So, your mom is human, but you don't know about your dad."

"Yeah," Lyn said as Clark and Umiko met on the back porch. "He's not in any of the pictures."

"Hence, Umiko's vampire theory." Greg smiled and waited for Lyn to sit before he took his own seat.

"Something like that."

Clark and Umiko came back into the house.

"She wanted to come with us to talk to your dad, but she's got tutoring sessions all day. She offered to cancel them, but I assured her we weren't going alone," Umiko said. "She gave me money for lunch and made me promise to bring Clark over to meet her."

Clark put down his coffee and wiped his hands on a paper towel.

"Not now." Umiko sat at the table and doctored her coffee. "Hey, why are there coffee drips on my plate?"

Lyn and Greg shared a look and a laugh.

Lyn reached into her pant's pocket and fished out a folded green bill. She handed it to Clark. "Gas money."

"You don't have to…"

She waved him off. "This road trip is my thing, you've offered to drive. Gas money is the least I can do. Thank you."

"Actually, that 'thank you' is the least you could have done." Clark smiled at her. "But thanks." He slid the bill into his front pocket.

CHAPTER SEVENTEEN

To Lyn, it looked like a big red, white, and brown boat on wheels. The rust explained the squeak and squeal of metal grinding on metal as the door opened and closed.

Clark put the key in the door lock and turned it. It made a clunk as the metal lock moved out of place. He opened the door, which sounded like it objected, tilted the black vinyl seat forward and offered his hand to help Lyn into the back seat. "You'll want the blanket under you. The upholstery is not in the greatest shape." Clark said, motioning to a flannel backed fleece blanket spread across the back seat.

"What is?" Greg said as he walked to the other side of the car.

Lyn spread the fleece blanket across the back seats and sat down. She could feel breaks in the vinyl through the soft fleece, but the double layer of fabric dulled their edges.

"I rebuilt the engine," Clark answered Greg's rhetorical question. "It was in pretty bad shape. Now, she purrs like the Mustang she was almost 60 years ago." Clark tossed Greg the keys, over the roof of the car.

"On the outside, she looks her age." Greg unlocked the car

and pulled open the door. The door protested. "And sounds worse."

Clark pushed the front seat back after Lyn was settled and helped Umiko into the front. He closed her door and walked around to the driver's side. He hurried Greg into the back seat. "Just get in." He took the keys that Greg held out for him.

It took a moment for Greg to fold himself into the car, but once he got in, he had plenty of room as long as he kept his knees separated.

Lyn angled her body toward the middle of the car to keep her legs together and allow herself a little more room.

Clark tilted the driver's seat back and got in the car. He twisted the key in the side of the steering column and the engine turned over smoothly. "Hear that." The engine didn't purr, it roared. A deep rumble vibrated through the seats when Clark revved the engine.

"Sounds nice, man, when is she getting a facelift?" Greg smiled at Clark in the rear view mirror.

Clark's door complained as he closed it. "Probably next year. I haven't decided on a color. I could redo the red with white side stripes, or go black. It was originally 'Tahoe Turquoise,' but with tan interior. That's not my style. " Clark started backing down the driveway.

Umiko fastened her seat belt and Lyn fumbled around her shoulder for hers. "No seat belts?"

"Just a lap belt in the back. The front shoulder straps aren't market. They were added later."

Lyn clicked her single strap across her lap and pulled it tight. The buckle reminded her of airplane seats and she ran through airplane safety check in her head. Unfortunately, her nearest exit was out of reach. She'd need help getting out of the car.

"How much did you pay for it?" Greg asked and turned his head to look behind them as Clark backed up.

"Nothing." Clark pulled a photo from the visor and handed it back to Greg. "This is the original owner. The photo has been passed down with the car."

Greg looked at the man in the aged photograph, standing by a mint condition 1966 Ford Mustang Fastback, turquoise. "This guy looks like you, if you squint and tilt your head." He turned the photo over. *P. Clarkson '66.* "Your grandfather, maybe?" He handed the photo to Lyn.

She looked at the sleek new car in the photo. The thing she currently sat in was in no noticeable way to her comparable. She handed the photo to Umiko.

"Yeah. My mom's dad. I was named after him." Clark turned the wheel and started down the street.

Umiko took the photo and looked at it before putting it back into the glove box.

"We should add a picture. The four of us. It's not a family, but it's close." Umiko held up her phone for a selfie, and tried to get all four of them in it. Lyn only token participated. When Umiko couldn't make it work she settled on a photo of her and Lyn. Umiko posed and Lyn gave a small faked smile from the back seat.

Lyn was sure she was going to force them all to pose and smile for a round of photos later but for now Lyn stared out the widow and Umiko put away her phone.

"We'll get a group photo some other time," Umiko said.

Lyn smiled to herself and looked down the street. She noticed a muddy black jeep. She squinted her eyes to see who, if anyone was behind the wheel, but Clark pulled away before she could focus past the mud.

"I wonder if he'll follow us the whole way." Greg looked back at the jeep.

"Who?" Clark asked looking forward, then in his side mirror.

Umiko turned around and looked out the back window.

Lyn slid down a little in her seat, but the lap belt kept her from puddling on the floorboard like she wanted.

"Killian," Umiko grumbled. "What do we have to do to get him to leave you alone?" She said to Lyn.

If Lyn knew the answer to that, she'd gladly comply.

Clark pressed the brakes to stop at the stop sign. "I can let you out, you can take care of it now." He looked at Greg in the rearview.

"What about 'we' man, you have fists too." Greg faced his reflection.

"I'm a pacifist." Clark turned the wheel and pressed the accelerator.

"So, you're the chauffeur and I'm the heavy?"

"Yeah. I think that sounds accurate."

"Guys, we don't have to do this. Let's just go home," Lyn said. This day was already going to be difficult, she did not need Killian added to the mix.

"No!" Umiko said firmly and turned in her seat to face Lyn. Her voice commanded attention. "We are not turning around. We are doing this and we'll deal with assholes as we meet them."

Lyn was stunned. "You have never yelled at me before." Lyn paused and looked at her friend through narrowed eyes. "I don't think I've heard you say 'asshole' before either." She pushed herself back up in her seat and got comfortable underneath Umiko's gaze.

Umiko turned and pressed her back to her own seat. "Well, you've never needed it before and that is the best word I have to describe Killian."

Lyn could think of plenty of words for Killian, but Umiko was right. Asshole was a pretty good one.

Clark pulled into the gas station. Clark got out of the car and tilted his seat up to let Greg out, then walked around to open Umiko's door.

Lyn covered her ears to dampen the grinding sound.

"Can you grab me a big bottle of water and something healthy, please? Carrots or celery if they have it," he asked Umiko as he offered his hand to help her out of the seat and handed her the folded bill from his pocket. "Spend the rest on what you ladies want."

Umiko nodded and stepped toward the store.

Clark helped Lyn out of the back seat before he walked back around to the gas pump and slid in his credit card.

Lyn looked back to see Greg leaning on the trunk with his arms crossed over his shoulder as Killian pulled into the next pump.

Lyn quickened her step and caught up with Umiko before she opened the door to the small convenience store.

"Nice wheels. Looks like it came out of a junk yard," Killian said. "20 years ago."

Lyn stepped inside and let the door close firmly behind her before she slowed her breathing. She turned back and watched the three guys through the glass of the door.

Without sound it just looked like three guys talking cars. Greg actually looked like the dangerous one. His muscles tensed and ready for a fight.

Killian's movements were calm, confident. Clark just stood with his hand on the nozzle. He paid more attention to his car and the gas pump than to the person talking to him.

Greg, however, was glaring at the newcomer. His arms still crossed over his chest, he moved from the trunk to the back quarter panel of the mustang, closer to the gas pump and the threat. Lyn lost track of Killian for a moment when Greg stepped between her view from the glass door and the boy she was watching.

"What do you want?" Umiko's voice called from the cold cases. She was unconcerned with the events outside.

Lyn turned from her vantage point of the unfolding scene and helped Umiko make selections.

The girls gathered snacks. Waters for everyone, a bag of

chips, some nuts, two sharable candy bars and a small plastic container of cut carrots. Umiko inspected the carrots before handing them to Lyn to carry. They laid everything on the counter at the front of the store.

"I've called the cops before and I would do it again, except that boy's dad is always the one that comes out here." He placed the girl's items in two plastic bags as he rang them up. "Cop's kid." The cashier huffed.

Umiko and Lyn each added a few dollars to the money Clark had given them and paid the man behind the counter.

He took the money and gave Umiko the change. She pocketed the quarters and left behind the smaller coins.

The girls walked outside. Umiko, with a thin plastic bag of water bottles, in the lead.

"Hey, Lyn," Killian called over Greg's head.

Greg uncrossed his arms and walked around to Lyn's side of the car to open her door.

"Killian," she said as she tried to gracefully scrunch herself and the bag of snacks into the back seat.

Greg held the door while Umiko got into the car. When she was settled, he closed the door and walked back to the pump side as Clark finished filling the car's tank with gas.

Lyn saw Greg hesitate before finally turning his back on Killian and getting into the back seat.

"Where are you guys headed?" Killian asked.

"Road trip." Clark finished pushing buttons on the pump and folded the seat back into place.

Killian walked behind the mustang and trailed his hand over the flared edge as he moved toward the store front. He made eye contact with Lyn as he did. "She'd be hot if she weren't so scarred."

Lyn thought she noticed Greg flinch, but he was already trapped in the back seat of the car with her. He could not easily get to Killian, but he kept his eyes on the boy while Clark got back into the car and closed his door.

Clark drove out of the lot without comment.

They left Killian staring after them from the gas station.

"Do you think he'll follow us?" Lyn asked looking back. Killian smiled at her and waved.

"It doesn't look like it." Greg glanced over his shoulder as Killian stepped inside the small store. "And he doesn't know where we're going." He turned forward.

Umiko handed him two bottles of water. He passed one to Lyn.

Lyn faced forward in her seat and opened the bag of snacks searching for chocolate.

CHAPTER EIGHTEEN

*L*yn spent the next hour and a half staring out the car window.

She wasn't occupied with mapping their route. She heard Umiko's voice navigating but the 'fifteen more miles until we turn left' and 'turn right at the next intersection' barely registered.

She wasn't focused on watching their back either. Greg had that under control. He'd know if Killian decided to follow them. She felt the seat shift as he looked over his shoulder several times, but didn't once wonder what he was seeing.

Instead, Lyn obsessed over prepping for the conversation with her father in her head.

'Hi, I'm your daughter.' No, *he doesn't get to claim me after 16 years of nothing.* 'Hi, I'm your wife's daughter.' That's better. 'Maria has passed on.' Lyn shook her head. *That sounded stupid.* 'My mom is dead.' Too whiney? 'Maria died.' Short and to the point.

Lyn imagined him slamming the door in her face each time she said she needed his help. She winced the first few times. Enough that Greg asked if she was okay. When his voice finally registered in her ear, his hand was on her arm and everyone was looking at her. She nodded briefly and went back to starring out the window.

After she watched it in her head about fifty times, she started to get used to the image of the door slamming in her face. She wondered how it would compare to the real thing.

Lyn watched storm clouds roll in as they got off the interstate. They reflected her mood perfectly. The dark billowing mass, folding in and around itself. Lyn wondered if the clouds had lightning inside. Carefully pent up energy that could strike at any moment. Lyn did. She had the low rumble of thunder deep in the pit of her stomach, aching to be released.

Lyn leaned her head on the window and tamped the thunder down as best she could.

~

The address for Jonathan Michael Davis was a rundown duplex. The paint was faded and peeling after years of being hit by the harsh rays of the Texas sun. The bushes were mostly yellowed and dry, while the trees looked only slightly taller and parched.

Lyn imagined Ms. Evans tsk, tsking the state of this yard. She would have a grand time going after it with her hose. These looked like they could use a good flooding. Daily. For years.

Lyn stepped out of the car last, reluctant to move on to the door slamming phase. Her heart was racing. Her legs wanted to flee. A or B. She hoped it was A.

Side A had a cute little bistro set on the tiny patio and a ragged welcome mat in front of the door. She could make out floral curtains through the cracks in the window blinds. A feminine touch. *What if he remarried? Just because my mom never did, doesn't mean he wouldn't have. He's the one that left, after all. What if he left because he had another family?*

Lyn fell against Clark's car. She pushed the whirlwind of thoughts from her brain. She knew she wasn't making a lot of sense. Another family, now? Sure, it's been sixteen years. Another family when he left? She didn't know. She inhaled and pushed away from the car, staying close as she made sure her legs would hold.

Side B, on the other hand, had a bag of trash on the patio, and the blinds were closed up tight. There was no mat at all on the front step and the grass had washed away in spots to create a dry, cracked dirt layer on the sidewalk. The occupant was either neglectful or didn't care about the curb appeal. Maybe both.

"What's the plan?" Clark asked looking at Lyn.

Lyn straightened her spine and stepped away from the car so she couldn't use it as a crutch.

The group stood on the sidewalk looking at the house.

"We knock." Greg said and took a step forward.

Lyn stayed glued to her section of sidewalk.

"We can't all rush the door." Umiko stopped Greg and faced Lyn, pity on her face. "You have to be the one. We'll be here to back you up. I promise" The pity fled replaced by a cheerful smile as Umiko crossed her heart with her pointer finger. "You can do it!"

Umiko never met an obstacle that didn't bend to the whim of her excitement.

Alone? Lyn put her hand on the roof of the car for support because her legs, unable to sprint, threatened to quit.

It was warm for September, but she felt warmer. A bead of sweat trickled down her spine. *I shouldn't have worn black.*

"You can either knock on the door, or accept Ms. Evans as your new mom," Umiko whispered near her ear, cutting right to the point.

Lyn choked on air.

"Are you okay?" Greg thumped her on the back.

Lyn's eyes watered as she struggled to get a full breath between coughs to clear the obstruction in her throat.

After a few moments and worried looks from her friends, Lyn recovered and stood straight. She wiped her eyes on the sleeve of her shirt and started walking toward the door on A side. Would his new wife be understanding or furious? Lyn hadn't accounted for a wife or girlfriend in her conversation prep. Would she be the one to open the door in stead of her father? What would she say to his new wife?

"Um, Lyn, it's the B side." Greg pointed to the B side.

Lyn's shoulders sagged. Neglectful seemed more of a match to the man she imagined anyway. She walked up the B side driveway and was forced into the bare dirt beside a beat up pickup truck. The driveway was only wide enough for one car. In this neighborhood, having a driveway at all was a luxury. Most of the duplexes only had street parking.

She made it to the patio an hour later, at least it seemed so to Lyn who felt like she was moving through pudding. She turned back to her friends.

All three stood on the sidewalk by Clark's car. Clark leaned back on the passenger side of the hood and looked like knocking on a stranger's door to tell him she's his daughter was no big deal. Something he did so often that it was normal. Lyn guessed he had a handle on delivering bad news since he worked in hospitals and nursing homes.

Umiko's face shifted between excitement and anxiety. *At least she knows the score.* On the other side of that door was either a father who could come to love her, or a very good reason her mother never spoke of him.

Greg nodded at her, encouraging her to knock neither excited nor anxious. Steady and calm. She tried to channel his lack of emotions, but hers still resembled the rolling clouds over head.

Lyn took a deep breath, turned and knocked, as if Greg's nod had been a demand.

She heard a grunt and the clatter of bottles on the other side of the door. Her legs nearly bolted as the door opened.

"What?" the half dressed man on the other side barked at her.

Lyn stepped back.

What she could see of Jonathan Davis was rail thin and pale. She saw none of herself in his gaunt face. "Are you Jonathan Davis?" she asked, hoping she had the wrong house.

"Yes, what do you want?" Jonathan snapped at her through a small crack in the door. "I'm not buying anything."

"I…ummm." Lyn froze. This was him. This was her mother's husband. Her father. His brusk tone and demeanor disarmed her. Even the parts of the conversation she had practiced in the car fled her brain.

"Excuse me, sir," Greg said. He stepped up to put his hand on the small of Lyn's back, their shoulders touching. "My name is Van Gregar." Greg extended his hand. "This is Lyn Davis."

Lyn watched as a spark of recognition flared in the stranger's eyes. His face softened. His gaze pierced her eyes and traveled down her body and up again. She felt naked and looked away as a blush rose to her cheeks.

"Are you really her? My daughter?" He opened the door a little wider and examined her face. "You dress like Maria." His voice was less bark than before and more sad. "You kind of look like her." He examined her face. "The hair is different." He turned back to Greg. "What's this about?"

"Can we come in and talk?" Greg asked.

"No." The man closed the door in their face.

That was it. That was the door slamming in her face that she had played over and over again in her mind on the drive over. Lyn felt slapped by the door and the harshness of his one word. She brought her hand to her cheek as if she really had been slapped and stood frozen, looking at the closed door. Less than two feet from her face. Tears gathered in the corners of her eyes. After a moment, she hung her head and took a step backward.

Greg's hand on the middle of her back stopped her and he knocked on the door.

There was no answer and no sound from the other side.

Greg knocked again, harder. It sounded like a cop knock. A knock that you ignored right before the door crashed open and uniformed men with badges flooded into your home.

Lyn looked at the seriousness in Greg's face and posture and stepped slightly back in case he did decide to rush the door.

But this time, Lyn heard the sound of feet moving on the other side of the door. A moment later, it opened.

"You're not going to go away, are you?" Jonathan Davis asked. His voice was gruff and empty of compassion.

"No, sir," Greg answered with his military manners, his arms at his side. "She needs to talk."

Jonathan stepped between her and Greg, this time in a creased T-shirt. She started to fall off the concrete step into a bush, but Greg grabbed her arm to steady her.

"Running away won't help." Greg followed him and pulled Lyn gently along with him.

"I didn't think it would." Jonathan sighed. "There's a gazebo and a small park down the street. We can talk there. I'm not letting strangers into my house, even if one says she shares my name. I don't know who or what you are." Jonathan walked down the driveway and turned onto the sidewalk.

Greg linked Lyn's arm in his and followed. At the end of the driveway, he turned to Clark. "Will you and Umiko follow in the car?"

Clark nodded and opened the door for Umiko.

Greg and Lyn stayed six steps behind the man. "He's an ass and a half," Greg said.

Lyn stayed silent, her mind a flood of worry and other emotions.

"I guess I can understand him not wanting us in his house though. He doesn't know us and the numbers are skewed in our favor. We could kill him and steal his cat," Greg said.

"He said I looked like my mom," Lyn said. Jonathan didn't seem to her to be the cat type.

Greg nodded and picked up the edge of her thoughts. "Do you?"

"I used to think so, but not lately," Lyn answered. Her hand subconsciously went up to her hair. She kept her eyes glued to Jonathan's back.

"It's good that he recognizes her in you. He's more likely to talk to you than the rest of us, since you remind him of someone he knew." He paused.

She didn't fill in the silence.

"You've got to admit, I'm an intimidating person," Greg flex the bicep that was linked with Lyn's, "and Clark, well, he looks like death personified. Even Umiko looks dangerous, like a handful of sunshine and that stuff burns."

A nervous giggle escaped Lyn's throat.

Greg patted her arm and whispered. "I like making you laugh."

Lyn nodded. "Thanks for not making me do this alone."

"Are you kidding me? Umiko would kill me if I did. She'd burn me with her sunshine lasers."

Umiko waved as she and Clark drove past in the car.

Lyn smiled. "I'm going to tell her you said that."

"You want her to burn me to a crisp?" Greg asked. He put his free hand over his heart in mock pain. "I'm hurt."

Lyn and Greg walked on, keeping pace with the older man while also staying far enough back that their conversation wouldn't be overheard by normal ears.

"I don't know what to say," Lyn admitted. "Nothing I worked out in the car feels right." That wasn't quite true. Everything she thought of in the car sounded horrible, like she was begging. To Lyn, it sounded like a weak little girl needing a man, to protect her. It all left a bad taste in her mouth, even if he was blood related.

"Just lay it all out there. Complete honesty. Either he gives a shit, or he doesn't. It may hurt to find out which, but you don't have a lot of time to play around, right?"

Lyn nodded. She watched Jonathan turn onto a different side walk. He stepped into a gazebo that could use a coat of paint, but was otherwise in good shape. The green space around it was only that color because of the many weeds taking hold in the packed dirt.

A warm breeze wafted through the space, rough around the edges because of the storm brewing overhead.

Lyn caught the scent of azaleas and fresh cut grass as her hair blew in the wind. A sense of calm settled over her. She closed her eyes. *All or nothing.* The worst she could walk away with was the same as she arrived with, plus a bruised ego and worse self-esteem. *No big deal.*

Clark parked on the curb across the street. He and Umiko stepped from the car and crossed the street to meet Lyn and Greg on the sidewalk.

Greg released Lyn's arm. "You two go, we'll stay here," Greg said.

Lyn looked into his eyes and tried not to look like a deer in headlights.

He took one of Lyn's hands in his and held it. "Don't worry. Just get it all out, remember your timeline. We'll be there in a flash if you need us."

"Probably literally."

Greg turned to Clark. "Super speed?"

Clark shrugged.

"What happened to privacy?" Greg asked.

"I'm not asking. But I can still try to figure you out."

Greg turned back to Lyn. "You can do this."

She nodded, the butterflies in her belly fighting to get out.

He squeezed and let go of her hand.

Greg's hand was quickly replaced by Umiko's, as she took Lyn's hand and walked with her to the gazebo.

Jonathan waited on one of the built in benches. Umiko and Lyn sat on the one opposite the structure.

Lyn took a breath and gathered her thoughts.

Jonathan's eyes traveled around her face before settling on her lips. "How's Maria?"

"Dead," Lyn said. She wanted to hurt him, but the word sliced into her own heart too. She watched the emotions roll across his face. Shock, anger, sadness.

"I guess you're looking for a dad." His words sounded bitter in Lyn's ears. There was no comfort, no hope. They were uncaring and she felt each one slice through her thin skin.

A tear slid down Lyn's cheek, unbidden. "Did you love us at all?" Her words were tenuous. She wanted them to be steel edged with anger, but she couldn't hide her hurt.

Jonathan hung his head. "I loved her with everything I had."

"But not me." Lyn filled in. *At least I know now.*

"I..." he started. "You weren't mine."

Lyn blinked back the tears. "What?" The anger boiling inside of her pushed the tears away more effectively that her eye flutters. "I will not believe that my mother..."

"No. Not like that. I know she never cheated on me. I know she loved me." Jonathan shook his head. "I was there when you were... when Maria went into labor. I saw the baby she screamed into life. When the nurse brought you back into the room after whatever it is they do, baths and shots and whatever, you did not look like the same baby that left. The baby Maria gave all her strength and focus to bring into the world was chubby and pink, and had lungs that pierced your ears. The baby that came back was not. It was thin and pale and quiet. I knew it wasn't the same baby."

"The nurse told me I was wrong," he continued. "She blamed my doubt on being awake for over 48 hours straight, on the excitement of birth, on completely normal fears that parents have. She said there were no other babies born at the clinic that day. She said it was my baby and I needed to stop upsetting Maria." He pushed a tear out of his face, and looked at Lyn. "She was right about no other babies born there and then. Maria had insisted on using a mid-wife instead of an OBGYN. She had wanted to give birth at home, but I put my foot down, so we compromised on a small natural birthing clinic."

"My stupid foot. I was afraid that something bad would happen and I would lose one or both of them." Jonathan curled his hands into fists in his lap. "Something bad happened anyway, and I did lose both. Just not like I thought. Maybe if I had let her have the baby at home, it wouldn't have."

"What wouldn't have happened?" Lyn asked. Anger replaced by confusion.

Jonathan ignored her question. "I held you once. After you had eaten and Maria had fallen asleep. I picked you up from that plastic bassinet thing they put you in. You were so small. You looked frail, like I could snap you in half just by loving you. I was afraid I might drop you. Then you opened your eyes and I nearly did. Your eyes." He lifted his head and looked into Lyn's eyes. "Weren't real eyes, like you have now. They were the darkest shade of black I had ever seen. I knew then that you weren't mine, you weren't even human."

The air went out of Lyn's lungs. Umiko squeezed her hand twice in quick succession. Lyn turned to face her friend, whose whole face said I told you so until it saw the panic on Lyn's own. Umiko's hand squeezed again, longer this time.

Lyn took her next breath. A deep intentional breath. One that did little to soothe the rip in Lyn's core.

Lyn leaned forward, her head closer to her knees, her breath caught in her lungs. Umiko had been right. And with that simple acceptance Lyn no longer knew who or what she was. She could no longer hold on to humanity. She longed for her mother to tell her she loved her, that she would always love her and that she was hers, no matter what anyone else said. No matter what her DNA looked like.

"Maria wouldn't hear it, of course, she was already in love with you." Jonathan's words dripped with aggression.

"So what am I, if not human?" Lyn asked without picking up her head. Her voice pitched higher. *And who are my real parents. No! Maria Davis is my real mom. The only mom that matters.*

"Hell if I know. I hired a private investigator, behind Maria's back. I wanted to find our real baby so she'd believe me. Of course, she found out anyway. She kept track of the finances and I could never lie to her. She said I could either accept that you were our baby or get out."

Lyn took another breath, slow and steady. In and out. She was counting her inhales and exhales trying to find the involuntary rhythm that would keep its own pace. Breathing was supposed to be easy. It wasn't supposed to need a conscious effort. Lyn knew this from last year's biology class, from life, but she didn't trust her own body right now.

Lyn's hard earned breath brought with it the smell of decay and the faint trace of skunk.

"Did the investigator find another baby?" Umiko asked.

"No." Jonathan shook his head. "The last I heard, he had leads he was going to follow up, but then he dropped off the radar. He quit returning my calls. I received a final invoice and a copy of the file in the mail about a week later. I called the number on the letter head. The guy that answered the phone told me that Parks had died in a car crash and that he would not be taking up the job. I was angry and didn't pay the bill but I never heard back from the guy. I searched the whole file for a location on my daughter, but he hadn't found any definitive proof that there even was a second baby." He paused and shook his head. "I still don't buy it."

"He thought it was possible, but couldn't prove it," Umiko said.

Jonathan nodded.

Inhale. Exhale. Lyn thought to herself. "You said I looked like her, maybe I am your daughter. Maybe that's why he couldn't prove anything." *Inhale 2, 3. Exhale 2, 3.*

His eyes traveled over Lyn's face. He shook his head. "If you've come here hoping to find a dad. It's too late. Maria is dead. You just lost the one person in the world that loved you over everything. Even if I thought you were my kid, I'd be a horrible person to let you watch me die too."

Umiko's arms wrapped around Lyn's shoulders, but Lyn hardly noticed. She felt numb.

The air stilled, the birds stopped chirping. Lyn's world collapsed in on itself. Her mother was gone. The only other blood relation she knew of, just told her he didn't think he was, and, to top it off, he had stripped away her humanity. *Slim hope to ultimate destruction in six point two minutes.*

Thunder rumbled in the clouds. A lightning strike lit up the darkened sky.

CHAPTER NINETEEN

*L*yn sat frozen on the bench of the gazebo with her eyes closed. Her head between her open hands. Her mind reeled. Her chest pounded. Her lungs ached.

Only Umiko's arm draped over her shoulders, anchored her to the here and now. Her mind was lost in a sea of rumbling clouds. She waited for them to release their burden. For tears to fall, for a scream to rip through her lungs and throat or for her heart to give a final shuddering thump.

Another lightning strike and corresponding rumble ripped across the sky. Her ears listened for the pitter patter of rain drops. None came.

Instead she heard the rattle of a muffler. Her heart thumped, then paused.

Time seemed to stand still.

The only mark of time passing was the sound of the muffler getting louder. Closer.

"What in the world?" Lyn heard Greg say from the sidewalk.

Lyn lifted her head with her next pulse beat and she and Umiko turned to look at him.

"How did he find us?" Greg said as he jogged across the

street and traced his fingers along the rear of the car. He stopped near the passenger side and slid his finger over the same spot a few times before he squatted down.

Greg picked something off and flung it to the ground. He stomped on the thing and twisted his foot in one spot. He ground whatever he had found into the asphalt as the Jeep turned onto the street.

Killian was behind the wheel and a set of muscles rode in the seat beside him.

Lyn couldn't think of the guy's name. All of Killian's cronies looked the same to her. Biceps that strained shirt sleeves, missing necks, and shoulders that rivaled a bear's. Walking, talking intimidation.

"What's going on?" Jonathan asked as he stood up and went to stand on the steps of the gazebo. Umiko and Lyn remained sitting. Lyn's eyes frozen on the scene unfolding in front of her. Her pulse began to quicken.

Clark stepped up the steps and introduced himself to Jonathan.

Lyn thought that this was not the time for such things, but Clark, for all his black clothing and death metal band shirts, was the best mannered person she had ever met.

"Lucky you," Lyn said to her not-father. She plastered a fake smile to her face that was all fake and zero smile. "You can meet my stalker." She saw the look on his face. "You've missed out on a lot by leaving us." Lyn stood and watched the Jeep pull up on this side of the curb, blocking the route to the mustang and cutting Greg off from her view.

"How did she die?" Jonathan asked out of left field.

Lyn's brain changed gears but she didn't turn her gaze from Killian and his sidekick. She knew what Jonathan wanted to know. "From a brain injury that she should have survived. She slipped and hit her head." Lyn shook hers. "That's all. It was just a stupid accident."

"Gregar?" Killian said with a friendly tone as he leapt

down from his jeep. "What are the odds of seeing you in this neighborhood?" His voice feigned interest.

"Killian, what are you doing here?" Greg's voice, not so sugar coated, mirrored the threat in his posture.

"I was visiting my grandmother and thought I saw my good friend Lyn's bodyguards." Killian made a movement with his head and his cohort jumped out of the jeep and moved toward the gazebo. "Don't worry your pretty little head. I'm just here to say a quick hello."

"She's not going anywhere with you."

"You think I'm here to kidnap her?" Killian feigned hurt feelings with the same hand to the chest motion Greg had used earlier.

"Am I wrong?" Greg asked. "Isn't that what you just told your crony to do with that twitchy head thing you did? Get the girl?" He paused. "Well, I am not going to let you."

"I have business with Lyn that is none of yours." Killian squared himself to Greg. His back to Lyn.

"Does she know that?" Greg asked as he crossed the street in front of a moving car. The car slowed suddenly and the driver leaned on his horn. Greg didn't break his eye contact with Killian as he moved and the car drove past.

"I feel like I have made my intentions clear, but I admit, she might need a formal invitation." He moved to include Lyn in his peripheral vision, while still keeping Greg in his line of sight. "Lyn," he called. "We have something to discuss. In private."

"Wow, you didn't trip on that mouthful of bullshit. I'm impressed," Greg taunted. "I don't care, why you are here, Killian. You are not taking Lyn anywhere."

"I just want to take her for a run, Gregar. No harm in that. She enjoyed it this morning."

"Listen carefully. She is not going anywhere with you." Greg stepped up to Killian. The jeep between them and the curb.

Killian showed his teeth in a creepy version of a smile. "Go ahead, I know you want to say it. Over your dead body."

"Will he actually kill the guy?" Jonathan asked from his vantage point in the gazebo

Clark and the girls, focused intently on the barely audible conversation between Killian and Greg, startled to the sound of the voice nearest them.

Jonathan's normal volume pulled their focus from the fight that was about to start.

Clark thought before answering. "I wouldn't put it past him, but his dad can't keep him from trouble out here. We aren't in his jurisdiction anymore."

"What are they?" Jonathan looked at the two boys.

"Cops' kid and a military brat. I don't know what branch."

"Human?" Jonathan asked.

Clark shook his head. "The guys in the jeep are shifters."

"Werewolves?"

"There are lots of shifter types, but yeah, I'm fairly certain these are wolves. Dangerous ones. Greg can take a serious beating, but he's not invincible." Clark summed up Killian and Greg. "I helped set his nose on Thursday." Clark pointed at Greg. "You can't even tell now."

"You don't know what kind of creature your friend is?" Jonathan asked.

Clark turned to face Jonathan. He looked down on the man both because of his height and his comment. "I know that he's taken more than one beating for your daughter and he's about to take another. I suspect he'd do a whole lot more than bleed for her if the circumstances demanded. That's all I need to know about my friend."

Lyn let Clark's pride in Greg wash over her.

"And the friendship part is recent." Lyn heard Clark mumble under his breath.

Clark turned to face the sidekick, which had closed the

gap between the sidewalk and the gazebo. "Look dude, let's not get physical. I'm sure we can negotiate a deal. Lyn's choice of course, she's not property to be traded."

"You loved her?" Jonathan looked back at Lyn.

Lyn's eyes welled up with water. She wanted to stomp her foot and scream at the world. She didn't want to talk about her mom. She didn't want to be the prize in a fight. The last straw was this stranger asking her questions like he might actually care. Tears fell from her eyes. "You really think I'm a monster?" Lyn's shoulders sagged.

Umiko stepped forward and put her arm around her friend. "Yes, she did. She still does. More than anything," she yelled at him. "They were inseparable, and Maria would have done anything to protect Lyn." Umiko's voice flared with a fierceness that made Lyn cry a little more.

Jonathan nodded and passed Clark to meet the big guy on the sidewalk. "You watch the girls."

"I'm not sure that's a good idea." Clark tried to stop him, but Jonathan brushed past.

He turned from Clark to the stack of muscles. "I think you should go back where you came from," Jonathan said to the jock bearing down on them. "I'm having a moment with my daughter and you weren't invited." Jonathan planted his feet and blocked the big guy's path to the gazebo entrance.

The muscle turned away from Lyn to face this new threat. Albeit, a frail and pale one.

Lyn was struck by Jonathan's words. He had called her his daughter. Maybe he did care about her. Or he cared enough about Maria, to learn to care about Lyn. She allowed herself a little glimmer of hope.

Lyn and Umiko huddled in the back of the gazebo while Clark stood guard at the entrance.

Lyn couldn't watch both fights at once. Not with any real attention.

She tried to find Greg, the boy who would more than

bleed for her. What did Clark mean by that? Would Greg go so far as to get himself killed for her? Why would he do something stupid like that?

Greg was still in the street with Killian. Lyn watched as the shifter threw the first punch at Greg, who dodged and pulled Killian off balance with his own momentum. Killian was only off guard for a moment though, when he regained his center of gravity, the pair circled one another.

Killian threw two more punches, while Greg guarded his face and danced around the threat. Killian regained his footing from the last failed punch and when he turned, Greg's fist connected with his cheek.

Lyn tried to keep an eye on them but a grunt pulled her back to the closer fight.

She turned her attention as the sidekick feinted a rush and Lyn thought he was headed for Clark and the gazebo. She pulled Umiko back to the rear railing. Jonathan was out of his depth. He held his ground for now, but Lyn didn't think the puny little man would hold against the muscle he was about to face off with. If the muscle could land one good punch, Jonathan would be out for the count. Jonathan had to keep moving, keep the muscle occupied, while not letting an angle to the gazebo appear or his opponent would simply rush it.

Muscle man was relaxed, unconcerned, he lifted his fists and Lyn held her breath. She wondered why he didn't just walk through the smaller target.

The sound at the sidewalk pulled her focus back to fight between better matched opponents.

Both boys had traded a fair number of punches. Lyn could make out a matching set of cuts along both boys brow lines. In addition to the cut, Killian was sweating and his hair was a mess. Greg, however, looked less disheveled. Lyn didn't know for sure, but she thought Greg was winning. The look on their faces suggested as much. Killian snarled and Greg smiled as he stepped past another swing. Killian lost his balance and fell to the ground. He scrambled up and rushed at Greg.

Clark looked around. "Umiko, you and Lyn need to disappear." He stepped to them and blocked Lyn's view of the fight. He looked into Umiko's eyes. "You can meet us back at her dad's house, in the back yard, out of sight."

Umiko nodded.

"Good. Go, now, while they're distracted."

Clark turned back to the spot where Jonathan and sidekick collided. "Oof." Lyn saw Clark wince, but he stayed sentinel in the doorway. "Go. Please." He shouted.

Umiko looked around the small park. "I don't see a way out, do you?" Umiko asked.

Lyn wanted to look back. To make sure her people were standing. Part of her wanted to scream at them all to stop. To tell them she wasn't worth it. The dominant part wanted to run.

"Lyn," Umiko stage whispered.

Lyn let her dominant part take control. She looked around for an escape route. Somewhere to run.

The park was small, less than a half a football field long, not quite as wide and surrounded by oak and cedar trees. A few crepe myrtles spread throughout, provided shade cover but not much in the way of hiding places. It was also closed off on three sides by six foot tall wooden privacy fences. Backyards butted up to the park with houses beyond. The only ways out were over the fence or around the skirmishes, the latter unlikely to work.

"We could climb a fence?" Lyn climbed onto the bench and over the gazebo railing. She dropped down into a break in the surrounding shrubs and landed on bent knee to cushion her fall.

"I'm a swimmer, not a climber." Umiko followed Lyn. Jumping down in the same spot after Lyn had taken step back. Where Lyn had landed gracefully, Umiko fell to her knees and winced when one leg landed too close to a brittle shrub.

Lyn helped her friend stand, and looked for alternatives. If she got out of here, maybe the fight would stop before anyone could get too badly injured.

Umiko dusted off her knees, brushing dirt off of the fresh cut. She looked over the gazebo floor, through the rails. "They're distracted, let's just walk around the edge. I don't think I can climb."

"Okay, but run, not walk," Lyn said. Her fight response was drowned out by her flight response, as usual.

"Won't running be more likely to draw attention?" Umiko and Lyn stepped to the back of the park, near the fence line. Behind trees and somewhat out of sight. "We need to be sneaky."

The girls considered whether to walk or run as the sound of fighting continued. Either way, they'd be spotted, speed was trivial. Lyn took in the scene around them determined to find a solution. Maybe she should leave Umiko here. She'd be safe if Lyn were gone. Killian only wanted her. For what Lyn couldn't imagine.

Lyn couldn't see any of the fighting from behind the gazebo. She did see that Clark was no longer at his post.

"Look." Lyn pointed to a section of gazebo beneath the floor. "Clark said to disappear, right? I think we can hide under there."

"It'll be a tight squeeze, but I'm game. You first." Umiko crouched down as she made her way back to the gazebo and held some small branches out of the way

Lyn got down on her belly and army crawled under the gazebo where a section of lattice had broken away. Underneath, next to the bare earth, was cooler, but still warm, slightly muggy. It was also dirty and filled with things Umiko would hate. She looked behind her and just enough light filtered through the gaps in the floorboards that she made out her friend crawling through the hole.

"Please no spiders. Please no spiders," Umiko repeated under her breath and she found Lyn's hand to squeeze.

"I'm sorry. I can't keep the spiders away." Lyn squeezed Umiko's hand.

"Just lie to me okay," Umiko begged. "Be a friend and lie about there being no spiders or other creepy crawlies, or slithering animals under here with us."

"Umiko, there is nothing to be afraid of. I will chase off anything tiny that tries to eat you." Lyn squeezed her friends hand.

"Thank you," Umiko whispered and squeezed back. "Can you see anything?"

"Not from here, but listen?"

The girls heard grunts and what were presumably words, but they couldn't understand them. Lyn closed her eyes and concentrated. She heard someone fall and feet rushed to the gazebo.

"Where'd she go?" A stomp on the wood floor above them accompanied the question.

It didn't sound like Killian's voice so it must be the bonus muscle.

"I don't know, man. I was watching you beat on an old guy. She slipped past me." Clark's voice didn't betray anything different.

"Killian, she's gone," The muscle bellowed.

"That's August." Umiko whispered as low as she could.

Clark made a coughing sound and stomped out of the gazebo. Lyn was sure his footfalls were louder than they needed to be.

"Shhh." Lyn told her friend. She wanted to ask how Umiko knew the boy's name, but any sound could give them away. Especially if Clark moved away and couldn't cover for them.

"What are you talking about?" Killian shouted from farther away.

The girls inched forward. Lyn in the lead to move spider webs, and scare off anything alive. Umiko followed, staying as close as possible.

The first thing Lyn saw through the lattice was Clark's back. He was kneeling on the ground.

The second thing she saw was Killian's head and upper body whip around when Greg punched him.

Killian's hand flew up to the impact site. He let out a guttural growl at Greg. "You hit a man when he wasn't looking. That's not very honorable of you." He said through clenched teeth as he stood. Killian tensed his body, ready to pounce.

He kept Greg in his eye line and called to his sidekick. "Are you sure she's gone?"

"I don't see her."

Killian grumbled. "Can you smell her?" he called.

Muscles took a deep inhale. Lyn imagined his nostrils flaring with the effort.

Lyn and Umiko held their breath. Lyn had forgotten how obsessed they were with her smell. She should have left the park without Umiko, instead of trapping them both under the gazebo.

"Dirt, vegetation, blood, sweat, and fear. Maybe they ran for it while we were distracted." He took a second breath and walked around the inside of the gazebo.

"They can't have gotten far, let's go look for them," Killian said, keeping an eye on Greg and rubbing his jaw. "Nice hit, Gregar. But I'm going to find your girl."

Greg growled it was less animal sounding than Killian's.

Killian laughed. "Come on, August."

Lyn watched Killian back away from Greg and toward his jeep. Muscles followed, reluctantly, his eyes searched for her as he walked. Greg stood his ground, but looked spent. Clark was still kneeling on the ground. *Did he get hit?*

Lyn held her breath until the jeep's engine revved and pulled away from the curb.

"Where's Jonathan?" Lyn asked Umiko in a whispered voice. "Where'd he go?" *I must get my run and hide tactics from him.* Lyn thought. Her emotions ran from worried to content. At least he wasn't hurt. She didn't like the idea of people getting hurt because of her.

Then she saw Jonathan's boots, toes pointed up and to the sides, dead weight. She followed the line of his legs behind Clark's hunched back but couldn't see Jonathan's head. She tried to get up and hit her own head on the beam above. "Shit." Lyn pressed on the spot of her head that had connected with solid wood. The zap of nerves clamped her jaw and a tingling sensation flooded her body.

"What's wrong?" Umiko looked in the same direction Lyn had been looking.

"I've got to get out of here." Lyn started crawling backwards. Her knee pressed into something hard.

"Ouch," Umiko squeaked.

Lyn lifted her knee.

Umiko moved her hand to her mouth. "Ugh." She spat out dirt as she tried to get out of Lyn's way.

Backing out of the small space was harder than getting in. Lyn kicked and growled. She grew frustrated with every second she was trapped.

"You're scaring me, Lyn." Umiko shimmied as far from Lyn and the way they had come as she could to let her friend pass.

"I need to get out." Lyn's foot kicked and connected with a loose piece of lattice. It broke free and flew out from the gazebo frame. The hole was wider now, and more sunlight came in.

"Lyn, it's okay," Umiko said.

Lyn turned her eyes to her friend. They burned in her skull.

Umiko shrank back and stayed quiet.

Lyn army crawled backwards out from under the gazebo.

Once she was clear, she jumped up and ran around the side of the structure. In her haste, she collided with Clark, who toppled out of his kneeling stance and landed with his butt flat on the ground next to Jonathan's prone form.

"I think I hit my head," Jonathan said to her. He did not open his eyes.

Clark stood and left her alone. "Umiko?" He moved in the direction Lyn flew from. Calling for her like a game of hide and seek.

The sight of her father laying prone on the ground with a head injury brought back other terrible memories plus ones she only imagined. "Don't you dare die." Lyn pounded the ground by her father's body.

"It hurts. Like a freight train ran me into the ground. But I don't think I'm going to die from it." He reached out his hand to hers.

Neither did her mom.

"I can't handle someone else dying because of me." Lyn's eyes leaked. She fought back the tears and focused on her anger. This was Killian's fault, not hers. She knew that in her brain, but her heart hurt too much to accept it.

"How's the other guy? Did I at least get as good as I got?" Jonathan blinked a couple of times, squinted and closed his eyes again."Wow, the sky is pretty bright."

Lyn looked up. There was no sun, there were dark clouds. Then she saw what he saw. Another flash of lightning lit the cloud like a brief flicker from a flashlight. There was still no rain. Just an angry electrical storm.

"The other guy walked away," Lyn answered Jonathan's question.

Jonathan sank into the ground. "I'm sorry, Maria," he said.

"Lyn," she corrected him. "Are you going to be able to get up?"

"Considering I see two of you, I think I need a minute." Jonathan stayed down.

Greg walked up. "Lyn, can Clark make sure he doesn't need an ambulance?"

His voice was low and controlled, like he was talking to a wild animal. His pitch soothed some of her anger. His melodic voice broke through her fear.

She nodded. Clark sat on his knees across from her.

"Damage report?"

"Shut it, Gregar. I am not one of your private security team," Clark said, but there was no animosity in his voice.

"Umiko?" Greg asked. "You're okay, right? Just dirty."

She must have answered with her head because Lyn heard the sound of hair move on shoulders. She heard the metal tinkling sound of Clark's wallet chain and Jonathan's uneven breathing. She heard Greg step through the dry grass toward her.

He was close enough that she could smell him. Sweat mixed with a coppery tinge. Blood. There was blood on her father too and on the ground here and closer to the street. There was blood on Umiko's hand and her knee. It was the only scent she could smell. The gentle perfume of azaleas was gone, so was the fresh cut grass, masked instead by the pungent smell of blood. Lyn's head drooped.

Everyone had been hurt, except her and Clark, and it was all her fault.

Clark stood up and walked over to Greg. Lyn watched the rise and fall of her father's chest and listened to heavy boot strike the ground. Eight steps. She thought Greg was closer than that, but she heard each distinctive step from Clark's steel-toed boots, and no corresponding steps from Greg's sneakers.

"His injuries aren't severe. He'll heal fine on his own,

given enough time." Clark's voice was calm and clinical.

Lyn remembered those same words in the same tone from the nurse at the hospital when her mother had fallen. They were lies.

"But, there's something more," Clark continued.

Lyn turned her head slightly to their conversation, keeping her head down and her eyes on her father.

"Do we need to call an ambulance?" Greg asked.

"It wouldn't help. It's not that type of more," Clark said.

Lyn heard the sound of Clark's pant legs rubbing against each other and a muffled whimper from Umiko.

"I have a first aid kit in the car. We'll clean up the cut," Clark said. "Can you wiggle your fingers?" Clark paused. "Good. It's not broken."

Lyn stopped listening to her friend's triage evaluation and instead focused on Greg's footsteps coming closer.

He placed a hand on her shoulder. "His injuries aren't severe." Greg squatted next to them. He used both arms to help Jonathan sit.

When the man swayed and began to topple over, Greg steadied him. "Just breathe."

Lyn heard Jonathan take a deep breath and she followed suit, closing her eyes.

"Good. Another."

Greg directed Jonathan's breathing until the man was ready to stand. He rubbed his hand between Lyn's shoulder blades and called behind her. "Clark, can you get his other side?"

Clark walked over and Lyn felt a hand in hers. Umiko held tight and helped lift Lyn from the ground.

"It can't happen again," Lyn whispered.

Umiko pulled Lyn into a hug. "You guys take him back in the car, we'll walk."

"Are you sure?" Clark asked Umiko.

"I'll be fine," Umiko said.

Lyn watched the two guys. She wouldn't have considered them friends two days ago, but they had proven themselves to be just that.

They carried the weight of a much older man between them and maneuvered him into the passenger seat of the rusted vehicle. Clark cranked the engine and drove down the street, while Greg jogged beside the car.

"Clark said his injuries wouldn't kill him, but that there was something else. What did he mean?" Lyn asked Umiko as she broke the hug.

The pair began to walk toward the duplex. Lyn's feet wanting to sprint ahead and get there before Clark and the car did.

Umiko slowed her. "Never scare me like that again," Umiko's little voice squeaked.

Lyn turned to face her. She saw the fear in Umiko's eyes, heard her increased heart rate, and smelled a sickly sweet scent beneath the dirt. "I'm sorry. I was worried that he was..." she cut herself off. "I didn't mean to scare you. I won't do it again. Please tell me what Clark meant?" Lyn begged. The nerves in her arm twinged in Umiko's grasp. She must have hit it on something getting out from under the gazebo.

"Clark thinks Jonathan has something else that is killing him. Something that's been working at it for a while."

"Like, cancer?"

"He's not sure."

"Umiko, is Clark a creature?"

"Yeah, but I don't know what. We haven't talked about that yet."

"I'm sorry. This is a horrible way to start a relationship. Fighting my battles and doctoring my...a stranger." Lyn paused. "I don't know what he is to me... nothing?"

"Your mom's husband. Or ex-husband." Umiko shrugged. "That's not helpful, is it?"

Lyn's lips curled into a forced smile. She thought about the many ways to explain relationships. She air quoted her next words. "It's complicated."

The girls giggled and the tension of the last few hours cracked.

"You look like you rolled through a dirt patch." Lyn said to Umiko.

"I think we did. I feel like things are crawling on me. I *really* want a shower. Do you think your... Do you think Jonathan would let us use his?" Umiko asked

"Did you bring extra clothes?" Lyn thought it was possible. Umiko was a pro at schemes.

"No, but I can at least shake these out. I think I would feel less itchy and I can make sure nothing is living in these but me."

CHAPTER TWENTY

When the girls got back to the house, Clark was waiting for them on the sidewalk by the car. "Are you two all right?"

They nodded.

Clark smiled. "Hiding under the gazebo was smart. Killian and his buddy didn't think of that."

"Yeah, well, it might have been smart at the time, but I think it was stupid. There's no telling what is in this shirt with me. I could use a shower and a change of clothes," Umiko said in a rush. She turned to Lyn. "No offense."

"It was pretty dumb. I think that other guy would have found us if Killian hadn't been so... Killian." Lyn sighed.

"Thank goodness for alpha male domineering," Clark agreed.

He lifted Umiko's hand. "We can clean this here." He opened a black tackle box that was already sitting on the trunk of the vintage mustang. He pulled out a pack of gauze and a small bottle of hydrogen peroxide. "It might sting." He cleaned the cut on Umiko's palm and made her open and close her fist several times before he moved onto her knee. "Lyn, do you have any scrapes we need to clean?"

Lyn shook her head. She didn't care about cleaning a small section of her skin. She wanted an hour long hot shower and fresh clothes.

"Can we go home now?" Lyn asked.

"But we didn't…" Umiko faced Lyn and tripped over her words. Her hands went to Lyn's hair.

"Don't you want a shower?" Lyn tempted her. "Warm water? Fresh clothes?"

"Umm." Umiko looked around and pointed at the car mirror.

"I know I'm a mess and that there are leaves and dirt in my hair, Umiko. I don't need to see it with my eyes. I can feel it." Lyn lifted her hand to her hair and pulled out a small brittle leaf. She briefly realized that was easier than it should have been.

Umiko nodded. "You should look."

Lyn rolled her eyes, but bent down and tried to place her head between the window and mirror so she could see her reflection. Clark turned the mustang's mirror to make it easier on her.

"What the hell?" Lyn's hand flew to her hair. Thin streaks of white shone through from underneath the brown and red. Like slivers of light through dark curtains.

The sky rumbled.

Lyn looked at her refection closer, turning her head left and right.

The brown hair, which she thought of as her own, was still there and still fractured in unstructured curls. The red highlights, Umiko's color, were well blended if unnatural. Lyn had thought it was a nice look, one that she could get used to in time. The new locks, however, were white as fresh snow and stark by comparison. The brown hair was a tangled mess but the white fell through her fingers without resistance. "This is…" She searched for a word.

"Cool?" Clark said with a smile.

"A clue?" Umiko offered.

"The worst hair style ever. It's different lengths and colors. I look like Frankenstein's monster's bride." Lyn leaned back on the car and sighed.

"Nah, hers was one big streak and stood up." Clark mimed. "Yours just needs a trim."

"On the bright side." Umiko put her fingers in her friend's hair. "The white looks tangle free." She pulled a leaf out of a white section and the silky hair flowed through it. She did the same with a leaf in the brown section and had to leave it there because the hair had it in a death grip.

"Sure, that's a nice perk. I can comb sections. But why is it happening? What on earth would cause my hair to change like this and so fast?" Lyn gathered the various strands and formed a quick and dirty pony tail on the back of her head. Most of the white was hidden among the reds and brown, but the ends were longer.

Clark and Umiko exchanged looks. They turned to Lyn and shrugged.

"No clue." Umiko took charge and drug Lyn to the front door of the B side of the duplex.

When they stepped up to the small porch, Greg came out carrying two full garbage bags filled with what sounded like glass.

"I opened the window blinds because there's no light. I don't think the electricity is on. Water works though. You can wash some of the dirt off your hands and faces but I wouldn't trust the towels."

"I can help with that." Clark went back to his car and retrieved a folded towel from his trunk. "Greg, you need any first aid before I put this away?"

"Nah, I cleaned up in the sink." Greg stepped around the girls and carried the bags to the end of the driveway.

Lyn looked at his face where she was sure Killian had broken the skin. There were no marks, and no swelling. She could see no physical evidence that he had been in a fight moments before.

Clark closed the trunk, first aid box stowed, and walked back up the path. He handed Umiko the towel and followed the girls into the house.

Inside, the duplex was dark even with the blinds open. Maybe Jonathan wouldn't be able to see Lyn's hair. She was self-conscious about her physical changes and more than a little freaked out. She knew Jonathan would just use the new look to confirm she wasn't his. That she wasn't human at all.

"Is there a bathroom we can use?" Umiko asked.

Jonathan was laid out on the couch with a plastic bag of something white on his face. He held his hand up and pointed behind him.

The girls walked in and closed the door. It was pitch black, with no windows. Lyn reached for a switch but it did nothing. Lyn sighed and opened the door. Just enough light came in so the girls could see their faces in the mirror. They tried not to touch anything more than they had to, but the half bath was too small for two people, especially with the door opened.

They maneuvered so Umiko was at the sink and Lyn sat on the closed lid of the toilet.

Umiko's elbow hit the corner of the door with a quiet thump. "Ouch." She sighed and turned the sink on to start washing her hands. The sight of the crusty bar of soap on the sink's edge was enough for her to decide to stick with straight water. She scrubbed for several minutes to make sure her hands were dirt free before she splashed water on her face.

"Hand me your shirt," Lyn said.

Umiko removed it and went back to her face.

Lyn shook the shirt out onto the floor. She would have taken it outside, but the floor needed to be swept and mopped anyway. She handed the shirt back to Umiko and they traded places. Umiko put her shirt back on and took

Lyn's while Lyn cleaned as much of the dirt off of her hands and face as she could.

Lyn brushed some dust off of her jean shorts and pointed to a spot on Umiko's. Umiko brushed the surface debris, but the denim held onto the ground in dirt.

"Better?" Lyn asked.

"I guess. It's not like I can clean my legs in a sink." Umiko resigned herself to the partial clean. "I don't feel anything crawling on me, but I want a shower, as soon as we get home."

Lyn agreed. "Let's go, then." They took Clark's towel and left the bathroom.

The guys were sitting in the living room. The front door opened for airflow and what little ambient light the storm clouds allowed.

"Do you still have the report from the investigator?" Umiko asked. She handed the damp towel back to Clark and said thanks.

Jonathan sat on the couch and Lyn could see that the bag on his head was filled with rice. No electricity, meant no ice packs. "In the TV cabinet." He pointed across the room.

Umiko opened a drawer and fished around.

Clark held his fingers to Jonathan's wrist for a minute before he stood over him to look at his head.

Lyn moved to the doorway and looked outside. The dark room felt confining to her. She wanted to be outside in the fresh air with the wind on her skin. She wanted to run. To find an open space and put her earbuds in and let go of the crazy.

"Do you know how long you have?" Clark asked.

Lyn came back to herself and turned to listen. Greg returned from taking the trash to the street and stood just behind her.

"The doctors said six months back in May." Jonathan found Lyn's face.

"Don't look at me like that. You and your friends can't save me, and I can't save you. You need to find a different option." He looked away. "Besides, I have no money, and why prolong it. I lost everything years ago."

"Gave up," Lyn said and crossed her arms over her chest. "You made a choice to give up everything years ago," she corrected him.

Jonathan dropped his chin to his chest and nodded. "I can't help you, even if Maria wanted it that way. I have an expiration date."

"You can sign some papers," Clark said. "To keep her from having to live with someone she doesn't know or trust."

Jonathan and Lyn turned their eyes to Clark.

"You can help her get emancipated. You're listed as her father on the birth certificate. You can sign the papers to make it easier on her. They may even rush the process with your terminal diagnosis. They did when my mom was sick."

Now all eyes turned to Clark.

"One day, we are all going to sit down and share some secrets," Greg said.

"I wasn't holding back. I thought Lyn just wanted to find her dad. I didn't think about the legal aspect." Clark shrugged.

"I'm sorry about your mom," Lyn said.

"I know you are, but it's okay. She's with my dad now," Clark said without an ounce of sadness in his voice.

A tear slid down her cheek. Lyn hoped that she would be able to talk about losing her mom without breaking apart one day.

CHAPTER TWENTY-ONE

"I found it!" Umiko said and held a manilla envelope up as a trophy.

Lyn jumped at her exclamation. Greg put a hand on her back to steady her and pushed her away from the open door.

"What do you have?" he asked.

Umiko used her hip to close the drawer to the TV cabinet and brought the packet to the coffee table. Greg moved a few pieces of junk mail and the TV remote out of the way, while Clark held his cell phone as a flashlight.

"What should I look for?" Umiko asked. "Do I just start at page one?" She picked up and scanned the first page, then put it face down to start a new pile.

"What are you talking about?" Greg asked.

Umiko rolled her eyes. "Long story, short. Lyn may have been baby switched. Jonathan hired a PI."

Greg turned to Jonathan. "Did the private eye find anything to support a switch?"

Lyn liked the way Greg didn't skip a beat. They didn't have to recap the entire conversation from the gazebo for him to catch up.

Jonathan shook his head. He groaned with the flare of

pain caused by the motion. He grabbed his head with his hand. "He thought it was possible, but couldn't prove it."

Lyn looked at the stack of papers and the envelope. Stack was an overstatement. This collection of paperwork seemed too thin to hold the all answers that Lyn wanted it to have. Whether or not she was switched? If so, who and where were her real parents? What type of creatures were they? Why had her hair started changing after all these years? How could she have lived as a human for sixteen years without knowing she was different? Why had her biological parents not tried to find her? Did they suspect the child that they raised was not their own?

"What made him think it was possible?" Greg continued questioning Jonathan as more questions piled up in Lyn's head.

"The midwife that delivered the baby." Jonathan put the rice bag back to his head and closed his eyes. "I can't remember her name. She worked in hospitals and clinics in several states that also had switching complaints. Nothing that ever stuck, but he said the coincidence was too strong to ignore."

Lyn moved closer and scanned the pages over Umiko's shoulder. "Who was the nurse?" She tried to find a single name in all the typed text.

"The same one who handed me the baby. The nurse that told me I was sleep deprived and not to worry. The one who took the chubby, pink one and returned with a thinner, pale, sickly one. I told Maria. I sent her a letter, when the PI told me that the nurse lived in a house near Maria."

Umiko put the sheet of paper she was holding face down on the second stack.

"What was her first name?" Jonathan asked himself. "It's right here." Jonathan tapped his temple. "It started with an A, I think. Ashley?" He put the bag of rice in his lap and turned his head to the ceiling, as if the answer would be written in the dingy paint. "That's not it." He shook his head. "Allison?"

Lyn's legs gave out. Greg caught her before she hit the floor. He steered her toward the couch. Jonathan made room for her.

"Alice." Lyn said as she fell back onto the couch.

"Yes! That's it!" He pointed at Lyn. "Wait, how do you know her name?"

"Why does that matter?" Greg asked Lyn. He squatted down in front of her.

"Ms. Alice Evans is the one who provided CPS with the paper that Maria signed to give her guardianship," Umiko said.

Greg turned to face Umiko, his hand rested on Lyn's knee.

"Lyn will have to live with her unless we find a blood relative," Umiko finished.

"Or get her emancipated minor paperwork filed," Clark reminded them.

Jonathan was silent.

"If she knew about the switch, she would have known I would fail. We only had 48 hours. Monday morning is the deadline. I can't find a completely different family by then. Even with this report." Lyn looked at Greg then Clark and finally Jonathan.

"If I say I'll sign the papers to help emancipate you..." Jonathan's question trailed off.

"If the father listed on Lyn's brith certificate vouches for Lyn's ability to care for herself. To essentially become an adult in the government's eyes, CPS should be satisfied, even if Ms. Evans has a valid document," Clark answered. "Ms. Evans can't object without giving away the baby switching theory. She'll risk implicating herself."

Jonathan nodded. "Okay." He paused. "But I don't understand why this nurse from your birth would be involved in your guardianship. Why does she even care, what is she to you?"

"I agree. There's something more than simple guardianship or even a possible baby switching going on," Greg said and looked at Lyn.

Lyn sighed. "She lives across the street from us…me. She's been my nurse for my entire life."

"Your nurse? As in yours alone?" Greg asked. "Why do need your own private nurse?" His eyes turned up to meet hers. He gripped his hands and used his elbows, braced on his knees, to keep his balance.

Lyn realized just how much she and Umiko had left out yesterday. Had it only been yesterday? Lyn put her head in her hands and leaned to prop her elbows on her knees.

"She's anemic, or Ms. Evans says she is anyway." Umiko's voice dripped with disbelief. "It sounds crazy to me. I mean, anemia. It's common. There are supplements. It doesn't required constant testing. It's not diabetes or anything. She could get a trained dog if she needed constant monitoring." Umiko looked at each person in the room in turn. They were all quiet. "Anyway, Ms. Evans gives Lyn some herbal stuff to take daily and draws blood sometimes, to test." Umiko placed the last word in air quotes.

Lyn leaned forward and picked up the manilla envelope. "I found an envelope like this in my mom's closet." She turned it over to read the addresses. To 'Jon Davis' from Parks Investigations, Inc. The same initials. P. I. I. Only now Lyn knew they weren't initials. "I think it's from the same person."

Greg turned to Jonathan. "Did you have the PI send the report to Maria?"

"No." He shook his head. "I didn't want her to know what I was up to until I had all the answers, and a lead on our baby. After she kicked me out, I thought it would be best to only take her concrete proof," Jonathan said. "He must have sent it on his own. Did she have letters too?" He looked at Lyn. "I sent them every year on her birthday."

Lyn nodded. "Yes, but most of the letters were unopened. The manilla envelope was still sealed, I think. I didn't pay much attention to it. I just threw it back on the shelf after we found what we were looking for." Lyn saw the look on Jonathan's face.

Jonathan sank into the couch. "I told her about the nurse in one of the letters. I warned her to be careful around that woman. That something didn't feel right. She probably just thought I was nuts."

Lyn sat back on the couch and closed her eyes. She focused on the beat of her pulse. "Maybe that is why my mom stopped letting Ms. Evans treat me. She must have known."

"Do you think your mom confronted her?" Umiko asked Lyn.

"If she did…" Clark trailed off.

Greg put his knees on the ground in front of Lyn and put his hand back on her knee. "Lyn, are you all right?"

"I. Can't. Breathe." She pulled air into her lungs and let it out again between each word, but the oxygen wasn't helping. Lyn squeezed her eyes shut and continued to hyperventilate.

"Panic attack." Clark diagnosed.

Umiko traded places with Greg and squeezed Lyn's wrist between two fingers. "I can't find it. Clark, you do it." She lifted Lyn's wrist to Clark who stood and took it in his.

"Do what? Umiko, what are we doing?" Greg asked.

"Sit, Clark," Umiko demanded. "Find her pulse, then tap it out for me. The same speed, but without sound. Here." Umiko made a spot on the table and sat on her knees.

Clark did as he was asked. Lyn's pulse was racing. He held her wrist in one hand and with the other, tapped the too fast beats on the edge of the coffee table with the pads of his fingers.

"Okay. I got it." Umiko picked up the tapping with the palms of her hands. "Lyn, focus." Umiko began to change the rhythm. "Clark, keep going until it slows back to normal."

"You think you can slow her pulse by tapping on the table?" Greg asked.

"I can if you're quiet," Umiko snapped. "She needs to be able to hear it." She continued her tapping.

Greg stopped talking and walked behind the sofa to stand at Lyn's back. She was on the verge of gasping for air. He placed his hands on her shoulders and watched Umiko's hands until he found the rhythm. He mirrored it with the fingers of his hands on Lyn's clavicle.

Lyn tried to drag in a breath and failed. Greg's hand on her collar made her stomach do a leap. She closed her eyes and felt the weight of his hands on her shoulders push her down. Into the couch cushions, grounding her.

She found a rhythm in her bones and focused all her attention on breaking through her oxygen deprivation and syncing to that slower beat.

It didn't stop the anxiety but the music overwhelmed her senses and she followed willingly. Her breath deepened, the oxygen finally reached her lungs.

"It's working," Clark whispered. He tapped her pulse as it slowed.

"Music is her kryptonite?" Greg asked.

"Music is the language her soul speaks." Umiko answered and slowed her beat a little more.

CHAPTER TWENTY-TWO

*L*yn's lungs relaxed, but her skin was still flush. Greg took his hands off her shoulders and she sank back into the couch, grateful for the darkness. She was sure a better lit room would give away the color on her cheeks.

"Where's your phone?" Umiko asked.

"I'm okay for now," Lyn said

Greg moved to sit on the arm of the couch beside Lyn.

Clark disappeared outside and returned with Lyn's purse, her bottle of water, and a bag of chips. He handed them to Lyn. She took a sip of water and placed her purse beside her on the couch.

"Music is her language? What is she?" Jonathan asked and moved further down the couch.

Lyn couldn't sink any deeper into the couch.

Greg, Clark, and Umiko turned as one and glared at Jonathan.

"She's Lyn Davis," Umiko said, her tone indicating what she thought of the question. "Same as she was five minutes ago. Same as she was sixteen years ago. Maria's only daughter and my best friend." Umiko punctuated the last few words.

Jonathan clamped his mouth shut.

A long silence followed and Lyn was back to wanting to hide from the awkwardness.

Greg spoke and chased the unease away. "It sounds like a long con. This Evans woman installed herself in Lyn's life from the very beginning. I'm assuming she wanted to keep tabs on her for some reason."

"Lyn's blood," Umiko said in an even tone.

"I don't think Ms. Evans is a vampire." Greg winked at Lyn.

Lyn pulled her phone out of her pocket and rummaged in her purse for her ear buds. She put them in her ears and turned her music on to a low level. She needed to hear Greg, but she also needed to fight the urge to flee.

"She was probably scamming Lyn and her mom with the anemia thing," Clark said.

"But look how pale I am," Lyn added to the conversation, her earbuds in place.

"Only a little paler than her." Clark pointed to Umiko.

"And maybe you're supposed to be pale," Umiko added.

"What I'm more worried about is the timing of recent events," Greg interrupted. "You said your mom had stopped letting Ms. Evans see you. After all those years, something changed. I think she did find out. Maybe from the report, maybe a letter."

"Anyway to know when she read the letter?" Clark asked.

Lyn shook her head.

"If she opened the right one recently," Greg mused.

"Or the wrong one." Clark added.

"It's only a theory, but maybe Lyn's mom got nostalgic. She pulled out the letters from her past, decided to open one maybe more than one," Greg said.

"The one where I told her about the nurse?" Jonathan asked.

"In theory, yeah." Greg nodded. "She starts to wonder if it's possible." He looked at Lyn.

Lyn turned the volume up.

"Not because she didn't love you." Greg's eyes held the hurt Lyn's heart felt.

Lyn nodded and closed her eyes.

Greg continued speaking to the group. "She stops letting Alice take Lyn's blood. The con woman confronts Maria, or vise versa. Alice either already had the papers or forged them," Greg said. "She's been around Maria for years, long enough to forge a signature."

"That make it sound like Maria's death wasn't an accident," Clark said.

"But it was." Lyn's eyes shot open and sat up. The movement cost her and she fought through the vertigo. "She slipped at work. Fell and hit her head. No one pushed her. Ms. Evans wasn't there. People would have seen her." He eyes moved from Greg to Clark. "Right?" she asked Clark.

Clark smiled at her and the pity that Lyn saw behind those dark eyes turned on the tears.

She leaned her weight on Greg's hip. She felt heavy. Like gravity was playing games and she now weighed 100 pounds more than she used to.

Greg put his arm around her.

"Lyn said it was a mild concussion and shouldn't have killed her," Umiko said.

Lyn sat silent, staring into her lap. She sorted through the info she knew and the theory her friends provided. She didn't attempt to stop the flow of water from her eyes, but she tried desperately to keep her breath steady.

"You think she killed my mom, somehow." Lyn felt herself vibrating with barely caged energy.

Greg squeezed her. Grounded her. Lyn focused on the weight of his arm and took a slow breath.

"We can't know for sure with what we have, but I can make a phone call. Get more info about Alice Evans. I don't think she can be trusted."

"Do it, please?" Umiko asked.

Greg nodded. "Take my place?"

Umiko agreed. Greg stood and walked out the open front door to stand on the front steps. Once outside, he dialed his phone and held it to his ear.

Lyn leaned into Umiko, but her friend was less solid than Greg. Lyn felt like she might push Umiko off the arm of the couch, so she sat up. Umiko held her hand and Lyn tried to focus on her friend's pulse. It was steady compared to her own. She tried to mimic it.

The sky rumbled and shook the ground.

Lyn stood up. "I have to get out of here. I'm hungry. I can't breath," she said as Umiko regained her balance. *I feel like I'm in a cage,* she added to herself. On one side she was blocked by Jonathan's legs, on the other Umiko's. She was just about to jump the coffee table when Umiko spoke.

"Okay." Umiko stood up and clutched Lyn's arm. "Let's go get some food."

"Are you willing to sign the papers today?" Clark asked as he found his feet.

"Don't we need a lawyer?" Jonathan asked.

"To make it legal, yeah." Greg returned and slid his phone back into his pocket. "But to get the ball rolling, all you need to do is write your agreement to the process, sign and date it in front of a notary. Lyn will have something for CPS, and if you kick it, or change your mind and decide not to help, she'll have what she needs," Greg said.

"You don't trust me," Jonathan said. Lyn could hear the disappointment in his voice through the panic of the blood rushing through her veins. She needed someone to move.

"I don't see how we can. You have a terminal diagnosis and this is too important," Clark answered.

Greg added. "We should cover our bases. I agree. I'll drive your truck if you're unable to with your head. Lyn can't afford for you to drive into a tree."

"You're blunt," Jonathan said.

"Yes, sir," Greg chipped the words. "I thought it better than delaying things."

"Fair enough." Jonathan stood up, then promptly sat back down onto the couch. "Not quite yet."

Lyn knew she wouldn't be getting out that way.

"Do you have any paper?" Clark asked.

"There's a notebook and a pen in that drawer." Umiko pointed to the other drawer in the TV cabinet.

Greg walked over and came back with a pen and a spiral bound notebook. "It's not ideal, but it'll do for a shield." He placed both items on the coffee table in front of Jonathan. "It doesn't have to be anything fancy, just state that you, as Lyn's father of record, allow Lyn to pursue an emancipated minor status. Don't sign it yet. We'll stop by a notary when we go get lunch."

Jonathan did what he was told. Greg read it and handed it back to Clark who was gathering up the papers on the coffee table. He placed the new addition into the manilla envelope with the PI's report.

"You don't mind if we take the investigator's report, right?" He held out his hand and Clark gave him the envelope.

Jonathan shook his head.

"Great. Let's go eat." Greg helped Jonathan stand.

The girls followed Clark to his car. He opened the door and waited for the girls to get in.

Lyn crawled into the backseat.

"Want me to sit with you?" Umiko asked.

Lyn shook her head. She fastened her lap belt and spread

her legs across the back seat floor board.

Umiko pushed the seat back and got in the car.

Greg and Clark spoke for a minute on the front lawn before they parted to get in their respective vehicles.

Lyn searched in her purse for her earbuds until she remembered she was already wearing them. She increased the volume and thumbed through the list of songs on her device. She landed on something slow and instrumental. A violin sounded in her ear. She sat back and closed her eyes. The music soothed her enough to sit in the back of the rusted boat of a car. Trapped. Again.

CHAPTER TWENTY-THREE

lark pulled into the parking lot of a P. Terry's Burger Stand and helped the girls out of the car. "Greg said we should go ahead and order. He wanted to stop by the bank and get Jonathan's signature notarized before he met us here."

Lyn, Umiko, and Clark stood in line to order. When they were finished, he paid and Lyn picked a table in the far corner, so her back would be facing a wall, and she could watch both doors.

"I'm going to go wash my hands with soap. I may even do it twice. Want to join me, Lyn?" Umiko asked.

Lyn looked at her blankly, but stood on shaky legs.

"Twenty-three," the voice at the counter called.

An elderly man on a cane started to stand up.

"I'll get it for you if you like," Clark offered.

"Please." The old man smiled and put his cane back on the chair arm.

Clark stood up the retrieve the older man's order.

Umiko and Lyn moved to the restroom to freshen up.

Umiko stood at the double sink and pumped soap out onto her wet hands. Lyn looked at her reflection in the mirror.

Her hair looked as if someone had scribbled over part and forgotten to color the rest. She removed the hair elastic and began pulling out several leaves.

Umiko dried her hands and helped. "It's going to need a brush." Umiko rummaged in her bag and pulled out a small flip open travel brush. She started running it through Lyn's hair from the bottom up and together the girls pulled out a handful of detritus.

When she was done, Umiko wet her hands and tried to scrunch the brown curls back into a curled shape instead of the frizz the brush created.

"It's fine. I'll just put it back in a pony tail." Lyn pulled her fluffy hair through an elastic band several times and washed her own hands. The hair now hung in tiers. The brown curly hair stopping before the straight red. The few stark white hairs ended two inches lower.

Lyn looked in the mirror and admitted that her hair, although three different colors and various textures, looked like someone might have gone to a stylist to get it done on purpose.

Umiko washed her hands a second time. This time up to her elbows. "I still don't feel clean."

"Well, you can't shower in the P. Terry's restroom. Come on."

When Greg and Jonathan arrived, half an hour later, the girls looked less like Pig Pen from Charlie Brown. Except for their clothes and lower body, which were mostly hidden below the table, they looked presentable enough to be sitting in a fast food chain with two cute boys and an older man.

Jonathan walked directly over to stand in line at the counter while Greg walked to the table.

He handed the large manilla envelope to Umiko. "That part's done. Anyone need a refill? More food?"

"I'm still hungry, I'll come stand in line." Lyn moved to stand up.

"Nope, it's on me," Greg offered. "What would you like?"

"Fries and a vanilla milkshake?" Lyn asked, her eyebrows raised.

Greg nodded.

"Please," she added when she remembered her manners. Greg had gone out of his way the last two days. She owed him and Clark so much. She realized she should have paid for their food. She began to rummage in her purse.

"If you're looking for money, you can stop. It's my treat," Greg said with a smile that could have been in a toothpaste commercial. The only thing missing was the gleam of light off the polished surface and the tink of the sound effect. "I'll be right back." He walked off to stand with Jonathan in line.

Lyn watched him walk away, her brain a flood of thoughts. She turned her eyes to Umiko. Her best friend was smiling her cheshire cat smile. If Clark had not been there, Umiko would have talked about how nice it was to watch a cute boy walk away.

"He's got a nice butt," Clark said.

Lyn laid her head on the table, heat rushing to her face.

Umiko kicked Clark's shin under the table.

He laughed. "Sorry, I couldn't help it."

Umiko changed the subject. "The hair thing is really kinda cool."

Lyn kept her forehead pressed to the table. She knew the blush was still on her skin and she didn't think she was needed for this conversation, anyway.

"You girls did a good job dying it," Clark said.

"We didn't dye it," Umiko said.

"What do you mean?" he asked.

"Wednesday her hair was brown, frizzy, and curly. All of it. A lot like her mom's. Thursday, there were red highlights. Today, it's this." Umiko ran her fingers through her friend's hair. "Do you think it's a creature trait?"

"Wait, does she really not know what she is?"

"No," Lyn replied into the table.

"Wow. That sucks."

"We're going to figure it out," Umiko said.

"Well, if it is camouflage, it's a bad one. I don't know anyone with hair that white," Clark said. "Her original hair was better at blending in. Even the red highlights are a natural color. This white has to be a trait. Part of what she is."

Clark considered. "Any other traits to consider?"

"Just the hair as far as I know, and she doesn't ever get sick."

"Why are you talking about me like I'm a puzzle to solve?" Lyn sat up and looked between Clark and Umiko.

Clark had the decency to look apologetic.

Umiko just shrugged. "Because we care," Umiko said.

"Well, stop caring, please, at least for a little while. They're coming over," Lyn begged.

Jonathan walked behind Clark and sat in the empty chair across from Lyn. Greg pulled a chair from an empty table and placed himself at the end. He passed Lyn a large bag of fries and a medium milkshake.

"Thank you." Lyn took a fry and let the salt melt onto her tongue.

"It's fine. I'll eat what you don't." Greg unwrapped his burger and took a bite.

The group finished their lunch in an awkward silence. Jonathan and Greg busy with their burgers, while Umiko and Lyn shared the milkshake and fries.

Clark looked from Umiko to Lyn and back, like he was still working on solving a puzzle. At least he was keeping it to himself.

After he wadded up the greasy burger wrapper, Jonathan excused himself to go to the restroom. When he was out of hearing range, the conversation started up.

"We should make sure he can get back to his house before we head home," Greg said. "We have what we need to hold off Ms. Evan's claim on guardianship. You can give it to the CPS person on Monday. Between the notarized paper, and the investigator's report, it'll at least buy you time. I can drive you to the office, if you need me to. After school or anytime, really." Greg shrugged. "I can miss a day of classes."

"We should make a copy first. Just in case," Clark added.

Greg nodded. "I already did. Sort of." He shook his phone. "I scanned it after the notary did her thing. It's not as good as the original copy, but at least we have something, just in case."

"The CPS lady will come by the house. She has several times. If she doesn't find me there, she'll call Umiko's mom," Lyn said.

"Oh crap, my mom," Umiko pulled out her phone and thumbed the screen.

"When do you think you'll hear back from your people about Alice Evans?" Clark asked Greg.

Greg shrugged. "I told them to be thorough, but if anything dangerous showed up to send it through immediately. I haven't gotten anything yet."

Clark nodded and reached for a fry.

Greg saw Jonathan coming back from the restroom and stood up. He gathered the trash, leaving the half bag of fries and what was left of the vanilla milkshake on the table.

Clark stood and wiped the table top with a leftover napkin. Umiko grabbed the fries and Lyn picked up the vanilla milkshake so he could finish the entire table.

"Are you okay to get home?" Greg asked holding out Jonathan's truck keys.

Jonathan nodded and took the proffered keys. "My vision is back to normal." Jonathan turned to Lyn. "I'm sorry."

"Thank you for signing the papers," Lyn said.

A silence hung in the air between them. An uncomfortable silence, like a deep and gaping chasm both were afraid to cross.

"Lyn or CPS will be in touch if they need you, about making it official." Greg held out his hand.

Jonathan shook it.

"Nice to meet you," Clark said and they shook hands as well.

Lyn didn't know what to do, so she stood there with her hands in the back pockets of her shorts.

Jonathan looked at Lyn. "It was nice to meet you. I'm sorry about Maria. Let me know if I can do anything else for her." He paused. "Or for you." He stepped toward the door. He turned back at the last minute. "If you ever find my real daughter…"

Lyn turned away and Jonathan didn't finish his statement. He walked out the front door toward his truck.

Greg pulled Lyn in and squeezed.

After a few breaths, Lyn pulled away and the four stepped out of the glass doors and watched Jonathan get into his beat up pickup truck. He sat in the front seat for a few minutes before he drove off.

"We need to go. My mom's worried. I didn't answer a few texts and she's a bit freaked out," Umiko said. "I told her that we stopped to grab something to eat on our way back."

"Let's go. We can talk more in the car," Greg said.

Lyn was just happy to be done with the hard part. She looked at the empty parking space where her father's, Jonathan's, truck had been.

"Lyn, you coming?" Umiko called.

CHAPTER TWENTY-FOUR

"She's going to want to ask a lot of questions," Umiko said as they pulled onto the street.

"That's not all." Lyn pointed out the front window.

Mrs. Clare was pruning the front bushes.

Umiko sighed. "I guess we're doing the meeting the mom thing."

Clark pulled into the driveway and was out of the car and to Umiko's door before she could open it.

"Sorry about the ambush," Umiko whispered as he helped her and Lyn out of the car.

"No worries," Clark said.

"You must be, Clark," Mrs. Clare said. She locked her pruning shears and placed them in her apron pocket.

"Yes, Ma'am. Clark Mannon. You know Greg." Clark turned to Greg, who was getting out of the other side of the car.

"I know of him. We've never been introduced."

Lyn noticed Umiko's mom give Umiko a look. She wasn't sure what type of look, but Umiko cut it off.

"We found Lyn's dad."

Lyn sighed as she was thrown under the bus.

Mrs. Clare's eyes turned to Lyn. The look she had given Umiko turned more to sadness.

Lyn looked sad right back.

Mrs. Clare nodded and changed the subject. "We can talk later. Anyone want cookies? Fresh baked."

Umiko and Lyn shared a wide eyed look.

"Shower," Lyn said. "I really need a shower."

"Right. Rain check?" Umiko said to Clark and Greg.

"Sure," Clark said. "Nice to meet you Mrs. Clare. I look forward to next time."

"Thank you for bringing them home safely," She shook Clark's hand.

"You're welcome," Greg said as he offered his hand. "Sorry we brought them home dirty."

"Why are they…"

"Come on, mama," Umiko said pulling the woman and her questions into the house.

CHAPTER TWENTY-FIVE

*L*yn slept at Umiko's house again that night, but excused herself from Sunday morning activities, in favor of a long bath in her own house.

She filled the large garden tub in her mother's bathroom with warm, almost too hot water and bubbles. She turned some music up on her phone, put a glass of cold water on the nearest counter and slid into the tub. Her buoyancy caused water and bubbles to drip over the edge and down the side of the tub to puddle on the floor.

Lyn melted into the water. She pushed the bubbles away from the spot her head claimed so that she could breath air instead of soap. She closed her eyes and let the music carry her thoughts away.

Music always helped soothe her worries. She wouldn't go so far as to say it 'was the language of her soul.' Lyn shook her head and giggled. Umiko had a flare with words at times. If it were up to Lyn though, she would have background music 24/7. Dancing was her secret pleasure. The music provided a sense of freedom and allowed her body to move and stretch without thought.

She blew away several bubbles that were swirling an inch or two from her chin and watched as they took flight.

Lyn relaxed deeper into the tub. She scooted forward and tilted her head back. When the top of her head was wet, she sat up just enough to keep her ears and nose above the water line. Bubbles tickled her lips and she blew into the water, creating a current that carried them away. She closed her eyes and let the music take over every thought.

The water warmed her skin for an hour before it started taking more heat than it was giving. The bubbles were down to scattered patches by then and her fingertips felt plump with moisture.

She wished the water would have kept its heat for longer. She didn't want to get out. Outside of the bathtub were responsibilities, and waiting for Monday afternoon, and possibly other shoes that wanted to drop. With her eyes closed, she wrapped herself in the last bits of warmth in the water. She imagined it warming and purred at the luxury of a simple bath, with no responsibilities, or worries, or shoes, dropping or otherwise.

"Just a little longer." She breathed across the surface of the water and the small ripples felt warmer against the skin on her chest. The warmth of the water near her hands, expanded to other parts of her body. She knew she was imagining it, but it felt just as nice as the real thing. She let her imagination run free while she could. Reality waited for her on the other side of the porcelain surface. She sank deeper into the water and used the tub as armor against the worry that would latch onto her beyond its rim.

The flesh on her ears began to burn. She placed a hand on her ear out of instinct. When she pulled her arm out of the water she noticed that the skin was not pale, it was bright pink. She pushed herself up. The motion moved the water and made the rest of her skin burn. She quickly jumped from the tub to the plush bath mat.

"What in the world?"

She faced the mirror over the sink. Her skin was a bright pink from her ears all the way down. It was a striking contrast to the pale of her face and the white of her hair.

"Shit."

The red was gone. The mouse brown curls, gone. Every hair on Lyn's head was a bright snowy white and hung down to her elbows. She never in her life had hair that long.

Lyn picked up the phone to text Umiko and heard a knock from the door downstairs. "Shit," she repeated and wrapped herself in a towel. Lyn reached in to let the water out of the tub and pulled her hand back before they made it an inch into the water.

It was ice cold.

Did she imagine the hot?

She looked back at her reflection. The red line still marked her skin. She touched it with a finger and watched the skin change color with her pressure. She was not imagining that.

Lyn took a single step back. Something strange just happened and she was at once curious and afraid.

Lyn heard the knock again and felt her pulse quicken.

"What the hell?" She took the towel and wrapped it around her head. She fumbled in her mom's closet for an oversized shirt and went down stairs without putting any underwear on.

CHAPTER TWENTY-SIX

yn ran down the stairs, hoping the knock was Umiko. She rounded the corner stair post, looked along the patio windows and through the back patio door but no one was there.

The knock came again. Lyn turned to the sound. Umiko wouldn't be at the front door and the CPS lady wouldn't come by until tomorrow afternoon. Lyn wasn't expecting anyone else.

Lyn's hands went to the towel on her head. She pulled the cloth down around her ears and tucked her hair underneath. She pulled the hem of the shirt as far down as she could. It definitely wasn't an outfit meant for greeting strangers.

Lyn stepped to the front door. "Who is it?" she called but no one answered. The window over the door was too tall to look out and the person on the other side had their back to the peep hole.

Lyn opened the door a crack. "Yes, how can I help you?" Lyn's heart skipped a beat.

Ms. Evans turned around. "Oh, dear, I must have come at a bad time." Her voice sounded like sugar on a cracker. Overly sweet and dry, crumbling almost. "Nothing for it, though." The lady took a breath and looked at Lyn. "You don't look too well. A little flush around the collar."

Lyn's hand went to her chest. She had forgotten about the color on her skin from the too hot water.

"Do you have a fever? I should take your temperature. I brought you a tuna noodle casserole. I didn't know if you'd be up for cooking yet, so I made extra and thought I'd bring it over. Should I put it in the kitchen? It's still warm, so I had to use my oven mitts. I can put it down on your kitchen counter though and take your temperature. You look flush. We wouldn't want you to get sick and miss school tomorrow. Your mom wouldn't be happy about that." Ms. Evans' words came out in a rush. She didn't wait for a response to any of her questions. She didn't seem to want any. "Make way. Hot dish." Ms. Evans took a step toward the door. She pushed it open with the back of her hand and forced Lyn to step away or get burned by the casserole dish.

"Gypsy, no." The neighbor's shouted as a golden retriever bounded over the small grassy area between the houses, right up to Lyn's porch. The dog started growling, a deep reverberating in your bones type of growl.

Ms. Evans took a step away from the door and Lyn noticed that she wasn't reacting to the sloshed white sauce on her wrist. *It must not be that hot after all.* Lyn thought. *Another con.*

Lyn looked in the direction the dog had come. Another retriever was pulling and straining against her leash. Mrs. Henesey was about to lose control of the second dog. "Let me get Romani in the car," she called, pulling the leash, "and I'll come get Gypsy. She's never bitten anyone, so you should be fine." Mrs. Henesey pulled on the leash. "No sudden movements, just in case. Lyn, can you get a hand on her? Try to calm her down?" Mrs. Henesey grumbled as she tried to push the massive hound into the car with her whole body. "They are both acting really strange."

Gypsy moved closer to Lyn and bared her teeth at Ms. Evans. She barked twice and started a long growl. She installed herself on the welcome mat, all four paws planted, and her back rigid.

Lyn peered at the dog. She must really be overheated because, to her, it sounded like Gypsy called Ms. Evans a bitch. Lyn shook her head. *That's crazy. Not the word choice, that was true, but the fact that there was a word at all. Dogs don't talk.* She needed to think and this noise and the uninvited guests were not helping.

The dog stood alert between Lyn and Ms. Evans and let out another series of threatening barks.

"Bitch. Bitch." Lyn heard Gypsy bark. She put her hand on the dogs rear end. She knew these dogs. She watched them when their parents went out of town. She walked them, took them to the park. She had never seen them act like this. She ran her hand down Gypsy's back and felt a tremor run through the dog. Her muscles were ready to spring. If Lyn had felt this type of tremor in her own muscles, she would be running by now.

"Maybe you should step back a little," Lyn said to Ms. Evans. "I don't think Gypsy is playing around at the moment. She's really agitated by something."

"Well," Ms. Evans huffed, "someone needs to keep a better hold of their animals." She glared at Lyn, the dog, and the neighbor in quick succession.

Lyn saw Mrs. Henesey try again to lift the second retriever into her SUV, but Romani was determined to come to her partner's assistance. "Bitch. Bitch." The second dog barked and slipped past its owner, who was forced to drop the leash or lose her fingers.

Lyn put her own fingers in her ears and wiggled them to try to dislodge any lasting bath water. "Ms. Evans. Please go home. We can talk later, after the dogs are gone," she shouted over the now doubled bark of the dogs.

Lyn saw the woman stomp her foot in frustration. Ms. Evans' lips moved but Lyn couldn't make out any of the words.

Lyn pointed her fingers at her ears over the barking dogs. "I can't hear." She moved her lips but didn't bother filling the shapes with sound. Greg had told her to avoid Ms. Evans anyway. The crazy dogs gave her the perfect excuse. She hid her smile and ran her hands along the dogs' backs. *Good dogs.*

Ms. Evans set the rectangular casserole dish on the patio and stepped down the porch steps backwards. She looked between the dogs and the dish of food, her eyes narrow.

Lyn thought she was either making sure that the casserole was safe before she left, or she was hoping the dogs would take the bait and eat the food instead of barking.

Gypsy and Romani ignored the dish and took a single step closer to Ms. Evans. They growled, exposing their sharp teeth. She huffed again and walked down the sidewalk and across the street to her own property.

Gypsy and Romani barked and stepped forward. Their teeth bared. Their noses pointed at the interloper. Their muscles tensed and ready to jump at any sign of danger. The barking trailed off, but both animals continued a guttural growl and watched Ms. Evans.

"I'm so sorry, Lyn." The neighbor stepped onto Lyn's patio from her side of the house and put her hand on the spot just in front of Gypsy's tail. Romani turned and bared her teeth at her owner for a split second before thinking better of it. "Nein!" Mrs. Henesey barked and Romani returned to her watchfulness.

Ms. Evans closed the door to her house and both dogs sat with a huff. When they turned their head to Lyn and their master, their tongues fell out between their happy jaws.

"You are so pleased with yourself, huh? Scaring off Lyn's guest," the neighbor said to her dogs.

"It's okay, Mrs. Henesey." Lyn reached out and scratched

behind Gypsy's ear. The dog pressed into her finger tips, deepening the scratch. Romani pushed her muzzle at Lyn's hand and tried to butt in. "I wasn't prepared for her visit anyway." Lyn pulled at the hem of her shirt before she used her free hand to pet the second dog.

"Indeed." Mrs. Henesey looked Lyn up and down. She turned her eyes to the pair of golden retrievers "They usually aren't so aggressive. I wonder what got them so worked up."

"Maybe it was the food?" Lyn suggested. Lyn scratched one dogs' ear with each of her hands. She leaned down to let them nuzzle her chin.

Mrs. Henesey eyed the foiled covered dish and her dogs.

"That's strange. Any food at their level, covered or not, is usually gone in seconds. They don't seem to care about whatever that is." Mrs. Henesey pointed at the dish of tuna casserole.

"Maybe they don't like tuna." Lyn shrugged. "When they were barking, did it sound like anything to you?" Lyn closed her eyes and mouth as the dogs' wet tongues licked her face. She pulled her head away to take a breath.

"You mean besides bad manners? All I heard was lawsuit if they had bitten her. Thank goodness they didn't. I'm sure that busy body would sue me in a heart beat." She clicked to the dogs and patted her thigh. "I'll let you get back inside and get dressed."

Lyn put her hand up and made sure the towel was still in place. "Thank you."

"Of course," she said as she clicked her tongue for the dogs to follow her off Lyn's porch. "Sorry again about the dogs. I just cannot imagine what got into them."

The dogs turned away from their owner and barked again at Ms. Evans' house.

"Nein. I don't like her either, but you can't eat her." Mrs. Henesey clicked a third time and the dogs stood to follow. Each nosed Lyn's hand for one last pet as they walked by.

Lyn waved to the pups as Mrs. Henesey put them in the car. They looked pleased with themselves.

Lyn stooped to pick up the casserole dish, trying not to let the baggy T-shirt ride up beyond her modesty. Lyn saw a flicker in the blinds on Ms. Evans front window.

Lyn closed the door with her hip and put the dish on the kitchen counter. She hurried upstairs so she could turn on the hair dryer and pretend not to hear if her nosy neighbor knocked on the door again.

She did not want to speak to Ms. Evans until after she had spoken to CPS, maybe not even then.

CHAPTER TWENTY-SEVEN

"Hello?" Greg called as he came in the front door after his morning run. He turned and locked the door behind him. "Anyone home?" He put his keys on a hook beside the door, and his wallet on a small half round table. He kicked off his running shoes and left them by the door.

No answer returned. His house was empty. His parents were already gone for the day. He had expected as much, but it was best not to accidentally come upon a Gregar in their own home. Things could end badly if you didn't announce yourself.

The smell of coffee still lingered in the kitchen. Greg's family ran on efficiency. He would find just enough coffee still in the pot to fill his cup.

Greg stepped into the kitchen and drank a full glass of water before he walked to the laundry room where he dropped all his sweaty clothes in the washing machine.

After their work days, his mom and dad would do the same.

Greg ran up the stairs, taking them three at a time. His thighs burned as he reached the top and turned into the bathroom.

~

*G*reg ran the towel once more through his hair and walked over to his closet.

His clothes were a collection of darks and neutrals. No prints, no funny pictures on T-shirts. Just utility and purpose. He selected a pair of lighter tan cargo pants from a grouping of tan cargo pants and a plain white T-shirt, just like the two plain white T-shirts next to it. Black crew socks, black boxer briefs, tan fabric belt. He tossed his selection on the bed and began to dress.

His phone rang as he went to put his first leg into the pants. He had turned the ringer on to make sure he didn't miss the call. He picked the phone up from his desk and slid his finger across to answer.

"Yes, sir." He answered the phone and listened to the voice on the other side of the line. "By 1800." Another pause. "I'll let her know, sir. I'll see you then."

His dad. Not the call he was waiting for.

Greg tossed the phone on the bed and continued to dress. After he fastened his belt and pulled the shirt over his head, he picked up his phone to check for messages. Lyn had not texted him.

He hadn't seen her on his run this morning either, even though he purposefully changed his route to pass her house.

He ran a comb through his hair, decided it didn't need product this morning, and went back down the stairs.

His phone rang on the third to last step. He pulled it from his pocket and looked at the ID. His mom.

"Yes, ma'am." Again he listened as the voice on the other end relayed the reason for the call. He nodded to himself, letting the voice finish. "Yes, ma'am. He said 1800. I'll be home." The voice said a few more words and hung up.

Greg poured himself the last of the coffee from the pot. He held a large plain white mug to his lips and took a tentative sip. It was the perfect temperature. No sugar, no cream. He preferred the bitter blend black.

Greg started cooking breakfast. Two eggs, over easy, a slice of toast with butter and three slices of bacon. He drank his coffee as he pushed things around in the skillets.

He slid the cooked items onto a plate and sat at the breakfast table. He punctured the egg yolks with his fork and watched as the yellow ran over the edge of the egg whites and continued around the edge of the toast.

He wondered what Lyn was eating for breakfast.

He poured another glass of water from the pitcher on the table and cut a slice from his egg. His forkful was halfway to his mouth when his phone rang for the third time.

He shoveled the bite into his mouth and stood long enough to get his phone out of his pocket.

"I've got some news." The voice on the phone said.

Greg swallowed his first bite of breakfast. "Good. Hit me," he replied.

"Alice Evans is an alias. One of a few I've managed to find so far. None of which have a very good backstop. All of them worked in hospitals, specifically maternity wards and birthing centers. But we can't find a record of any degrees. Her references are solid, but her education has holes. It could be that they are so old, that her records weren't fully digitized."

"How old?" Greg leaned back in the high chair. He gave his entire focus to the voice on the other end of the line.

"That's strange, actually. All the aliases are the roughly same age, early 30's, but span at least 50 years. This woman, if they are one person, doesn't age like normal. If it's not the same person, it's huge coincidence."

"So, she's a creature?"

"Looks that way."

Greg heard a shuffle of papers from the other end of the line.

"Does your dad know I'm doing background checks for you?" The voice on the phone lowered.

"No," Greg replied.

"Greg, you've got to stop doing this to me," the man on the other side of the call groaned. "I'll call you back. He just walked in."

The phone call disconnected and Greg set his phone beside his plate. He took a bite of his breakfast and waited for the call back.

"A creature. Who hangs around babies, newborns, and doesn't age normally," he said aloud to himself and dipped his bread in the yellow egg sludge before taking a bite. "She could be a vampire. They've been known to acquire a taste for infants." He thought about what Lyn said about Umiko's obsession with vampires and smiled to himself before shaking his head. "Lyn's not acting like a vampire victim. She's breathing and she's not enthralled. If she were she wouldn't be trying so hard to get away from the woman."

He ate another bite of egg and stared at nothing in particular. The age thing had him stumped.

He ate the last bite of his breakfast before the phone rang again. He held it to his ear with one hand and picked up his plate with the other.

"Hello."

"Your dad just put me on a job, I can't keep at this one, but I wanted to tell you the rest of what I found first."

"I'm listening." Greg set his plate in the sink and waited.

"She's not registered as a creature, none of the aliases are. Alice Evans has no driver's license, no arrests. But each of the hospitals she's worked for has been investigated for neglect."

"What kind?"

"The kind where babies might have gone missing or got mixed up."

"That fits with what I've learned. So, there's no record of what type of creature she is?"

"No, but if you can get me a set of characteristics, I can run it through and see what pops. Right now, all I have is age thing. So, vampire is high on the list."

"No. We can strike off vamp. What age is listed for the Alice Evans alias?"

"Her birth year is listed as 1954. So she'd be 65 or so. The photo in the file is about 20 years younger than that. "

"What? That can't be right."

"Sure it can, the photo is from employment date."

"No, not the photo. If she is the woman I'm thinking of, she's early 50s at the most, more likely late 40s. Are we are sure the alias' are all hers?"

"We have photos from the employment badges. We ran them through the computer. Different hair and eye color, but the basic facial bone structure is the same. Like I said, it's either one hell of a coincidence, or the same person."

"Thanks. Send me what you have. I'll get back to you." Greg pulled the phone away from his ear.

"Greg, hold up."

"Yeah?" Greg asked moving the phone back.

"If she's not a vamp, my next two choices would be fairy or witch. Don't make any deals and... if she's a witch..." The voice on the phone trailed off.

"I'll be careful." Greg ended the call. He washed his dishes and placed them in the drying rack to drip dry.

Both witches and fairies can change their appearance. Greg leaned back on the countertop. His mind processed what he knew for a fact and extrapolated what he could from there.

Greg discounted the idea of Alice Evans being benevolent and ran through the traits that would make her a threat. He wouldn't need to protect Lyn from a nice fairy or good witch, and being prepared was better than underestimating his opponent.

A deal with a fairy was binding with severe consequences

for non-compliance on both sides. They had mostly natural types of magic, elements, plants, animals.

A witch however, was a wild card. There were so many types and so much overlap that you couldn't pin down exactly what you were up against until you faced it and survived. The survival was the kicker.

Not even his people were immune to magic. Heightened strength and reflexes, yes. Taller and more robust, sure, but magic could still kill.

A fairy on the other hand, wouldn't directly hurt anyone. That didn't fit with the situation, if Greg assumed she killed Maria and/or the PI, and Greg thought it was too coincidental to discount. Fairies preferred a good game of cat and mouse, preying on the weak and stupid, and giving them just enough rope to hang themselves. This con felt more hands on, so that left witch.

Greg took a deep breath.

Witches were a different beast entirely. The bad ones obliterated the idea of a nice witch millennia ago. Forcing the whole species into hiding or face angry humans with torches and archaic witch finding tests. As far as a witch was concerned, humans thought it was better to burn it than to take a chance and die from it.

Of course, times were changing. The good witches were the first to come out. They led the charge for equal tolerance, and other marginalized creature groups followed suit. Race, gender, species. It was all coming out into the open now.

Still, there were homicidal witches, just like in the human population at large. Homicidal witches were more dangerous than homicidal humans, though. Witches could strike from afar, a single hair or discarded fingernail, a few words and… well, accidents happen.

"Accidents happen." Greg finished his coffee, and quickly rinsed it out before he placed it in the drying rack. He grabbed his keys and his wallet from beside the front door and left through the garage after arming the alarm system.

Greg grabbed a second helmet from a row hanging on a peg board in the garage and clipped it securely to the bike. As he cranked his bike, he thumbed his phone and held it to his ear.

"Lyn," he said and paused for her to speak. "I have news, but not over the phone. I'll be there in three minutes."

He would normally give a girl more than a three minute warning, especially this early in the morning, but he had a bad feeling and he didn't want to take a chance.

CHAPTER TWENTY-EIGHT

yn hung up the phone and looked herself in the mirror.

"Three minutes?"

She unwrapped the towel from her head. White. Whiter than the towel, which looked almost yellow next to Lyn's hair now. She ran her fingers through a few strands. They came out smoothly, no tangles and already dry.

"Well that's helpful. I guess." She stared at herself in the mirror. Taking in the transformation. "Three minutes," she reminded herself.

She quickly put her hair into a pony tail and marveled at her ability to do that in seconds. Her old hair necessitated spending hours trying to get tangles out of it first. Maybe the white had its benefits. She looked at herself in the mirror. "Why is this happening?"

She heard an engine pull up to her house, she looked out her mother's window onto the driveway below. Lyn saw a motorcycle. Its rider in a dark red helmet, T-shirt, cargo pants and heavy black boots.

She rushed into her mom's closet, threw open a drawer and pulled out the top pair of underwear. Black lace. She tossed it in the back and chose another pair. Still lace, but pink this time, and looked like it would cover more of her backside than the other pair. She stuck her legs in one at a time and pulled them up. They fit. Lyn lifted a bra out and decided to go without. She was not as endowed as her mother. She yanked a shirt off a hanger at random and grabbed a pair of jeans.

The doorbell rang as she was stuffing her legs into the worn denim.

She looked at herself in the mirror one last time. Her hair fell onto the sleeves of a well worn 'Nevertheless, she persisted' shirt. Lyn felt like a fraud, but the clothes fit like a glove.

On her way downstairs, she grabbed a ball cap that said 'girls rock' in gothic letters and slid it onto her head. She pulled her pony tail through the hole in the back.

Lyn opened the door, but before she could say anything, Greg stepped in, forcing her away from the door in his haste. He closed the door firmly behind him.

"What's wrong?" Lyn asked as he turned from the door to face her.

"I think she's a witch," he whispered in her ear.

Lyn's butterflies returned as his breath caressed her ear. She was aware that he was standing less than an inch away. *What?* She wasn't thinking as fast as Greg and her brain wasn't making the connections it needed to make, especially since Greg's body was pressed against hers. "Who?" she whispered back. She wondered if her breath on his cheek made his mind jumbled as well.

"Alice Evans. You said she was your nurse. Has she been in your house?" His breath on her ear made her skin flush.

Her nerves flared. She stepped back, the spell broken. "Of course, but not since my mom's accident," Lyn said without whispering.

"Good, but not great. Grab your stuff and let's go. I'll buy you breakfast. Coffee?" Greg closed the distance and kept his voice low.

"I already ate." Lyn didn't back away. She had a powdered donut from a bag chased with orange juice that should have been poured down the drain last week. She rethought her refusal. "But I could go for something else. Are you sure you need coffee, though?" Her voice was low, just above a whisper.

Greg took a breath. "We can go anywhere you want, but I have intel that you need to know and this is not the best place to discuss it."

"O-kay." Lyn's pulse started racing. She'd never seen Greg this high strung. If he was panicked. Things must be bad. "I'll get my keys." She grabbed her house key from beside the door leading to the garage and checked her pocket for her phone.

"Do you have an alarm system?" Greg asked. He looked around at her walls.

She nodded.

"Use it," Greg said.

Lyn didn't hear demand in his voice, exactly. More like a strong request. She complied and keyed the passcode into the panel in the hallway. When the beeping started, Greg opened the front door. He exited first and Lyn closed and locked the front door behind them.

It was a bright, sunny day outside. The storm from yesterday didn't bring a single drop of rain or a reprieve from the heat. Today's forecast called for hot. After a certain point, the numbers didn't matter anymore. It was all just different degrees of hot. Moderately hot, very hot, instant burn hot, and hotter than hell hot. Today was in the instant burn range. Lyn looked at her pale arms. Sunscreen should probably be a daily thing.

Greg propelled her to his bike, handed her a helmet and picked up his. He put his helmet on and flipped up the visor.

She froze in the gaze of those blue eyes.

"I've never…" Lyn hesitated. She thought through all the 'Share the Road' safety signs and the myriad of accidents involving bikes that she had heard about. Almost always fatal and never good for the exposed rider.

"Are you scared?"

Lyn straightened up. "No." She lied.

Greg motioned her over with his hand. He pinched the brim of the 'girls rock' cap and slid it off her head. His eyes lingered on her hair as her pony tail slid through the cap.

"I like your new look. Did you do it this morning?"

"Something like that." Lyn had been worried about what people would say when they saw it. She looked at the honesty in Greg's eyes. "Thanks," she added.

Greg handed her the cap and placed the helmet on her head. He tightened the chin strap and lifted the visor.

"Too tight?" he asked.

Lyn shook her head, which now sat twice as heavy on her shoulders. She shoved the cap into her back pocket as far as she could, which wasn't far. She pulled it out again and tried to…she didn't know what to do with it.

"We've got eyes on us." Greg took the cap and threw his leg over the body of the bike.

Lyn moved to turn.

"No, don't let on that you know. Climb on behind me and hold tight." He tucked the cap into his own, deeper, back pocket. "Don't make large movements. I need to compensate for your weight. I can't do that if you move too fast. It's all about balance. You're a dancer, you're good at balance." He paused to let her settle on. "Close your eyes if you need to. There's a headset built in. We can talk if you want. I'm going to take us somewhere close, but out of the way. Someplace I know we won't be overheard. I'll make you breakfast, if you want. The kitchen is stocked with junk food too. All the chips and granola bars you can eat."

"What about Umiko and Clark?" Lyn asked as she lifted one leg over the seat of the bike and sat down.

"We'll text them after we get there." Greg cranked the engine and Lyn grabbed his sides with her hands. He moved her arms to hug his torso. "Tighter. It's easier to feel the shifts in balance and I don't want you falling off when I turn. You can't hurt me. And close your visor. Bugs do not feel good hitting your face at speed."

He closed his visor and put his hands on the handle bars.

Lyn closed her visor with one hand and shimmied forward until her front was pressed against his back. She could feel the ridge of her cap between them. She returned her arm to his middle and squeezed his torso as he backed out of the driveway and drove down the street. As he turned, she saw Ms. Evans glaring at them from inside her front window. The blinds snapped shut.

Lyn shivered.

"You okay?" Greg asked.

Lyn heard his voice through the headset. "I do not like that woman. She gives me the creeps."

"She should," Greg said as he accelerated down the street.

CHAPTER TWENTY-NINE

After ten minutes of watching cars pass way too fast and taking turns that made her feel like she was going to fall, Lyn was more than ready to get off the bike. Her hands made fists in Greg's shirt and she felt his stomach pull away from her nails.

"Close your eyes," he said in her ear.

His voice in the helmet mic was not quite as intoxicating as the real thing. Especially not when her stomach was debating mutiny.

She squeezed her eyes shut and willed herself to relax. The motorcycle took a bump and she slid forward another inch. Lyn counted her breaths and imagined the wind caressing her instead of pulling at her. An old friend welcoming the attention and extending an invitation to lend her speed.

She would have put her head on Greg's back and hid, but the helmet was bulky and the bumps made it bounce. She would leave a bruise on Greg's back and give herself a headache in the process.

She decided to keep her head up but her eyes closed and did her best to hide from the wind behind Greg's broad shoulders and helmet. She tried to concentrate on something besides the asphalt going by beneath her at 50 miles per hour.

She was on the back of a motorcycle, going she didn't know where, with a boy she had only been friends with for two days, but made her stomach turn inside out when he stood too close and whispered in her ear.

She had known him longer than that, of course, just like everyone else at school. He spoke to her in the halls and had distracted Killian for her on many occasions. But she had learned a lot more in the last two days. The biggest surprise was that he considered her a friend. That he cared about her. Why else would he have helped her yesterday?

Umiko did it out of some vicarious desire to find her own dad. Lyn could understand that and would do the same for her one day, but not for another four years.

Greg on the other hand, as far as she knew, didn't have ulterior motives.

She, Umiko really, had placed her challenges at his feet and he had gladly picked them up. She wasn't used to trusting many people and she found it odd how easily she had started to trust Greg.

The only other people she trusted were her mom and Umiko. Once, she thought she could trust Ms. Evans, as far as a person can trust a home care nurse that poked and prodded and came at her with needles. Not with all her secrets, but she at least trusted her to have Lyn's well being in mind.

Unfortunately, that trust had been built on a lie.

If Clark and Greg were correct, Ms. Evans had been conning Lyn and her mother since the beginning. This mysterious motorcycle ride to 'somewhere safe' had her worried about what she didn't know about the woman who had pretended to care about her.

Lyn's mind spiraled to the next level.

How many other people only pretended to care? The CPS lady? She probably had more kids on her schedule than just

Lyn. Lyn Davis was just a name on a checklist that needed checking off. Greg? Was he just pretending? Was she just a damsel in distress to him? Someone to feed his need to be Sir Gregory, Knight of Cedar Oaks High. Maybe he didn't actually care about her and her troubles anymore than he would have for any other of Killian's targets. She just happened to be the only one at the moment, so Greg could devote all his time to her.

Lyn felt the motorcycle slow and turn. The wind no longer flowed around them and the hot morning air settled on her skin. Lyn's knees felt the muscles in Greg's thighs tense and relax as he put out his feet. The rumble of the bike's engine stopped and the bike with it.

Lyn heard the sound of a garage door behind her.

"You can let go, we're here." Greg's voice said in her helmet.

Lyn felt Greg's shoulders shift against her chest as he lifted off his helmet. She opened her eyes.

They were inside an old fire station. The light and heat of the outside world slowly faded away as the garage door met the ground.

The corrugated metal roof was two stories above their heads. The only light in the room came from large rectangular windows set in the top of concrete walls over the large, now closed, garage doors. The dimness and height of the interior allowed for a cooler temperature. It was almost chilly with the large overhead fans rotating. A stark contrast to the world outside.

"What is this place?" Lyn unclipped the helmet she was wearing and slid if off her head.

Greg held his helmet in his lap. "It used to be a firehouse. It's one of a few secure locations around town that my dad's company uses. We know it's not bugged by anyone else. There are security cameras around the outside, monitored 24/7."

"So, someone knows we're here." She looked around for the cameras, but didn't see them.

"Yeah, but they're with me. You're safe here." Greg assured her.

Lyn was aware of how close she was sitting to Greg and she scooted back before she stepped down from the bike. He followed after and took the helmet from her.

"My house isn't safe?" Lyn asked. She felt the rhythm of her heart pounding in her ear. Whether it was from the motorcycle ride, the situation, or being alone in a cold dark space with Greg, she didn't know.

"I couldn't be sure." Greg shrugged. "Sorry, if I scared you." He placed the helmets on the bike's seat and stepped away from her. One arm crossed over his abdomen. "There's a kitchen, fully stocked." He turned to a door in the wall of the big open space. "Would you like something to drink?" He moved to the door, his back to her, his arms at his side.

"Yes. Water. Thanks."

Greg's hand pushed open the door.

"How do you… What do you…" Lyn tried to call but stumbled over her thoughts. "What are you?" She settled on one of many questions running through her head. Questions about Ms. Evans, about Greg, about who was monitoring the cameras, why it all mattered? What it had to do with her? She settled on the one thing that mattered to her most, right at that moment. The answer to which would help her know if she could add him to her short list of trusted people. If he was pretending or not.

Greg looked at her from the open door.

She turned her head when his gaze made her anxious. Maybe that wasn't the best question to lead with. "Sorry, that was rude."

Greg shook his head. "I'm just trying to figure out where to start."

"Me too." Lyn's muscles were tense. Her body still

vibrated from the motorcycle's movements. She would have loved to run and she could have in this space. She turned back to face him.

"I promise to answer all your questions in just a minute. I'll grab some waters and be right back. Don't leave."

Lyn heard a pleading in his voice. She nodded her head.

Greg stepped through the door and it swung closed behind him. Lyn heard his phone buzz and Greg say hello, but she couldn't hear the rest of the conversation. She was left alone in the cavernous space with all the unanswered questions floating through her brain.

CHAPTER THIRTY

*L*yn ignored the questions piling up in her brain and looked around the firehouse.

She stretched out her arms and turned.

The open space was nice. Not as nice as a green space with trees and open sky, but nicer than inside of a motorcycle helmet. This space was even larger than the auditorium stage. Lyn imagined three fire engines parked side by side with plenty more room on the outer edges. There was a pole in the back corner, near a bank of open metal lockers, but the uniforms and other gear were long gone.

She pulled her phone out of her pocket and texted Umiko. She made a couple more finger taps without waiting for the reply and music bloomed through the speaker. Soft at first, until she turned the volume up.

The acoustics in the large space were better than she expected. She maxed the volume and closed her eyes. She let the music fill the space of the firehouse and drown out the pulse beats in her ears.

She focused on the beat and changed her breathing to match. She worked out some of the tension in her arms and legs from her first motorcycle ride, Greg declaring her house unsafe, and Ms. Evans glaring at her from the window as she left.

Her body shivered as she remembered that glare. She forced the memory from her head by filling it with a better one.

Her bath that morning had been wonderful, at least until it superheated for no reason. Lyn tried to push that memory away too but her brain was filled with all the things that had gone wrong.

There was the surprise visit from Ms. Evans, the neighbor's dogs seeming to talk to her, and Greg's insistence that she get out of her house with only three minutes notice. Her nerves were getting on her nerves.

She'd been high strung for days now, weeks really. Ever since her mother's accident. She ran. She danced. She took long baths but she couldn't seem to get a handle on her anxiety for long. It seemed that every question answered led to another. Every roadblock she thought she had passed, just led to more.

Who or what was Greg? Why did his dad have a company that needed a safe house? Was Ms. Evans really a witch and what did that mean for Lyn? Questions upon questions filled her head space but fled in the presence of the music taking over.

Lyn let out a long breath and allowed the music to seep into her bones. She tried to get the music to soothe her fired up nerve endings. But it wasn't working this time.

Her pulse was still faster than the music. She opened her eyes to see if Greg had returned.

And her heart skipped a beat. Her pulse was still thundering, but a smile spread across her face when she thought about Greg.

He grounded her better than music. She remembered his hands on her shoulders. The firm but gentle tapping of the beat on her clavicle that helped her out of her panic attack yesterday. She remembered him standing close this morning, and the feel of his breath on her ears.

Butterflies built in her stomach and she ached to flutter along with them.

Lyn took a few tentative dance steps. The music's tempo rose, and her arms begged to do the same. She let them. She closed her eyes, no longer caring if Greg saw her dancing. She was pretty certain he already had. She allowed her body to move as it wanted, trying to spend the energy building up inside of her. Trying to force her pulse to slow.

She danced away the unknowing and reveled in the memories of the way Greg made her feel. She let herself be carried on the rhythm of the music, all self-consciousness abandoned.

The song faded out and she stopped dancing. The butterflies had abated for now. She adjusted the volume on the phone speaker and sat on the ground with her legs crossed like she remembered from kindergarten.

She listened to the sounds of the space and the barely audible music from her phone. The vibration in her muscles was calmer and she felt a modicum of safety. She sat with her hands in her lap and her legs relaxed. She located the sound of a drawer opening and closing again.

The squeak of a door hinge signaled company.

"I told Clark to let Umiko know you were with me. They're going to meet up for lunch, sooner if he can get off of work early," Greg said as he opened the door with his hip. His hands were full with two bottles of water and a few packages of snack foods.

"I texted Umiko." She pulled out her phone and checked for messages. She didn't find one, but if Umiko had a lunch date, she was probably preoccupied with getting ready for that.

Lyn turned her torso, stretching her back as she watched Greg walk a few steps behind her and bend to pick up something from the ground. He brushed it off on his pants leg and handed it to her. "You dropped this."

It was her ponytail elastic. It must have fallen out when she was dancing. Her hand went to her hair to quickly make a new one.

"You can leave it down," Greg said, "if you want to."

She stopped wrapping and allowed the white hair to fall to her back. She put the elastic around her wrist. It was stretched enough that there was no worry of it cutting off any circulation. Her mom had a pet peeve about hair bands worn as bracelets.

"When did it turn?" Greg asked freeing his hands of the various food stuffs.

"In my bath this morning. I don't know why it's happening." Lyn started to look away when the flood of anxiety threatened to over take her. Instead, she looked at Greg. His smile disarmed her. He wasn't concerned about this new development. He was curious.

"What's changed?" Greg sat cross legged in front of her. His knees inches away from hers but further from the ground. He looked uncomfortable.

"What's changed?" Lyn repeated the question. She didn't know where to start. A lot of stuff had happened recently. She started to bark that her mother had died, but she stopped herself. She knew he wasn't trying to be mean. She looked into his eyes and found only kindness. He was making an effort to come to her, even though sitting on the floor cross legged looked awkward for him. She let out a deep breath and with it her anger.

"I'm eating funeral food. I'm stressed out from things I don't know and didn't know I don't know. I'm not taking my medicine. I apparently look like the sun is afraid of me. The water went cold and hot again. I nearly burned my skin in the bath. AND you haven't answered any of MY questions." She looked at him in the wake of her verbal release.

Greg straightened his legs and leaned back on his hands. He was non-plussed.

"Point taken," Greg said. "My dad runs a private security firm. He has access to military style equipment, but more cutting edge. The safe house is maintained by us, but used by government types too, under our purview. The security is top notch, the passcodes update almost daily. The call I received when I got here was the monitor on duty asking if I needed anything. Since it's empty, only our guys are monitoring it. They know me. I'm the boss' kid. My turn for a question?"

Lyn nodded.

"Meds? You and Umiko said you had some herbal thing you take daily?"

Lyn voice was more steady when she replied. "Yeah, some herbal concoction that Ms. Evans made for me. It's supposed to help with my anemia. A few days before my mom died she poured the last bottle down the drain."

"I'm glad your mom poured it out. Don't eat or drink anything that woman gives you."

"She brought a casserole this morning, even the dogs didn't bother eating it."

"Dogs?"

Lyn held up two fingers. "That's question number two."

Greg smiled. "You're turn, I guess."

Lyn smiled and answered his question anyway. "The neighbor's dogs got loose. Gypsy and Romani. They started barking at Ms. Evans on my porch." She giggled. "It sounded like they were calling her a bitch." The sound replayed itself in her ear. The giggle froze in her throat. "Wait. You said Ms. Evans is a witch."

Greg nodded. "It's our best guess. We ruled out vampire."

Bitch, witch. Lyn said the words in her head. Could the dogs have known? She shook her head at the thought. She was just being silly. Dogs didn't talk.

Lyn and Greg shared a smile. "We? Meaning you and Umiko?" Lyn asked.

"No. A buddy of mine. He works on the intelligence side of private security. The company has access to a lot of world data and our ears are in a lot of intelligence chains. Given enough time, I have the resources to find out anything about anybody."

"I remember. You had him look into Ms. Evans."

Greg nodded and sat up straighter. "Right! That's what I need to tell you about. Alice Evans is an alias." Greg started. He peeled back the foil lid of an apple sauce cup and offered Lyn a spoon. He gave her all the intel her had gotten this morning. "Where were we? That's three for you, I think. My turn. Do you know how old Ms. Evans is?"

"Late 40s, give or take. What does she want with me?"

"I don't know. The other aliases only stuck around long enough at their jobs to be cleared of the baby switching allegations. Each entire alias drops off the grid after that. Maybe because of the pressure she felt the need to move on. You were different somehow. Alice Evans stuck around. The authorities never got involved here. Jonathan, didn't complain to them or they didn't take him seriously. He hired a PI instead," Greg said.

"And the investigation died when he did," Lyn supplied.

"Which I'm not sure is a coincidence anymore."

"You think she had him killed?"

"I think she caused his accident, and not in person. Hence witch."

"Do you think she wants me dead too?"

Greg shook his head and relaxed a little. "No, I think she wants something else from you. Something in your blood. It all comes back to the strange anemia treatment. Umiko's right, it doesn't fit."

"You think the meds were part of it. Why? To control me?"

"Yeah, but there are other ways of doing that. If your hair

started turning when you stopped taking the meds, maybe they're related. Anything else funny start happening around that time?"

"Not that I can think of. Clark thought the changes in my hair might be a camouflage wearing off."

Greg scratched his bare chin. "Interesting. Tell me more about your hair."

"It's hair. For my entire life it was the same color as my mother's, but her curls were prettier. Mine looked more like they were struggling to be curls. After she died, they got frizzy. I thought it was stress. Last week, in the middle of Geometry, Umiko noticed red highlights. The same color as hers. Then the white started appearing. A few strands at first. Today, all of it." Lyn put her hands behind her neck and pulled out, letting the white hair fan out and down her back. She still wasn't used to being able to do that without tangles grappling her fingers.

"Chameleons blend into their surroundings. It's fascinating to watch. There are videos on the internet."

"I'm not a lizard," Lyn said.

Greg laughed. "Fair enough."

"And I wasn't blending into my environment."

"No, you were blending into your support network." He cocked his head to the side and looked at her hair. "I'd be interested to know if it reversed if you took the herbs again. Would your hair turn brown and curly like your mom's or red and straight like Umiko's? I'm betting it would go red." He looked Lyn in the face.

Lyn watched as the color in his face drained.

"But don't, okay. I don't want you to take anything from that woman." Greg sounded worried. "We'll figure you out another way, if you even care."

"Umiko does." Lyn sighed. "It's her pet project. This whole, 48 hours to find a guardian thing only put it on the back burner." Lyn remembered Umiko's face from yesterday, when her dad had said the baby he held was not human. When he had pretty much confirmed Umiko's theory that Lyn was a creature. "She'll pick it up again soon, I'm sure."

Greg nodded. "But do you care?"

Lyn shrugged. "It might be nice to find my real family. To find out where I belong."

Greg didn't comment.

A phone buzzed.

Lyn and Greg both looked at their devices.

"Not mine," Greg said.

"It's Ms. Evans." Lyn showed Greg her phone display.

He sat up straighter. "Answer it and put it on speaker."

Lyn did and held the phone up near her face.

CHAPTER THIRTY-ONE

"*L*yn, dear, this is Ms. Evans." The sickly sweet voice on the other end of the phone made Lyn's skin crawl.

"Hello?" Lyn said.

"Hello, dear. I'm glad I caught you," Ms. Evans said.

Lyn took advantage of the pause, she knew it was a fleeting opportunity. "How did you get this number?" Lyn asked.

"Your mom gave it to me. She wanted me to have it in case of emergencies. She was a smart lady, your mom. I'll miss her terribly."

Lyn doubted that was true. "And this is an emergency?" She asked.

"Well, not exactly. Okay, maybe just a little. I've been trying to meet up with you for a while. Your mom said you were busy with some sort of summer school project, then the poor thing had her accident. I wanted to talk to you both about some odd test results. It's not something we should talk about over the phone, dear, HIPPA and all. You understand. Can we meet? I'll make you a nice lunch."

"I'm busy, Ms. Evans." Lyn cut in before the older woman finished the last syllable of her word.

Greg motioned for her to draw out the call.

Lyn wondered what he was listening for. She sighed and tried to think of a question to ask that she could fake interest in. Exactly the opposite of what she was. "Which test?"

"One of the blood tests, dear. The last one. I ran it twice, of course, to check the results. It wasn't conclusive, but it looks like we need to make some changes to your medicine. It's not working like it was before. You've probably noticed a difference. Anyway, we can adjust the dosage to get back on track."

"What do you mean, it's not working like before?" Lyn asked, genuinely interested this time. She realized that if she asked something simple, the talkative woman would draw out her answers. Lyn hated the way Ms. Evans spoke. She never gave a simple answer when a thousand words would do the job. Lyn sighed and looked at the phone. Maybe the woman was just lonely and needed someone to talk to her sometimes, like Clark had said about the nursing home residents.

"Well, dear, you looked paler than normal when I came to see you this morning. Have you been taking the drops I gave you last time? Of course, you wouldn't stop, you know how important they are. Silly of me to question you. But that's why I think we need to increase your dosage. Go ahead and take another dose when you get back home and I'll bring over a new bottle with a different iron concentration. When do you think you'll be get back, dear?"

"I'm not really sure, Ms. Evans. I'm at the library." The lie came easily to Lyn's lips.

"I saw you drive away on the back of that death machine. Your mother wouldn't approve. She wouldn't want you to have an accident and die because people didn't see you on that thing. 'Share the Road' is catchy, but people don't pay enough attention. Always on their phones these days. Who was the boy? Anyone I know? Did your mother like him?"

Ms. Evans paused. "Hmmm? Lyn?" Ms. Evans fished for answer.

Lyn lowered her voice. "I really shouldn't be using my phone in here. The librarian is strict. You wouldn't want me to get in trouble, would you?"

"Of course not. You're right. Just tell me when to expect you for lunch, dear. We can talk then."

"I can't make it for lunch, Ms. Evans." Lyn shook her head. *This woman will not take no for an answer.* "My project is due tomorrow, early."

"So soon? Okay, dear. How about dinner? I made up another lovely casserole. Did you put the one I gave you in the fridge? You can eat it later in the week. This one is much more food than I can eat alone. There is plenty to share and don't worry, I'd still have leftovers. I tend to make too much. It'll be nice to have someone else to feed." Ms. Evans drew out the words.

"I've already got plans," Lyn said. The woman's slow speech was grating on her nerves. She looked at Greg, her eyes pleading. He nodded. "Sorry, the librarian is coming over. I've got to go, bye." Lyn hung up without waiting for the woman to speak.

"What was that about?" Lyn asked. "Why did I need to keep her talking? You weren't trying to trace it were you?"

"No, it was a long shot, but I was trying to see if she would let something slip. Did she say anything that made you question her motives?"

"Just the thing about you."

"What about me?" Greg asked.

"That my mom wouldn't approve of me on the back of your motorcycle. That's not right. Well, maybe she wouldn't approve of me on the *back* of it. But she wouldn't disapprove of motorcycles in general."

Greg's face scrunched up in a question.

"My mom had her own motorcycle, in college. We were

going to take a motorcycle safety course together, we even talked about getting me one when I started college."

"Anything else?"

Lyn played the conversation over in her mind. "I didn't have a summer school project. I didn't even take summer school. Why would my mom have told her that?"

"A throw away excuse maybe. The same reason you used the library. To get out of something she didn't want to do." He smiled at her. "You are a pretty good liar. It rolled off your tongue just as smoothly as the rest of your words."

Lyn wasn't sure if that was a backhanded compliment or not. "So, my mom didn't trust her."

Greg shook his head. "No. I'm sure of that now, and I don't trust her either."

CHAPTER THIRTY-TWO

"What happens now? I can't stay here." She flung her arms out to encompass the space. "And I no longer feel safe at my house." Lyn crossed her arms over her chest. "Thanks for that, by the way." She tried to put a little levity in her accusation but failed. She laid back on the cold floor, extending her legs straight. They bumped into Greg's and he shifted to lay beside her.

"I'm sorry," Greg said. "Do you have any other family, grandparents, aunts, uncles?"

Lyn sighed. "If I did, I wouldn't have had to hunt down a father that I'd never met."

"Right."

"I wish time could just stand still for a moment. Long enough for me to catch my breath and wrap my head around all the new stuff happening." Lyn closed her eyes and counted her breath. The need to run, to catch up, to do something called to her.

Greg stayed silent.

Lyn moved closer. She pressed her arm and shoulder into his until she could feel the heat radiating off of Greg's body.

After a moment, he found her hand and held it. Everything else vanished except the butterflies. She closed her eyes.

~

After an hour of laying on the cold concrete floor, Greg's phone buzzed. Lyn opened her eyes when she felt the vibration in her thigh and caught a blur of motion above them. She blinked and it was gone.

Greg pulled his phone out of his pocket and put it near his ear. "Wait, what?" He moved from laying to standing in one graceful motion.

Lyn was left cold on the ground.

Greg looked down at Lyn. "Yeah, she's with me."

Lyn stared past his shoulder. Her eyes tracked a lone monarch butterfly.

Greg turned away from her and the butterfly fluttered away.

Lyn tried to hear the person on the other end of the phone, but she couldn't make out anything. Greg must have had the volume turned low.

When Greg ran his fingers through his hair, she sat up. Her muscles tensed. Something was wrong. Again.

"What?" she said to Greg, her nerves fraying. "What is it?" she pleaded.

Greg turned and extended his hand to her. She took it and rose. He held the microphone of his phone away from his lips, but kept his ear to the speaker. "Umiko was supposed to meet Clark at the park for lunch. She didn't show so he went to her house. He says Umiko's mom was home. It took him a while, but he finally got her to say that Umiko was with you. He left wondering if he and Umiko had gotten their wires crossed, but that didn't sit right, so he called her. No answer. No replies to his texts either."

Lyn pulled her phone from her pocket and pushed the two

buttons it took to call her BFF. It rang three times and her friends' voice came on the line. "Hi!" Lyn was relived until the voice kept going. "I'm so sorry I missed your call. Leave a message and I'll call back as soon as I can." She held the phone down at her waist level and stared at it.

"It went to voicemail. She's never let my call go to voicemail. She even answered it in church once. We both got a lecture that day about appropriate calling times." Lyn hung up and texted her friend.

She typed three letters. *MMQ.* Lyn looked at Greg. "She'll text back when she gets it. She knows it's important. She'll also head to my house as soon as she does."

"Why your house?" Greg asked, a slight hitch in his voice.

Lyn heard the hitch. It was subtle, like he tried to mask it, but Lyn knew he was worried.

"It's what we do. MMQ means 'meet me quick.' If I send it, we meet at my house. If she sends it, we meet at her house. Unless we amend it with a different location." She searched his face. "Did I just make it worse? I did, didn't I? You don't think she's safe there either." Lyn paced a small section of the large warehouse. She put the nail of her left pinkie between her teeth while she thought. *Skate Park.* Lyn keyed the word into her text message and hit send.

She held the phone at her side, clutched in her fist and turned to face Greg. "Greg, I'm worried about her."

"I know." He reached out to touch her.

She dodged it and took a few steps one direction, then turned and stepped back. Lyn's legs ached to keep moving. A run would be ideal, she settled on pacing.

Greg put his phone back near his cheek. "Clark, did you hear Lyn?" He paused to let Clark answer. "Go to the skate park. She didn't answer Lyn's call either, but she'll go there as soon as she gets Lyn's messages. Either there, or Lyn's house. We'll go to the skate park first. It'll take us about 20 minutes." He paused. "Clark, Ms. Evans can't be trusted. She's a witch."

Greg listened. "Details later. Any chance you're immune?" He was quiet for a moment. "Damn." He was quiet again. "No, I'm not either." He nodded. "Okay. Be careful. We'll get there as soon as we can. Text me if she shows up."

"Me too." Lyn shouted but Greg had already disconnected the call.

"Do you think she's okay?" Lyn searched his face for answers that he didn't have.

"Any reason Umiko would lie to her mom about being with you?" Greg asked.

"There's only one reason I can think of, and he just called." Lyn's brow creased. "Umiko doesn't usually lie to her mom." Her breath caught in her throat. "Something has to be wrong, why else would she lie this time? Greg, we have to go. Now."

Lyn bounced on her feet and watched as Greg started a new text message. She watched as he entered her number and one she didn't know. "We'll use this to communicate." He typed up a quick message and hit send. Lyn's phone pinged. She cleared the message notification.

Greg walked over to his bike and handed Lyn the second helmet. "Let's go find Umiko."

CHAPTER THIRTY-THREE

A rumble built as Greg opened the large garage door.
She didn't remember the sound of it opening being so loud. "It needs some oil," Lyn shouted over the growing sound.

A thunderous crack vibrated the aluminum panels.

"That's not the door." Greg pointed to the growing gap. A river of water was flowing into the french drain just beyond.

"Rain? But it was sunny an hour ago." Lyn walked over to stand with her arm extended out into the falling water. "The forecast said it would be cloudless and hot."

"Maybe it will stop soon? Either way, this isn't going to work," he said.

"What won't work?" Lyn turned on him.

"With the fresh rain on the street, your inexperience at riding, and my inexperience at having you on the back on my bike. It's too dangerous."

"No, we have to go. We have to find Umiko!" Lyn stomped her foot and splashed water up her jean leg.

Greg shook his head. "We also have to be safe about it."

Lyn stomped her foot again, getting her pants legs more wet. She growled and looked out into the dark sky. "No." She said and stepped out into the rain. She stuck her hand out and the water flowed over her fingers and gathered in her palm. "I need to know she's safe." The rain plastered her hair to her head and started on her shirt. She looked at Greg.

Greg stepped out from under the dryness of the building to stand beside her. "I know." He pulled her close and looked into her eyes. "We just need to think of a better way." He pulled her back into the building and out of the rain as a flash of lightning lit up the sky. He brushed her hair from her face and turned her chin to look at him.

"You can't ride in this?" Lyn questioned him.

"I can, but it will be hard to control the bike until the rain washes away the oils from the road. But I can't do it with the extra weight. No offense to you." He looked into her eyes. "I'd be focused on you and compensating for the few pounds you add and not the road where I need to focus. Plus, you kind of hurt me last time." Greg lifted his shirt.

Lyn glanced at his abs and took in a breath. There were two barely noticeable matching set of half moon marks on either side of his chiseled middle.

"This is after it's healed. You'd like motorcycle riding even less while being pelted with rain. It hits like razors." He smiled. "A lot like your nails actually."

Lyn reached out to touch the marks on his abs. "I did that." She tried to line her fingers up with the marks. Her nails were trim. She wasn't sure how she was able to mark him, but the scars lined up perfectly. "I'm so sorry."

"No worries." Greg put his shirt back in place and Lyn noticed dull blood flecks and ragged holes in his white shirt.

He must have tried to clean up when he had been gone so long before. But the holes didn't mend so easily as his skin. They looked like a small knife blade had stabbed him repeatedly. "I heal fast. But I cannot chance riding in the rain with you on the back yet." He took a deep breath and stepped in to Lyn. "I won't risk you getting hurt."

Lyn's phone buzzed in her pocket. She stepped back and read the notification on the lock screen.

"No. No. No." She said emphasizing each word with a stomp. The third stomp lined up perfectly with a crash of lightning.

"What?" Greg asked.

"Umiko. She returned my message." She showed him the phone screen.

"SOS," Greg said out loud. "Any alternative meaning I should know about?"

"She needs us." Lyn's muscles were vibrating. She looked around for something to throw or hit. There was nothing within easy reach except for Greg. She looked out into the rain. Lyn sank into her heels and tensed her thighs to push off from the ground but Greg grabbed her hand before she could.

"Look at me."

She reluctantly turned to face him, but her eyes still darted around his face, around the large expanse of room and back out into the rain. She needed a way out, a way to get to her friend.

"Lyn." Greg squeezed her hand. "Look at me, please."

She tried. Her eyes slowly settled on his.

"Good, now do you trust me?"

She thought about it. He had answered all her questions, except one. She still didn't know what type of creature he was. But she didn't have time for that now. He had never given her a reason not to trust him. He was a good guy. His nickname was Sir Greg for a reason. Right now Umiko needed him to be her knight and he would be, she was sure of it. She nodded.

"You'll be safe here. I promise."

"What?" Lyn pulled her hand away. "No. I'm going."

"Lyn," Greg's voice was calm, like he was taking to a wild animal. "I can go faster without you and focus on Umiko." He took her hand again. "We both want me to find her. I will, but

I need to know you're safe. Do you promise not to do anything stupid?"

Lyn nodded.

"Say it."

"I won't do anything stupid, but you have to find Umiko."

Another crash of lightning and the building rumbled, along with Lyn. She couldn't tell if the butterflies were from the eyes staring into hers, or the anxiety of what Umiko's SOS text might mean. Probably both. Lyn felt like she might throw up.

Greg released her hand and stowed her helmet in a compartment on the bike. He put his own on his head. He reached in his back pocket and handed Lyn her 'girl's rock' cap before straddling the bike.

Lyn gripped the cap, her knuckles turning white.

"There is a phone in the kitchen," Greg pointed to the door he had used earlier, "if you dial 0, you'll get the office switch board. If you need anything, use it. They'll help and call me, if necessary. You're safe here," he said to her before he put down his visor and started the engine.

His masked gaze disarmed Lyn. She could just about see her reflection in the sheen of the visor. Only her reflection was not what she was used to seeing. She had forgotten about her hair. "Just go, find Umiko," she shouted at him before she turned away. She didn't know if he could hear her through the helmet and over the rain, but she needed to yell it if only to soother her own nerves a tiny bit.

Greg drove a circle around Lyn, turning his bike around in the dry space before heading out into the pelting rain.

She stepped to the garage door and watched his progress. She gasped when she saw him fishtail over a slick spot at the end of the driveway. When he was out of sight, she opened her phone and texted Umiko back. "On the way."

She stared at the phone, hoping for a reply. One didn't come.

Be safe. She said it to herself, but meant it for everyone. Umiko. Greg. Clark too, if he needed it. They were all important to her now. She needed them all to be safe and she needed this whole stupid thing to be over.

The butteries in her belly turned into a low grumble. Her fear turned to anger. Umiko needed her. She might be in danger and Greg was driving too fast in the rain on two wheels to find her while Lyn was hiding in a safe house. Lyn kicked and her foot splashed water. She let her anger bubble up and rush past her lips. She didn't know where she was and a stupid storm was keeping her from going to her best friend. She threw her cap on the ground with all the strength she could muster. It didn't even make a satisfying thump.

"You could have done this yesterday," She yelled at the clouds.

The sky flashed brighter. Moments later thunder grumbled above her.

"Don't talk back to me." Lyn stepped out into the rain. Her hands made fists and she thrust them out to the side of her legs as a sound erupted from her throat. No words were sufficient, but her vocal cords didn't need any. The inarticulate sound they made carried all her fear and anger.

The sky heard her. The rain fell on Lyn's upturned face as soft snow.

Lyn looked around. Her throat sore from screaming and her eyes wide. A shiver went down her spine. She held out her hands. Tiny flecks of snow landed on her upturned palms. Rain fell and thunder rolled, but in the inches beyond her skin, it was quieter and softer.

She doubled over and emptied the contents of her stomach, which was immediately washed down the drain by the rush of rain water.

A text message buzzed her phone. She rinsed her chin with rain and looked at the screen. "911." It was from the unlabeled number in the group text with Greg. "Clark."

Lyn pushed her hair out of her face.

She looked around for her cap and put it on her head to keep most of the rain from her eyes. She put her phone in her back pocket and made sure her keys were in her front. When she was done, she ran.

This run was wild, uncontrolled. She didn't have a path to follow or a playlist to keep her on task. She didn't know where she was, she only knew she had to get to the skate park, fast. Lyn ran as quickly as she could in the same direction Greg had driven. She searched for smells and sounds that could help her recreate the direction she had come. The rain was masking both.

She cursed herself for having closed her eyes like a scared child on the drive over and not checking her phone's map before running out into the rain. But she ran and followed her senses the best she could. She had to trust them to get her to where she needed to be. She didn't have an alternative or any more time. Umiko needed her.

CHAPTER THIRTY-FOUR

*H*alf an hour later, Lyn made it to the skate park. Rain flowed down the concrete ramps and collected in the bottom of the bowl. Scraps of trash bobbed as raindrops landed and pushed them around.

It would dry out in the heat and the sun, either that or the concrete would soak it up, but for now, Lyn estimated it was at least ankle deep.

Lyn was out of breath and her sides hurt. She placed her hands on her thighs and took deep breaths, wincing with the expansion of her lungs and the strain on her abs. She had never run that fast in her life.

The realization invigorated her. She knew what those mothers who could lift a car off of children felt. If Umiko was trapped under a car, or even a bus, Lyn felt like she could lift it.

She looked around the park. Her view was blocked here and there by empty half pipes, quarter pipes, and a few scattered trees.

She moved over to one of the concrete tables. The rain was cleaning a sticky brown flecked milkshake stain off the surface.

She looked around to get her bearings.

This table was the same one she and Umiko had been sitting at last year when Killian spilled her strawberry milkshake. Lyn's eyes narrowed at the memory as she stomped onto the top of the table. *Asshole.*

Lyn's view was less obstructed here, but there was no sign of Umiko or Clark. There were no cars or motorcycles in the parking lot.

She didn't imagine she could have run faster than Greg on his bike, so he must have been here and gone already. She hoped he had found Umiko, but she wouldn't stop worrying until she saw her friend with her own eyes.

She imagined Umiko sitting on her porch waiting for her. She'd act embarrassed by all the fuss, but secretly be excited by the same. Maybe Umiko would be in Lyn's back yard. That was a better place to find her. Ms. Evans wouldn't touch her there. She'd be safe from the witch. Or would she? Could Ms. Evans cause Umiko to have an accident? Like the PI and her mom? Lyn let out a pained scream.

Lyn jumped down from the table to the bench and down again to the ground. She picked up her foot to run to her house, but on her first step forward her legs turned to jelly. She nearly went down, instead she managed to land on the very edge of the concrete bench. Her tail bone shuddered with the unexpected impact.

Her break had cost her momentum and her legs screamed in defiance.

Lyn groaned in frustration. A lightning strike cracked and sounded so close that Lyn fell to her knees. She dug her fingernails into the packed ground, scooped up clumps of dirt and threw them with a growl that would have cowed wolves.

She stood up and attempted a speed walk. Her legs fighting her with every step until she slowed to a crawl. She was so close and the last half mile was mocking her.

She didn't have the adrenaline to run, much less lift a bus or fight a witch.

Tears threatened to join the rain coursing down her face.

There was no short cut between the skate park and her neighborhood. Fences and houses bordered the park on the side closest to her street. She would have to go all the way around to get home.

lightning lit the sky like a giant question mark. Thunder answered.

Lyn took a deep breath. She shook the water from her hat, wiped her face, and steeled herself to walking.

When she passed the park's playscape, she gave into to her legs' demands and stopped to stretch them out. She closed her eyes and breathed into her muscles, trying to rejuvenate them for the last push.

She had lost enough time.

Greg should have found Umiko by now. They might even be on the way back to the firehouse for Lyn.

She pulled out her phone to check for messages. Rain splashed the screen that mocked her with its absent notifications. She turned the ringer on and the volume to max before she put it back into her pocket in a poor attempt to keep it at least a little dry.

The hairs on Lyn's arms tingled and she spun around.

Someone was watching her.

There were no kids or parents on the playscape. There wouldn't be, not in this weather. Lyn turned more slowly and looked for the eyes she knew were there.

She spotted three guys sitting on a metal bench under a nearby pavilion.

"Lyn, you look awful," Killian called out. He was dry underneath the metal roof. His arms crossed, his body leaning on one of the poles.

"Like a wet dog," one of his henchmen added and elbowed his friend.

"What's with the hair?" the third asked slapping his buddy's elbow away.

All three laughed.

"A wet dog with ghost hair."

"Yeah, we can call her ghost."

Lyn wasn't going to stand there, in the rain, while they taunted her.

She channeled all her fear and anger into a single sprint and charged at her bullies while a terrifying scream ripped from her throat. She would finally stand up for herself and end this now.

Killian grabbed her hands as they went for his throat. "I'm stronger than you." He said through clenched teeth. His lips curled up in a smirk.

Lyn felt the strength he had to exert on her wrists to keep her from connecting with his skin. She flicked out her fingernails and satisfaction settled over her as they scraped against his throat.

"But please, continue," Killian said. Lyn heard the strain in his voice as he used all his might to keep her from doing worse than surface scratches.

Lyn pushed forward and forced Killian to fall onto a bench still gripping her wrists. A distorted smile flashed on his face, made even creepier by a flash of lightning behind her.

CHAPTER THIRTY-FIVE

*L*yn jumped as the sound of thunder ripped across the sky and pulled her attention away from her struggle.

Killian used her distraction to right himself and thrust Lyn back, off the edge of the concrete foundation. She fell to her butt in the mud.

Killian's two cohorts grabbed her arms before she could scramble away and lifted her to standing. They pulled her back onto the concrete foundation of the pavilion and held her tight, one arm per person.

"You shouldn't be out in a storm like this," Killian said.

Lyn's phone rang. The sound reflected off the metal roof, surrounding them.

"Do you want to get that?" Killian rubbed his neck where Lyn had managed to swipe him with one of her nails. He looked at his hand. "You drew blood." His face waffled between anger and amusement.

Lyn watched his nostrils flare. The phone rang again.

"Shut that off," Killian yelled as he walked over to the edge of the pavilion and used rain to wash the small trickle of blood from his neck and hand.

One of his cronies pulled the phone out of Lyn's pocket and handed it to him.

Killian glanced down and read the screen out loud. "Alice Evans." He stepped toward Lyn.

Lyn tried to yank her arms free of the two football players. "Please let me answer it?" Lyn begged.

Killian held the phone up so that she could watch as he declined the call. "Oops? Wrong button." Killian's expression mocked the apologetic words. He slid the phone into her front pocket.

Lyn spit in his face. Anger and energy coursed through her body. She didn't know where it came from, but her muscles were no longer tired from running, she was energized and ready for a fight. She imagined Killian as the bus she would have to lift to recuse her friend.

Killian lifted the hem of his T-shirt and wiped his face without taking his eyes off of Lyn's.

The phone rang again.

Lyn stared at Killian. He stared back.

Another ring, but neither broke eye contact. A third trill and he pulled the phone out of her pocket. Killian turned it so that Lyn could read the cracked screen. "Is this important?"

Lyn struggled to free her arms. She knew better than to ask to answer it. She glared at Killian, and wished her eyes could convey the pain she wished upon him at this very minute.

He took a long breath. Lyn noted the slight smile on his lips. He was enjoying this.

The phone rang for a fourth time.

Killian lifted it, his eyes locked on Lyn's and swiped to answer. "Sorry, Lyn can't come to the phone right now. She's a bit held up." He disconnected the call without waiting for a response from the caller.

"Now, maybe, we can have little time for ourselves," he

cooed in Lyn's face. The gentle softness in his voice a contrast to the mischief in his eyes.

He was so close to her that Lyn smelled the bacon cheeseburger he had eaten for lunch. She thrust her head back and quickly forward, hitting her bully's chin with her forehead.

Lyn recoiled from the pain. She remained on her feet only because of the muscled guys holding her up.

"That is not a move for the untrained." Killian rubbed his chin and took a step back. Just out of Lyn's range. "I have to say, though, I like seeing the fight in you."

The phone rang again. Killian growled as he read the name on the screen. "This Alice bitch is getting on my nerves." He looked at Lyn, his eyes narrowed. "Get rid of her."

He accepted the call and put it on speaker.

"Lyn," The voice on the other end was not the sickly sweet voice of a friendly neighbor calling to check on her. It was livid. "I have something you want." Ms. Evans clipped the last of her words.

"Let her go!" Lyn shouted and tried to pull away from the two football players holding her arms. She pulled hard enough that one nearly lost his grip, but he redoubled his efforts and held her firm.

"I'm sure we can come up with some sort of deal." The voice on the phone shifted. It lost some of the anger and took on a little sweetness. "Come by the house and we can talk. I'll make cookies." The last statement was recognizable as the Ms. Evans she was used to and Lyn had to remind herself that it was a lie. The statement, the voice, the concern. All lies.

"I already told you," Killian interjected, "she's busy, right now."

"You listen here." The red hot angry version of Ms. Evans' voice returned. "You stay out of my business, wolf." Lyn heard the spit fly out of Ms. Evans' mouth over the phone, as she enunciated the last syllable of the threat.

"She's mine," he growled into the phone and disconnected.

It rang back immediately. He answered it, and put it back on speaker. "I said back off."

"Lyn?" It was Umiko's voice shaking with fear.

"Let her go," Lyn growled, she shook one arm free and grabbed the phone. She held it like a bomb. Her hands shaking.

"You come get her." This time Ms. Evans disconnected the call.

"What the hell have you stepped in, pup?" Killian asked as he took the phone and his crony got Lyn's arm back under his control.

CHAPTER THIRTY-SIX

$\mathcal{U}$miko had wanted to tell her friend to run, but her voice betrayed her. She was only able to say Lyn's name before her voice faltered. She struggled against the ropes that held her arms to the plush armchair. The weave of the decades old fabric chafed the skin under her thighs as she tried to wiggle free.

Clark was tied to the chair opposite her, his mouth still gagged.

Umiko watched his facial muscles as he worked to clear it. His dark clothing was in opposition to the floral fabric of the arm chair. Like Death himself was forced to sit in a flowering garden having tea with an irritating queen.

This queen needs taking down a peg or four. Umiko glared at Ms. Evans.

"What do you even want with her?" Umiko asked. She wanted to keep the crazy woman's attention on herself and not on Clark's progress.

Umiko turned when she heard Greg start to stir from his landing spot beneath a section of fallen bookcase.

Umiko had been shocked when Ms. Evans threw him into the book case the moment he came through the door.

It had happened so fast that Umiko had not seen the woman move. She, instead, had watched Greg arc through the air and crash into the bookshelf, taking the bottom half of the shelves down with him.

Umiko was sure that Greg had broken several bones, simply because who wouldn't have when met with wood at such force. The older lady was deceptively strong.

Ms. Evans flicked her finger and another shelf broke free of its pegs and dropped its load on his head. "Why won't you stay down, boy?"

Umiko's eyes went wide. When she watched Ms. Evans throw Greg into the book case earlier, she thought the woman had just gotten lucky. But it wasn't luck. It was something else. A creature trait.

"You *are* a vampire," Umiko said as she watched Greg crumble under the avalanche of splintered wood and books. She could barely make out the rise and fall of his chest, and he was unconscious, again.

Ms. Evans began to laugh. "Worse, sweetie." She made a swiping motion with her finger in Umiko's direction.

Umiko didn't know what just happened.

Umiko tried to speak but her voice betrayed her, again. There was no sound. She opened her mouth to scream, but the sound didn't reach her ears.

"Quiet, girl, I need to think." The jittery woman paced the section of floor behind the couch.

Umiko's eyes followed her, willing her to be the type of person who thought out loud.

It only partially worked.

Ms. Evans grumbled to herself, but Umiko couldn't make out what she was saying. She caught a word here and there. Binding. Tincture. Deal. Dead.

"I don't know what this is all about," Clark said as he shifted his mouth free of the gag.

Umiko watched as Ms. Evans flicked her finger in his direction, then, more forcefully, her whole hand.

"But we can work something out, no one has to die," Clark finished. The gag hung limp around his neck.

Ms. Evans made a motion with her hand as if to slap Clark from across the room, but nothing happened. She gasped and froze. She stared at her hand and her eyes turned to slits.

Umiko watched as the woman stomped over and slapped him with her hand and what looked like all the force the older woman could muster. Clark's head twisted from the impact. Umiko tried to call out, but her voice didn't make a sound.

"That stupid woman! This is all her fault." Ms. Evans picked up a vase of fake flowers from the coffee table and threw it at the fireplace between Umiko's and Clark's chair.

Umiko winced as glass shards stung her bare skin and blood welled up from the tiny scratches.

"If she had just let it go, trusted me. But, no," Alice said. "What tipped her off? What made that woman suspicious and keep me from the child?" The old woman started pacing again, ignoring her captives. She rubbed at her forehead. Her volume lowered and she mumbled to herself again.

Clark and Umiko looked at each other. He smiled at her and Umiko felt a tiny bit safer in that smile.

"Now look at me," Ms. Evans said.

And Umiko did.

"I'm all out. I should have started taking more sooner. Stocked up."

Ms. Evans' hand flicked to the bookshelf. Umiko's head turned, expecting another shelf to fall, but nothing happened.

"Now the power is gone. Even my own." Ms. Evans pulled at her hair. Some of it came away in her hand. "My hair!" Ms. Evans put her hands to her face and felt around with her finger tips. "My beautiful face!"

Umiko wasn't sure beautiful was the right word. Ms.

Evans make-up was running in such a way that it made her face look 10 years older and almost melted.

Ms. Evans sighed. "I'll have to make a new deal." She pivoted and started walking back the other direction. "The girl will have to hold up her end, just like with her mother." She looked at Umiko. "Her real mother. Not the one I gifted her to." She dangled the phrase like a carrot for a donkey. "Lyn is no longer hidden, not since she stopped the tincture. Was that your doing?" She watched Umiko's face. "They will find her, you know. They'll come for her without me and my magic." Part of Ms. Evans' face smiled. "Lyn needs me to protect her."

Umiko closed her eyes and turned her head from the grotesque sight.

"This wasn't supposed to happen. You weren't supposed to happen." Ms. Evans thrust her fingers in Umiko's direction. "How did you get past the binding? Lyn's only connection was supposed to be Maria. Keep Maria happy. Stay hidden. Play human. But you. You probably put ideas in her head. Did you put ideas in Maria's head too? Make her doubt me. Ruin my deal."

Ms. Evans fixed her eyes on Umiko. She was close enough that Umiko noticed her enlarged pupils and spider lines of blood vessels in the whites of her eyes.

"I noticed her hair changing. You didn't think I would," Ms. Evans said. A calm coming over her words. A stark contrast to the rush of panic moments before. "I guess I could thank you for the visual clue. Your color is quite distinctive." The woman reached out to touch Umiko's hair. "But the binding is wearing off now. She's not taking her meds like a good little girl."

Umiko attempted to pull back. She tried to yell. *What deal? What were you doing to Lyn?* No words came out of her mouth.

Ms. Evans retreated from Umiko's side .

Umiko watched as the woman's head cocked to the sides as if she was listening to something.

"It was a good deal," Ms. Evans said. "A solid deal and I kept up my side. I made sure she stayed hidden. It was working until Maria..." Ms. Evans eyes went glassy. "It wasn't my fault." The panic settled back around the woman's words. "I'll tell her. She'll have to understand that."

Umiko tried to follow the ravings.

"Her mother will blame me. I'll blame the human woman. Tell her I took care of it. I just have to get Lyn back on the binding drops." Ms. Evans punctuated the word by pounding a fist into her open palm. "I'll bind her to someone else. Someone less suspicious than Maria. One I can more easily control. Maybe myself." Ms. Evans smile came back. "Maybe if I bind her to me, I wouldn't need to take her blood. Maybe I can figure a way to use her power without it." The aged woman looked to the ceiling and then shook her head.

Umiko tried not to look away from the creepy face. She was reminded of movie portrayals of junkies. The far away look in their eyes. The jittery mannerisms. The way they ran words together that made absolutely no sense to any one but themselves.

Ms. Evans looked away from Umiko and began pacing again. "I have to be careful about the wording." Ms. Evans voice returned to a mumble.

Umiko looked at Clark. His eyes looked back. She smiled, but he didn't return it. A heartbeat later, she realized he was looking past her. She turned.

Greg was watching Ms. Evans with one eye. The other was caked in blood and swollen shut. His top arm, the one that took the brunt the falling books, lay limp at his side, swollen. The angle looked all wrong.

Great. She thought to herself. *Our hero is broken. His sidekick is a pacifist and I can't get out of this stupid chair.* She silently growled and struggled against the ropes. They seemed to just get tighter.

She considered changing, but she was fully dressed and her selkie traits would be of no use here except to give her secret away to a lunatic. She was helpless.

"That damn wolf is keeping her from me!" Ms. Evans screamed.

The sound forced Umiko to turn back to the older woman. It was his voice that she heard on the phone. She wasn't just imagining it.

Killian has Lyn!

Umiko struggled against the ropes. She couldn't depend on Lyn to get her out of this. Her friend had her own set of troubles at the moment.

Umiko glanced at her phone on the low coffee table. Next to Clark's. They were of no use to her. She hoped Greg still had his, but he couldn't make a call if he passed out again. Did he make a call before he came in? Was help on the way? Even if he did, it wouldn't help Lyn. Umiko needed to get to her phone, better yet, she needed to get to Lyn.

Ms. Evans threw another vase of fake flowers. "I need my magic. I need Lyn's blood." This time, the vase hit the mirror above the mantel.

Umiko closed her eyes and turned away from the breaking glass and shards of raining mirror. She felt a cut open up on her face and a warm slow trickle begin.

Ms. Evans turned her crazy, wild eyes to Umiko.

Umiko shuddered and a piercing pain flared in her arm. She looked down at the pain and saw a piece of mirror standing straight up. The shard was roughly knife shaped. An inches of reflective surface faced her.

She blinked.

It blinked back.

A tear slid down Umiko's cheek.

"You." Ms. Evans eyes were glued to the mirror shard and

the blood leaking for Umiko's arm. "You aren't human either."

Umiko's pulse quickened.

Ms. Evans looked at Greg.

Umiko followed her gaze. Greg had shut his eyes again. Umiko, with tears flowing and a silent sob, hoped he was only pretending unconsciousness.

"You can't fight me." Ms. Evans stepped closer to Umiko and grinned.

Umiko squeezed her eyes shut and screamed, as loud as she could, as she took in the full brunt of the woman's psychosis. A tiny squeak was all that came from her open mouth.

"Where is my bag?" Ms. Evans turned around in her living room, searching. She retrieved a black medical bag from the kitchen counter and placed it on the coffee table next to a candy dish with ancient looking candies that were probably all stuck together, and a set of black pillar candles. She sat on the couch, unzipped the case, and laid out an array of medical equipment.

Umiko opened her mouth and screamed as loud as she was able. The squeak that came out was little more than a mouse's twitter.

Ms. Evans spread out a blue cloth on top of which she laid a rubber strap, a syringe in a sterile paper cover, and a vial to collect blood. "If Lyn won't cooperate. I'll have to get someone else's blood until she does. What special skills do you have?"

"Umiko won't consent." Clark said.

Ms. Evans glared at him. "She's afraid of needles." His voice was calm. "Look at her, she's terrified."

Umiko nodded her head, emphatically. Tears fell from her face. The wedge of mirror in her arm shifted. Her breath faltered.

She wasn't scared of needles. She was scared of the needle

wielding junkie, but Clark must have said it for a reason and she would play along.

"I don't care if she's scared," Ms. Evans said.

"You need her to give of her own free will. It's more potent that way, right?" Clark paused as the witch's eyes settled on him.

When he had her whole attention, he spoke again, more quietly. "It's not going well for you. Your power is spent. You can't take chances." Clark said. "When Lyn gets here, she and the authorities could squash you like the old decrepit lady that you are."

Ms. Evans snarled.

Old? Umiko wondered if Clark had hit his head. Umiko looked at the woman, her head tilted to the side. Umiko could see it. The state of the woman's face wasn't all make-up related. The deep lines around her eyes, the slouchy chin skin. The way the old woman's shoulders slouched forward, causing a curve in her upper back.

She is old.

"Care to make a deal?" Clark offered.

Umiko looked from Clark to Ms. Evans. She didn't know what game he was playing, but Ms. Evans was taking the bait. Umiko chanced a look in the other direction.

Greg probed his broken arm with the fingers of his other hand. He winced when he got to the tender spot, but gripped it. Umiko's voice let out a squeak. She cut it off with pinched lips and turned her head. She didn't want to watch her friend set his own broken arm.

"What do you have to offer me?" Ms. Evans asked. She sat back on the couch, her ankles crossed, with a needle in one hand, staring at Clark.

Clark sat up straighter in his chair. He leaned forward as much as he could with ropes tied around his chest and looked straight at Ms. Evans. "I..."

Umiko heard the deep velvet caress of his words, she wanted nothing more than to listen to him.

"…walk the line…" he paused.

Ms. Evans leaned forward.

"…between life and death."

Umiko pushed against the ropes binding her to the chair.

Clark continued. "I hold council with the after." He paused, dragging his words out.

Umiko thought he was either buying time, or doing a good job at marketing. Even she wanted to hear his next words.

"I speak on behalf of the dying." He paused. "Yet I remain untouched by decay." Clark's eyes flashed in the firelight.

Umiko blinked. She looked from Clark to the unlit fire. Her brow creased and she looked back at Clark. He winked at her.

Umiko turned to Ms. Evans. She had the unwrapped but capped needle resting on her lower lip. The old woman was considering Clark's offer.

Umiko took a breath. She hoped she was reading Clark's theatrics correctly.

"No!" She tested her voice. The words were a squeak, strained. She tried again. "Clark, no." Her voice sounded strange, like a door hinge unused for decades, but she had words. "Clark, you can't." Umiko laced her words with a sad keening, easier done because of the creak her voice happened to be composed of at the moment. "She'll use your power against us." Umiko struggled against her ropes. She didn't have to lie about trying to get free. She used it as a distraction in case her words weren't sincere enough. "Don't do it." She jerked at the ropes and the slice of mirror in her arm jerked with her. Umiko winced and screamed out with the fresh wave of agony.

Umiko knew that shard of glass needed to stay in her arm until the paramedics arrived. She silently thanked the swim coach for making sure the team was first aid certified. Umiko took a breath and watched the mirror.

The mirror watched her back.

Ms. Evans sat forward, uncrossed her legs and moved to the side of the couch closer to Clark.

"Freely given?" Ms. Evans asked.

"Freely," Clark repeated. The velvety softness of his voice calmed Umiko, who momentarily forgot to struggle.

Ms. Evans plunged the needle into his vein.

Umiko locked eyes with Clark. He winked at her again, the fire-like flicker absent. She looked back at Greg. His arm didn't look as contorted, but the pain showed on his face. He nodded at Umiko.

CHAPTER THIRTY-SEVEN

*L*yn struggled against her captors. "Killian, I have to go. You can punish me later. You know where I live. We go to the same school. You'll have plenty of opportunities to make me wish I were dead."

Killian looked at her.

Lyn saw his puzzled expression. "I have to help Umiko. You can bully me later. Your whole crew too. Whatever you want."

"Bully?" Killian asked.

Lyn noted a flicker of doubt cross his features before it was replaced by arrogance.

"Who do you think you are? You don't get to make the rules." Killian sniffed. He stepped closer to her. "Your scent..." He paused to take a breath. "What are you, Lyn Davis?"

"What are you talking about?" Lyn asked.

"I can smell you." He reached out and touched her hair. "I can smell the shampoo you use. The food you eat." He pulled his fingers gently down the length of Lyn's hair.

Under different circumstances, his touch would have felt nice.

"This isn't bleach." He sniffed again. "A year ago, you smelled like iron and sulfur. You smelled horrible, like confinement, but there was something underneath, something more familiar. You smelled like a long run and a rain storm."

"Whatever." Lyn barely controlled her eye roll. "I need to go, Killian. My friends need me."

Killian took another long sniff this time from her neck and face. "You smell like wet dog."

"Thanks," Lyn said. Sarcasm dripped from her lips. She struggled against the biceps that held her tight. "Let. Me. Go." She ripped one arm free and the crony holding it yipped. The sound caught her off guard. It was the same sound a kicked dog would make, not the beefy football player that took pleasure in making Lyn's life hell. "Sor…" she almost apologized.

Killian put his hands around her neck and lifted. "It's time we finally find out what you are."

Lyn's stood on point, using her ballet skills to continue breathing. She brought her hands up to wrap around Killian's wrists, her nails dug into his skin.

Killian looked at them and smiled. "The long run." He set her down and in one swift motion, he took his hands off of her neck and grabbed her wrists. He held them in front of her face. "Do you have anything more than claws and a call, pup?"

Lyn looked at her nails. They were filthy from digging in the dirt, but they were also longer, and sharper. Thick with a slight curl at the end. Her breath faltered as she saw how similar they were to the nails on Killian's hands.

"No! I am not like you!" she yelled in his face.

"You are more like me than you realize." He smiled.

"I don't have time for this," she snarled and pulled straight down on her hands, putting as much weight into the maneuver as she could. She curled her fingers as she did so and used her nails to scrape Killian's skin.

"You're one of us and you will submit." Killian bared his teeth as he let go of her wrists.

Lyn flinched at the sight of their sharpness, but she recovered her wits and bolted left. Killian followed. The cronies remained under the pavilion while Killian chased Lyn in the rain.

Lyn ran past the bright colored playscape, past the huge rope sphere jungle gym, past a short playground rock wall, and toward the entrance to the park. She would have to make it all the way to the street before she could get around the row of houses standing between her and her friends. But at least her legs were working again.

Lyn didn't look back, she didn't care what Killian and his cronies did, she just had to outrun him and get to Ms. Evans' house to rescue Umiko.

Lyn heard a pained growl behind her and she put more speed into her run.

Lyn tripped as something pulled on her ankle. She landed face down on the ground. She clawed her nails into the ground and struggled pul herself farther. To keep going. To get away.

Sharp pain pierced the skin of her ankle in three distinct places and a slight warmth spread around them. She stopped struggling. The sharpness faded, but the pain lingered. She rolled over to face the threat.

A wolf straddled her body between its four legs. Its warm breath blew the hair from her face. The wolf put one front paw on her chest. Its claws pricked the skin through her wet shirt just below her clavicle. The paw's heaviness pinned her to the ground. The weight of the beast could easily break a rib. She tried to move, but the claws pierced deeper into her skin.

"Killian?" Lyn looked into the wolf's eyes. She wasn't sure how much humanity to expect when he was like this. But she found something familiar. "Please? I really can't do this right now."

In her frustration, she threw her head back and it connected with the hard ground. Her eyes lost focus and she closed them against the rain and the pain.

A strained breath later, she turned her head to the side so water would not go up her nose.

The wolf breathed her in. A sound started deep in its belly. It grew in timber and resonance until it lifted its head and it escaped full volume from his throat.

Fear tingled over every inch of Lyn's drenched skin.

Another bolt of lightning illuminated the sky. The thunder echoed.

The tiny hairs along her arms stood up as if she had been struck by the primal force of nature.

he wolf stood over Lyn. His fur matted to his skin by the rain. He shook and the rain water flew from his pelt in an arc around his body. His ears twitched forward then back. The ground trembled and grew, like an earthquake building power. The vibrations turned into foot falls as the wolf stepped off of her.

No longer trapped beneath fanged fur, Lyn scrambled up. She turned to run, but a ring of muscles surrounded her.

She could not name a single person who stood in the circle, but she knew they were all on the football team.

Killian's crew stood shoulder to shoulder around her and the wolf.

"Cut it out!" Lyn yelled and rounded on the team. She made eye contact with every one of her captors, looking for the weak link.

They didn't flinch.

Lyn let out a long growl of frustration and the team took a collective step back, but the circle stayed intact.

"Enough!" She rounded on the team. "I'm wet. I'm muddy. My friend is in trouble." She made fists at her side. "I don't. Have. Time. For your games." She howled. The last word packed a punch and made more than one team member brace himself by stepping back and low as if at the line of scrimmage.

"You sure about this?" one of the circle asked and looked at the wolf.

The wolf snarled at the speaker.

The speaker crossed his arms. The wolf starred him down.

The speaker lifted his hands in surrender. One of the guys that had held Lyn earlier offered clothes to the wolf.

Killian's wolf form turned to face away from her and she sensed a tremor in the group.

She scanned the faces that made up the circle keeping her from Umiko. She heard a murmur and strained to make out the words.

"We don't change in front of others."

"She's not an other. She's a shifter too. Can't you smell it?"

"Maybe she'll change in front of us. She's pretty."

Lyn turned to the last voice, and its owner had the decency to look embarrassed.

"Lesson number one," Killian's voice said to her. He zipped up his pants and turned to face her. He took the shirt and his henchmen stepped back into the circle. The second crony, the one Lyn had torn herself free from, was holding his wrist with a towel. A bright crimson smear stood out against the white terry cloth fabric. "Learn to get undressed fast. Shifting with your clothes on makes the shift even more painful." Killian stood in front of Lyn with his shirt in his hands.

"I'm not one of you!" Lyn shouted in his face. Her hair hung heavy with the rain, her clothes clung to her skin.

Killian pulled his T-shirt over his head and shook some more water out of his hair.

"She's right. The mixed breed isn't…"

Killian crossed the circle in two steps. His face inches from the dissenter's. The rest of the statement died. The two locked eyes. Killian's muscles tensed.

Lyn had seen that stance before. She stepped away, backing into the player that had called her pretty. She sidestepped, hitting a second player. He put a beefy hand on her shoulder and she looked into his face. He winked at her and pushed her one step forward before removing his hand. Lyn turned back to Killian.

Both guys were holding their ground, but the dissenter broke eye contact first. Killian took the win and faced each member of his squad in turn. "If anyone here can tell me what she's mixed with, we can have that discussion." He paused. Then waved his hands. "Anyone?"

The circle took a collective sniff. Lyn's entire body tensed. She was already on edge because of the time being wasted with whatever this show of testosterone was. With the added attention of the surrounding guys, she felt fully aware of the closeness of her wet clothes. She was essentially standing in a ring of hungry looking, well-muscled, adult males, and she was lunch. She crossed her arms over her chest feigning defiance while still looking for an opening in the circle.

"Well?" Killian asked.

No one spoke up.

"Right, then until we do know what she's bred with, she's pack."

A grumble swelled from the crowd.

"Lowest of the low, of course." Killian ceded, his hands in the air by his face. "Honorary only. Pending proof of loyalty."

Lyn's annoyance and frustration bottomed out. Her eyebrows rose as she took in what Killian said.

He stared at her and the silence between them stretched. Lyn met his eyes and held it. She knew the entire pack's eyes were on her.

Lyn tried to figure out what just happened. Did the guy who had bullied her and made her life hell for a whole year just include her in his boys club? Did he offer his help? His whole gang's help?

"Now, pup." He held her gaze. "What kind of mess did you step in?"

Lyn didn't trust him, not by a long shot, but her friend, maybe friends, were in trouble. She was up against a witch and she didn't know what that meant. Greg had been worried. He made her promise not to do anything stupid.

She wondered if this counted. Teaming up with bullies. If it did, she would just have to break the deal. She would use every tool at her disposal and she had just been presented with seven very sharp weapons.

"Ms. Evans is a witch." The words tumbled out.

The wolves, in human form, grumbled. Lyn noted that some of the faces flared with anger. At her or her words, she wasn't sure yet.

The group listened without interrupting as Lyn told them what she knew.

"Umiko is being held captive. The witch holding her wants to make a trade. Me for Umiko. Greg and Clark went to find her, but I haven't heard from them since." Lyn let a single frustrated tear flow down her cheek and mix with the rain water. She wiped the tear and rain from her face and continued. She told the team what she and her friends suspected, that Ms. Evans, the nosy woman who lived across the street from her, was responsible for her theoretical swap the night she was born, had convinced her mom of an illness, and had been dosing her with herbs and taking her blood for sixteen years. Lyn thought about censoring her speech, but she had everything to lose and no time to pick and choose her facts. She told them everything she could remember about Ms. Evans.

They listened politely to every word until she punctuated

her explanation with her last statement. "I think she killed my mom." Even with the rain, she felt her eyes fill with water, but she was quick to brush it away. She already felt vulnerable in the middle of a group of guys easily twice her weight and a head or two taller than her. She would not cry here.

The whole circle growled, showing off sharp canines.

"I do NOT like witches," one voice said above the snarl and the rest echoed the sentiment.

"A vote," Killian said.

The circle of football players turned as one and looked at him. Killian laughed. "Just kidding. No Vote." He turned to Lyn. "This pack will help rescue your friends. For a price."

The hope that had built up inside of Lyn burst. It was just another game to him. Another way for Killian to make her miserable. Another carrot on a string that he dangled in front of her only to rip it away when she reached for it. She couldn't hold back the tears but she reached for the anger as well. "Never mind." She wasn't going to play that game anymore. "Get out of my way."

She moved to push through the circle. It bent around her fury, but held fast. Lyn beat her fists against the mountain in front of her. The mountain wrapped his arms around her and squeezed before letting her go. The guys to his right and left patted her on the shoulders.

"Ask the price, pup." Killian raised his voice to her back.

"Why?" she snapped and spun around, unabashed by the tears. Her white hair whipped around and lashed the three pack members that had tried to console her. She took a step and thrust a finger into Killian's face.

He didn't flinch.

"Why should I? So you can hold the locker combination just out of reach? So I have to beg to do the one thing I NEED to do." Lyn paused and lowered her voice. "Is that what you want? Me to beg?" She glared at Killian through the water in her eyes. "Fine. I'll beg. Tell me what you want from me,

Killian Jacobs. What is your price? I'll pay it. For Umiko." She hung her head.

"You have to kill it." Killian's voice was low, but firm.

She blinked and looked up. "What?"

"To be fully accepted as pack, you have to prove that you are one of us." Killian said. "We'd kill anyone or anything that killed a member of our pack. A death for a death."

The pack murmured their agreement.

"Do you not think I would wring that woman's neck if she hurt a hair on Umiko's head? Do you not think I am angry that she stole my mother from me?" She glared at Killian.

"I don't doubt your anger, Lyn Davis. I've seen it." He put his hand to his neck and smiled. "It's sharp." He pressed his finger to Lyn's chest. The smile gone. "I doubt your resolve." He tapped his finger. "You fold under pressure." He tapped again. "You run when things get difficult."

Lyn brought her hand up to catch his next poke, but it didn't land.

"I've watched you run for a year. You never once stood up for yourself." He smiled at her. "Until today."

"If you get me close to her, I'll put the witch down." Lyn's words came out firm and she stared into Killian's eyes.

Killian nodded. He flicked a finger at the circle.

A rumble started in the belly of one pack member and grew until the entire pack let out a sound that would have had smart people running in the opposite direction.

Several of the pack hooped and hollered and flexed their muscles. It was exactly like what Lyn imagined the group would do before a football game.

Or it was until someone bent over with his back to Lyn and unzipped his pants.

The circle let him pass before Lyn got a face full of football player butt.

Lyn heard another pained growl.

"Do you have a plan?" Killian asked.

Lyn shook her head.

"How far can you shift? Claws are nice. Teeth are better."

Lyn shook her head again. "I'm not one of you," she repeated more meek this time. She wished Killian would listen to her.

"We'll see," Killian countered.

CHAPTER THIRTY-NINE

Killian stared at the girl in the middle of his pack.

Lyn Davis faced him unafraid.

She had had the nerve to spit in his face. She drew blood. Twice. Her claws worked fine. Killian grinned and looked her up and down. *I've been trying to break you for a year, and this is closer than you've ever been.*

Her self-protective instincts were starting to kick in. She was angry and lashing out. She would have tried to break his finger if he had poked her once more. He was sure of it.

But he had charged her, full wolf. He had broken her skin. Breathed down her neck. Threatened to break her ribs. Nothing had happened.

He had wanted to use her fear and anger to force the change. He thought today would be the day that she would break free of her cage. To fight back.

Instead the girl had run, on two legs, like she always did. Slow. He barely spent any energy catching up to her. Clothes off, shift, leap.

His shift was all instinct now. It still hurt, but it was fast. His muscles and bones were used to the intense shift of features. The knees were the worst part and even that was tolerable to him these days.

For children born to it, the shift was hard to suppress. Fear, excitement, worry, all conducive to the change in most bred werewolves. All things Killian had thrown at her from that first day he smelled her at school.

He remembered her scent. The scent of a caged animal. One caged so long, that she was content to stay confined. Her scent was mixed with anxiety, fear, and other puzzling scents that he couldn't place but wanted to figure out.

The challenge of her scent had become his obsession. Maybe now, he would finally understand them.

But first, he needed to free her from that damned sulfur smelling cage.

He stepped close and took a deep breath. The metal smell lingered. The smell of cages and traps. He had tried to force her instincts to kick in, but she had lived as a human too long, her animal nature was locked up tight. Even still, he was surprised that she had not changed even once in sixteen years.

The first time is wild, uncontrollable, scary. Killian remembered. His dad had cornered him in the shed, only he hadn't known it was his dad at the time. 5 year old Killian had peed himself. The wolf growled and Killian felt the same sound build in his own chest, responding to the wolf's call. After the sound broke free of that little boy's mouth, the wild took over. No one could have stopped it. The blood thirst, the anger, the heightened sense. They overwhelmed everything. Even the calming voice of a loving mother wouldn't have broken the spell. Not that Killian's mom would have stopped it. Both his parents were full blooded wolf and his first shift was a right of passage. One he had to go through in order to learn control.

One that Lyn was way overdue for.

Killian smelled how close she was to breaking free.

The price the pack asked would unlock her shift. Her first kill. The blood of her enemy. Avenging her mother. Lyn would be overwhelmed by her wild instincts.

She might be able to deny that she was one of them now, but when she came face to face with the life that had ended her mom's and threatened her best friend's, she would fine tune her rage and the blood spilled would call her wolf.

She was just as much predator as he was, he was sure of it.

"You *are* one of us," he whispered in Lyn's ear.

She stepped back into the circle of muscle.

"But we don't have time for arguments, or training." Killian turned and walked away from her.

The circle opened.

Propelled by the guys at her back and sides, Lyn followed Killian to the pavilion.

CHAPTER FORTY

The team gathered under the pavilion. The opposite direction from where Lyn wanted to be. Away from Umiko.

Lyn chanced a look over her shoulder. Maybe she could try to run for it again. She looked to her left and right.

Lyn was flanked by guys who could run her down on two legs and she suspected they were faster on four. She had no choice but to wait for a better opening.

The guys wrung the water out of their shirts, brushed it from their skin, and shook their hair out. They gathered around one of the metal tables talking amongst themselves.

Killian walked to one end and Lyn was led to the other.

"When Scout gets back we'll have a better grasp of the situation," Killian announced and the table quieted down.

"Where did he go? How does he know where Umiko is?" Lyn asked as the two guys flanking her sat.

"He's our best tracker. He'll find her," one of the faces answered her question.

Lyn turned to face her house, even though she couldn't see it from here. She started to review her options.

"Lyn," Killian's baritone voice snapped at her.

Her thoughts vanished and she faced him across the table filled with Killian's fan club. They were all watching her, but it was different than in the hallways at school. She didn't feel like prey now.

Killian looked her straight in the eyes. "You need to tell us what you know."

"I already did." Lyn balled up her fist and shouted at him.

"No, you told us a story, a compelling one. Now, we need tactical knowledge." Killian said.

"What type of witch is she?" one of the faces called out.

Lyn turned to the voice and shrugged.

"What skills does she have to use against us?" another asked.

Lyn looked blankly at the new questioner. "I didn't know she was a witch until a few hours ago." Lyn hated the sound in her voice. She sounded drained. Like she had already been defeated.

Scout walked up to Killian on two legs, fully clothed. He began to whisper.

"To the pack." Killian told him.

Scout stood at the empty seat to the left of Killian and addressed the gathered pack members. "The old woman is home. There are three other people with her. She definitely smells like a witch. Like dirt and scorched earth, but she also smells like death. She was rambling. I couldn't make out her words because they were jumbled. They didn't make sense. She sounded crazy but worse, desperate."

"There was blood in the air and sweat. There must have been a fight. The hero was in there, but I couldn't hear him. The red haired girl is scared. I heard her shout something to the other person. I couldn't get a read on the last one. But his voice sounded hollow. I wanted to stay and listen, but I knew I had to get back here fast."

Scout's eyes met Lyn's.

The hero and the red-haired girl. Greg and Umiko. The

third must be Clark. "Killian, we have to go." Lyn pounded her fist on the metal table so hard that her hand throbbed as the vibration rippled up her arm, but she refused to show weakness by shaking out the pain.

Killian didn't move, he looked at her and calmly asked, "Have you been in the house?"

"Yes," Lyn barked. "It's an old lady's house. Ugly floral print furniture, fake flowers, yada, yada, yada." Lyn stepped back and two arms shot up from the guys seated closest to her.

They grabbed her arms and held her in place, only using as much pressure as they needed. Lyn stopped and they let go. She didn't doubt they would be after her and drag her back if she ran for it.

Lyn looked over her shoulder. "This is a waste of time."

Killian sighed. "The front door opens to…?" He prompted Lyn with a flourish of his hand.

She took a deep breath. "It's a one story house. There is an office to the left of the door. It's a straight shot past the open dining room and the kitchen, to the living room." Lyn closed her eyes and walked through the house in her head. Her pulse slowed as she did. A calm settled over her. "A hallway breaks off at the kitchen that leads to a bathroom, two bedrooms, and the laundry room. The kitchen and living room are open. The living room has a back door. It leads to the yard. The master bedroom is down a short hallway to the right of the living room."

"Garage?"

Lyn opened her eyes. "Never been in it, but it should be off the same hallway with the secondary bedrooms. Maybe through the laundry room?"

"Okay. Steve, August, and Flynn will go in through the backyard." Killian turned to them. "Jump the fence and stay quiet. Wait for my signal."

Three heads from Lyn's end of the table nodded.

"Flynn, you get Umiko out. Steve and August will cover you."

"Where do I take her?" Flynn asked.

"Away, I don't care. Some place safe, but nearby. Lyn will flay you alive, if you stray. Just stay with the girl and don't let her do anything dumb."

Flynn looked at Lyn and nodded.

Lyn wished his look would have meant something to her. Like that she could trust him to take care of her best friend.

The truth was that she didn't know anyone at this table beyond that they were normally mean to her. The fact that they weren't being mean now confused her. It was like her whole world was reordering itself without consulting her.

Lyn didn't know what she was, who she was, or where she fit in.

Lyn shook her head.

"Lyn, focus." Scout had walked to stand by her side. She recognized his scent from school. Cedar.

Lyn turned her attention back to Killian.

"After that, Archie, Mike, and I will go in the front. Once we're in, Mike, you take the office. Archie, you take the first hallway. Clear them both and cover my flank. I will go straight through. We want to surround them as much as possible."

Two more heads nodded.

"What about the hero?" Michael asked. "Will he fight with us?"

"Probably not, but he'll fight with her." Killian turned to face Lyn across the table. "Who's the third person? The hollow voiced one. What is he? Will he fight? "

"Clark won't fight. With or against you. He's a pacifist and, as far as I can tell, human," Lyn said.

Killian looked at Scout who shook his head. "There are no humans in that house, I'm sure of it."

"Wild card then." He looked at August. "Cover Flynn and

the girl first, then get Clark out. If he won't go, that's his call. He's not important."

Lyn started to object to Clark's importance, but had a more pressing question "What about me?"

"You are going to give the witch exactly what she wants." Killian smiled.

Lyn's phone rang.

"Tell her you're on your way," Killian said before Lyn even looked at the busted screen.

CHAPTER FORTY-ONE

*L*yn stepped up to the front porch and knocked on Ms. Evans' door. The thump of her pulse in her temple kept time with her breaths. She had no thoughts, no questions. There was only the quick 1, 2 of the thump. Lyn inhaled and knocked louder with her exhale. Three times, with her pulse's beat. 1, 2. 3.

Lyn couldn't see the pack, but she knew they were there. After her last call from Ms. Evans, the team had reviewed their positions. Lyn had nearly shed a tear as she looked around the huddle.

From the inside, it was a family. A strange belonging.

As she stood on the witch's porch, she knew where each member of the pack was. She could hear them as if they were standing next to her. She wanted to scream at them to be quiet, but she'd just draw more attention to them and she needed to avoid that.

When there was no answer to her knock, she tried again. She closed her fist and held her arm above her head. She mimicked the way Greg had knocked on her dad's door yesterday. The knock that meant she'd be coming through by force if necessary.

She listened.

She heard the rain fall on the roof, and a thump, thump, thwack as three things hit the ground to the left and right sides of the house. Flynn, August, and the other one. *Umiko would know.*

The thumping of the blood flowing through Lyn's veins quickened. *Why isn't she answering the door?* Lyn considered ramming it, but what could Lyn's small frame hope to do versus solid wood. She growled at the lack of motion, and pounded a single fist on the door at head height with all the force she could. Nothing.

Lyn looked at the knob. She didn't expect the door to open, no one ever does, but the instinct to try was there. She wrapped her fingers and palm around the knob and turned.

The knob twisted freely and she pushed the door open while the hinges creaked. *Just like in horror movies.* Lyn mused. *Perfect.*

Lyn made a quick look at the street around her. The neighborhood was quiet. Eerily so. She watched a single car drive past the house, other than that there wasn't a single sign that anyone was out in the rain.

She wiped her feet on the mat out of habit. "Ms. Evans?" She said as she stepped through the threshold, fighting all her instincts to run the other way. Umiko was inside. Greg and Clark too.

Why was it so quiet?

She left the door open as planned and took a few steps down the hallway. "I'm here. Just like you wanted." She looked left, but the door to the office was closed. "We can make that deal?"

"No deals!" Lyn heard Greg's voice shout from the living room. She heard his sharp intake of breath and the resulting groan of pain.

She gave up her caution and ran past the office, the dining

room, and a hallway. She froze in the space between the kitchen and living room.

Greg lay on the ground in far corner of the living room, under a pile of books and pieces of book shelf. Umiko squirmed in one of the ugly floral print chairs in front of the fireplace, gagged. Clark sat still in the other chair, his eyes closed, a rope wrapped around his middle, and a while cloth tied loosely around his neck.

Ms. Evans stood up from Clark's side holding a needle filled with red liquid. Her back still to Lyn.

Lyn looked down at Clark's arm where a bead of blood was forming.

"What did you do?" Lyn asked. She moved toward Greg, before thinking.

Lyn stopped in her tracks, halfway to Greg. Lyn shook the thought from her head. She needed to stay in the game and stick to the plan. She needed to keep distance between herself and Ms. Evans.

Where the hell are they? She glanced at the back door.

"Clark offered." Ms. Evans singsong voice sounded far away. She mumbled a few words over the needle and a glow formed around the syringe. It flared blue for a moment.

"What..."

Ms. Evans turned the needle and plunged it into her own arm. The red liquid disappeared from the vial.

Lyn followed the glow from the needle up Ms. Evans arm.

Ms. Evans turned to face Lyn and froze. A long moment past before she spoke again. "I can still salvage this." Alice's voice broke.

Lyn recognized the sound of fear. Lyn must look awful if Ms. Evans was afraid of her. Her hand went to her hair.

It was dry, even though moments before she ran through the rain to Ms. Evans's house.

I wish the rest of me was dry. A shudder went up Lyn's spine and she involuntarily shook with the motion. Water splashed at her feet.

Ms. Evans took a step back. "You don't have to be here. The girl is coming, but you have to go. I can salvage the deal."

"Who do you think I am?" Lyn asked, confused.

As the glow spread up the woman's arm, there was a wild look in the woman's eye, like a TV junkie right after the long awaited drug of choice began coursing through their veins. Ms. Evans flexed her arm and the glow spread. A smile began to do the same on her face.

"No, Lyn, we have a deal," Greg said and tried to stand up. "Nothing stupid. Remember. You promised." He slumped back down.

The woman looked from Lyn to Greg and back again.

"I'm sorry," Lyn said to Greg without taking her eyes from Ms. Evans. "I already broke it."

"Lyn? Is that you?" Ms. Evans asked and glared at her through slitted eyes. She pulled the needle out of her arm and threw the syringe into the fire. She snapped her finger and the logs erupted in flames. A plume of purple smoke rose from the remains of the syringe. She flicked her fingers at the bookshelf and the last shelf of books rattled above Greg's head before it fell.

Lyn's hand went out as if she could stop the falling books from here. But the motion was futile. She gasped as books fell. Landing hard on Greg's head and arm.

"Not as potent, but it's better than nothing." She moved to look at herself in a fragment of mirror above the fireplace.

Lyn saw the distorted pout of a melted wax mannequin's face. "No rejuvenating effects. That's very disappointing." She turned to Lyn. "But, we can fix that. You're here now. Have a seat." Ms. Evans motioned to the couch. "Tea? Cookies?"

Lyn watched the woman from her spot between the living room and the kitchen, aware that her back was to the master hallway. Ms. Evans' make-up ran down her face, like she had stood in the rain for the past hour like Lyn.

Lyn hand moved to her hem with the intention of wringing out her shirt, but it was dry.

Her pulse sped up. *How am I dry already?* She looked down at the puddle of water on the wood floor at her feet and her pulse skipped.

She didn't have time for this. Lyn pushed the new development from her mind. She needed to focus on Ms. Evans and getting her friends out of this mess.

Lyn faced the woman, and moved to put a wall at her back. She inched closer to Greg in the process. "Let my friends go."

"Oh, I will," Ms. Evans sugary sweet voice said, "but we have a deal to make first." Ms. Evans smiled. "Don't we, dear?"

"I am not your 'dear'. I don't like you. I never have," Lyn snarled and moved closer to the woman.

"That's not very nice. What would your mother say about your behavior?" Ms. Evans paused and a smile spread over her face. "Maria, that is."

Lyn took a step forward and yelled. "You don't get to talk about my mother. You killed her."

"I had to, dear, she was being selfish. I needed you and she wouldn't let me see you anymore." Ms. Evans' lips formed a pout, like a three year old who wasn't allowed a cookie before bed. It was disgusting on her seeping features. "Besides, she was nothing to you."

"What are you talking about? And why do you need me?" Lyn asked as she took another small step toward Greg.

"Your blood. When I realized what it did…" Ms. Evans smiled her junkie smile. "It was an accident, the first time. I cut myself on one of your vials. When our blood mixed, it was like a warm summer breeze filled me. I felt stronger. Younger." The older woman filled her lungs with a look of bliss across her messed up face. "I gave you to Maria, bonded you to her to keep her from rejecting you and to hide you in plain sight. It was easy enough to do. I perfected the process here and there over the years. The bonding seals the deal, so to speak. You look like her, you know." Ms. Evans' eyes connected with Lyn's.

"Look like who?" Lyn asked.

"Your real mom." Ms. Evans smiled. She murmured something under her breath that Lyn couldn't make out.

Lyn couldn't move. *Like my real mom?*

A rush of fur and flesh flew from opposite directions.

Ms. Evans' eye slitted and she glared at Lyn. "You're tricky, too. Just like her." Menace filled her words. The arm that had been infused with Clark's blood lifted. It extended out from Ms. Evans' body and formed a sideways claw.

"I told you to back off, wolf," Ms. Evans shouted above the commotion.

Lyn tried to act, to get to Umiko, or Greg. But she couldn't get her feet to obey her.

"I told YOU she was mine," Killian answered. He stopped his motion, while the rest of the pack continued theirs.

Lyn felt her throat closing, she lifted her hand to whatever was tightening on her windpipe. She clawed at her neck and felt blood begin to trickle from the contact of her own nails. She felt nothing but the resistance of her own skin.

She stopped.

The floor was further away now and Lyn had to concentrate on finding her balance on her toes.

"Tell them to stop or I'll kill her," Ms. Evans said to Killian.

"You're bluffing," Killian countered.

"Freeze. NOW." Ms. Evans bellowed. Her voice, a deeper resonance than Lyn was used to, commanded.

Everyone froze in mid action, except Lyn. She used the limited motion allowed by the phantom grip to look around.

Flynn had Umiko over his shoulder and half way to the back door. She was holding something in her arm. Something sparkly. Flynn's foot lifted but did not connect again with the ground.

August was frozen with the claws of one hand stuck in the ropes that bound Clark. Killian was six inches from Lyn's back, his lips curled in a snarl, but there was no sound.

Ms. Evans stepped over to within a foot of Lyn and plucked a hair from Killian's head. She put it in an empty tea cup. "That will be useful later." She turned to Clark, her back to Lyn. "Nice trick."

Lyn tried to lash out at the woman, but it cost her her breath.

Clark shifted his arms back and forth and finished cutting the ropes on the August's frozen nails. "Doesn't work on me though. It's my blood after all." Lyn watched him take stock of the situation. He inclined his head at Lyn, then at Flynn and Umiko.

Lyn tilted her chin down. It was as much movement as she could manage with her neck constricted but it allowed her a full breath.

Clark nodded back and stepped past the pair.

"What are you?" Ms. Evans turned to follow Clark's movements. Her smile looked like a junkie fully invested in a good hit. "You're nearly as handy as Lyn here. I could figure out how to…"

"You'll find out what I am soon, I think." Clark stood up and moved to Greg's side. He looked at Lyn. "Don't let me stop you. She can't sustain it for long. Even I have trouble with the time part."

Clark squatted down and grabbed Greg's unhurt arm. He draped it around his shoulder and pulled Greg up from the debris. "We need to get out of here," Clark said to Greg.

"But, Lyn…" Greg objected, his eyes opened briefly.

Clark looked at Lyn. "She's got this under control. You'd just be a liability."

Greg struggled to stand on his own and wrench his arm away from the older guy.

Clark winked at Lyn. "Damage Report," he snapped at Greg in his best imitation of military command.

Greg stopped struggling and his training kicked in. "Broken arm, multiple head impacts, probable concussion."

Clark helped Greg walk around Lyn and towards the front door.

Time slowly resumed. Flynn's foot connected with the ground. Umiko began to scream.

"FREEZE," Ms. Evans yelled again. Clark and Greg ignored the command. August's frozen face was puzzled at his missing target. Flynn's once floating foot was now firmly pushing off the ground.

"3… 2… 1." Lyn heard Clark countdown.

Time clicked back into play.

In a blur of motion, Umiko was out the back door over Flynn's shoulder without a misstep. Clark and Greg hobbled out of Lyn's vision as the remaining pack, wolves and human, surrounded Lyn and Ms. Evans.

Lyn's spine straightened and she found her balance, held up by Ms. Evans' phantom wrist.

Her friends were away and safe. Lyn would have taken a satisfied breath, if she had been able.

The pack held position. Their eyes split between her and the witch.

Lyn knew they were waiting for her to fulfill her end of their bargain.

Ms. Evans arm bent at the elbow and Lyn struggled to keep her balance as she was moved to closer to Ms. Evans. "No closer or I will kill her." Ms. Evans's smiled through her melting face. "I can start again. There's plenty of creature blood in the world."

The pack growled.

"By the looks of it, you don't have time to start over. You smell like road kill left out in the sun too long." Killian wrinkled his nose at the smell.

"Be quiet," she hissed and used her free hand to backhand him, even though he was not near close enough to connect. "Let us pass. She's not one of you. You have no claim on her," Ms. Evans said. "I made a deal. I have to protect her. Hide her. It's my life on the line."

The pack called her bluff and blocked the way.

Ms. Evans squeezed her empty clawed fingers until her nails were biting into the skin on her palms. She watched the blood drip from her hand. She stepped closer and looked at Lyn's neck. "What? Why isn't it working? You should be bleeding, not me."

"About that," Clark called from the kitchen, "you can't kill her," he said to Ms. Evans. "I'm not allowed to end lives. I'm only a travel agent for those ending on their own. But I think you might have need of my services. Unless you already have someone coming for you."

Lyn couldn't see Clark, but she knew he was watching her.

"You don't have to do this." His voice took on a softer cadence. A sad one.

Lyn closed her eyes and ears to Clark's voice. She knew what she had to do, what she wanted to do. She smiled at the witch and struck out one handful of sharp nails. She raked them across the woman's neck, from ear to ear, in one smooth motion.

Ms. Evans hand gripped her own neck. Blood trickled between her fingers.

Lyn looked at her hand, wanting to see the satisfying sight of blood and skin underneath sharp claws.

Her fingertips were covered in blood with flecks of skin under the thin white human nails.

Lyn looked at the old woman. There was still blood, but she hadn't inflicted the mortal wound she had intended.

The pressure on Lyn's throat stopped and she placed her feet flat on the floor. Lyn took in a deep breath to replace the small ones she had been allowed to take previously. The air smelled of copper and sulfur. Fear and decay. Lyn almost gagged.

Ms. Evans laughed and looked at her barely bloodied hand.

A grumble started in Lyn's belly and grew until it drowned out the witch's cackle.

Lyn felt her teeth change shape and tasted her own blood on her lips.

"Kill it," Killian's baritone voice commanded from over Lyn's shoulder.

"Kill it,"a slow chant started among the two-legged pack members. The four-legged among them growled and bared their teeth.

Lyn blinked her eyes and her pulse synced to the beat of those two words as quick as it did to any drum.

"Kill it." The words echoed in her head.

She had made a deal with Killian.

"Kill it."

To be fully accepted as pack, she had to prove that she was one of them.

"Kill it."

They would kill the witch.

"Kill it."

She was pack. Pack obeyed Alpha.

She licked the tips of her now sharp canines and lunged at the woman, forcing her to the ground. Satisfied at the crack of bone hitting wood floors.

"Kill it."

Lyn straddled the woman's body. Her knees squeezed the

witch's hips so she couldn't easily throw her off. Lyn's hands pushed the woman's shoulders into the ground. Her claws punctured the skin of the woman's arms. Lyn snarled.

"Kill it."

Lyn closed her eyes. The witch had killed her mother. Had taken advantage of Lyn for sixteen years. Had kidnapped her friends and tried to use them as bait.

"Kill it."

If Lyn walked away now, the witch would kill them all. She couldn't walk away. She would not run and hide from bullies anymore.

"Kill it."

Lyn opened her eyes. She took the woman's skull in her hands and squeezed.

Ms. Evans skin was wrinkled, her hair brittle and a dull shade of grey, peppered through with white. She looked twenty or thirty years older than when Lyn had last seen her. It would be easy to crush her skull.

"Kill…"

The beat in Lyn's head faltered.

A second beat overrode the first. More complex. More intriguing. It called to her in a way the simple two beat chant did not.

Lyn's ears focused on the new beat, and the death chant faded to background noise.

Lyn looked at the face in her hands. A person. A lonely, desperate, crazy beyond measure person.

"Kill it."

A killer, the underlying chant reminded her. A strung out junkie.

An old woman, Lyn forced herself to remember.

Lyn didn't know what type of creature blood ran in her own veins. Killian said it was shifter blood. The pack said it was mixed. The old woman said she looked like her mother. Her father had too.

"Tell me about my other mother," Lyn demanded.

The junkie smiled. Her rotten teeth showing through her thin and cracked lips.

Lyn might not know who or what she was, but she knew she was not like Ms. Evans. She was not a killer. And she was not like Killian. She was music. Lyn's nails withdrew and her teeth returned to normal.

"Kill it," Killian said in her ear. "You can't be pack unless you prove yourself. We kept our part of the bargain. I got you close. We rescued your friends. You owe us." His breath caressed her ear. "You have to do the rest."

Goosebumps spread from the flesh of Lyn's ear and down her neck.

"Kill it," Killian demanded.

Lyn took a deep breath to steel herself to do what she had to do and smelled Killian's last meal. She pulled her right arm back, folded her fingers inward and punched the woman in the face.

The way the old lady's head flopped to the side, unconscious, satisfied Lyn for the moment. Michael and Scout each took one of the woman's shoulders.

Lyn caught a fleeting smile from Scout. *When had he gotten here?*

Scout nodded at her.

She trusted that nod. He and Michael would make sure Ms. Evans stayed down.

Lyn stood and turned to Killian. The music still flowing in her bones. "I am not one of you," she said calmly while meeting his eyes.

"She killed your mother. You are alone, and it's her fault. You have no one. Without us, without pack..." Killian said.

"I have them." Lyn pointed in the direction of the music.

A rhythm, like a calm heart beat, spilled out of a cell phone lifted high above Greg's head. He and Clark stood in the space between the kitchen and the living room.

Clark smiled at her, a bit of pride in his features.

Greg lowered the phone and held out his hand.

Men in dark military gear filtered in and around the group.

"Bind her hands and mouth," Greg said to them without looking away from Lyn. "She's weak, but don't take chances. And see to her wounds."

Lyn hesitated to put her bloodied hand into Greg's clean one.

Greg made the decision for her and took hers, gore and all.

"You'll need us. You have no idea how to control your shift," Killian taunted her. "You'll end up hurting yourself or someone you care about."

She ignored Killian. "What will happen to her?" Lyn asked Greg.

Greg walked her out of the house.

CHAPTER FORTY-THREE

yn and Greg stood on the porch of Ms. Evans' house. The rain had stopped and the sun was threatening to make a show for the last few hours of the day.

Lyn rested her empty fingers on a damp bush near the steps. Lyn brushed her hand across the bush and the scent of rosemary wafted up and toward her. Her mother's favorite scent.

Killian startled her by coming out of the house and stepping too close. He took a long sniff of Lyn before Greg pushed him off the porch.

"We're not done," Killian said as he turned and walked away.

Greg's eyes stayed on Killian's back while he spoke to Lyn. "Alice Evans won't bother you again. She'll be registered, of course. Face a trial, like normal. In the end, her own kind will have a big say in what happens. But I doubt the Witch's Council will take kindly to her. She'll be made an example of."

"Witch's Council?"

"Politics is not your thing, is it?" Greg said.

She shook her head. "My mom was my thing. She worked

in a hospital. She saw a lot of pain and despair. We pretended the world didn't exist outside our house. I think she sheltered me from a lot."

"I think that was her job." Greg squeezed her hand.

"I mean really sheltered." She turned to look up at him.

Greg nodded. He pulled her to the side of the porch, so men in military uniforms could enter the house with a gurney.

A uniformed man, flanked by 2 men in black shirts and tan cargo pants stepped from a hummer parked on the curb.

"Heads up. Parental ambush twelve o'clock," Greg said quietly to Lyn.

"Van," the man addressed Greg and turned toward Lyn. He stood on the ground at the bottom of the steps. Lyn, four steps up, was eye level with him. "Lyn, right?"

"Yes, sir," Greg said.

"I'm Colonel Gregar," the man said to Lyn.

A uniform came out of the house.

"Excuse me for one moment," Col. Gregar said and walked to the other side of the porch.

"Sorry," Greg whispered to Lyn.

Lyn nodded and tried to listen to the colonel's conversation.

"Wait until the girl leaves," Greg's dad said quietly and the uniformed man went back into the house.

When his dad was done talking to the uniform he turned back to Greg. "There will be a debriefing, of course." The man's back was straight, his shoulder back. He looked like a brick wall and showed all the emotion of one. The man's face was a slightly older version of Greg's and completely blank.

"You'll need to answer some questions too." He looked at Lyn.

"Can I speak to her?" she asked. She wanted to find out what Ms. Evans knew about her mom. About her.

Colonel Gregar shook his head. "I'm afraid that won't be

possible, Ms. Davis." He looked from his son to Lyn. "Will you be joining us at dinner tonight?"

"Um." Lyn fought to find words.

"Not tonight, sir." Greg rescued her.

Greg's father nodded and turned to his son. "Not my place." He stared at Greg for a moment then lifted his hand to shake. "1800. You know how your mother values punctuality."

Greg dropped Lyn's hand long enough to shake his dad's. The man walked back to his desert brown Hummer consulting with his men.

"Was that…?" Lyn hesitated.

"Yeah." Greg grinned. "I think he likes you."

She looked at Greg like he had green horns growing from his head. "I did not get that at all."

"He invited you to dinner and cut me right out of the equation." He paused.

Lyn's eyes followed the Hummer as it turned at the end of the street.

Greg reached for Lyn's hand and pulled her closer.

Lyn looked up into Greg's eyes and her stomach growled.

"So, how about dinner?" Greg asked. "Just the four of us?"

"Your mom and dad?" Lyn stepped back.

Greg laughed. "No." He turned her around and pointed across the street.

An ambulance's lights flashed, but the siren was silent.

Lyn ran down the stairs and around the military uniforms standing between her and her best friend. She grabbed Umiko in a bear hug, barely avoiding the EMT examining her forearm.

"Did you know Scout's older brother is an EMT?" Umiko said before Lyn squeezed all the air from her lungs.

"Are you okay?" A guy in a paramedic uniform asked her.

Lyn nodded her head.

"Good. Scout will be happy to hear that." The EMT stepped back. "Umiko, though, is going for a ride. Get in." He helped Umiko in after stabilizing the mirror shard and closed himself in the back of the ambulance with the girls. "We're going to make sure this doesn't move, while my buddy drives. You'll probably be in and out with a few stitches."

Lyn heard the siren come on and felt the ambulance move.

"I'm Jake, by the way," the EMT said.

CHAPTER FORTY-FOUR

Umiko's mom met them at the ER which, lucky for them, wasn't busy. A few stitches and a lot of talk about being lucky and they were sent home.

Lyn pulled an old T-shirt from the recesses of her closet over her head and gathered up her dirty clothes. She heaped two laundry baskets and set them at the top of the stairs. She rooted around for a pair of gym shorts but all she found was a pair of middle school branded shorts. She groaned and slid the slightly too small in the waist shorts over her hips. It wasn't like anyone was going to see her.

Lyn carried one basket at a time through the kitchen and into the laundry room. She dumped the baskets out on the floor and started sorting darks and lights. She put a load of lights in the washing machine and set the dials.

She opened the dryer and was reaching in to pull out the fresh smelling clothes when she heard a knock at the door.

She reached into her non-existent pockets, looking for her phone that she must have left upstairs. She glanced out the back windows as she moved through the house. It was dark out, but just barely. Maybe 9 o'clock?

"Who's there?" The last time she had to ask that question

it was the neighbor who did indeed turn out to be feasting upon children's souls... okay maybe blood... and maybe feasting wasn't the right term.

"Greg?" she called out loud, she didn't know anyone else that would turn up at her door after dark. "Clark?"

The door knocked again.

Lyn shook her head and tried to drive away her automatic anxiety response. The witch was in custody. Her friends were safe. And not every door knock meant something bad was going to happen.

Lyn unlocked the door and opened it a crack. "How can I..."

Lyn was pushed out of the way before she could finish her question.

"We have unfinished business," Killian said as he and his pack barged into her house.

Lyn watched as the team split up. "Wait, where are you going?"

Two guys went into the kitchen like they were invited. Michael and August, maybe? Lyn heard kitchen cabinets opening and closing.

Two more walked past Lyn and up the stairs. Steve and Archie, if Lyn remembered right.

The last two, Flynn and Scout, plopped down onto the couch and turned on the television.

"What is this about?" Lyn put her hand on her hip. She feigned nerves of steel when her pulse was threatening flight.

"To be fully accepted as pack, you have to prove that you are one of us," Killian yelled over the volume on the TV as he closed and locked the front door.

Lyn made a note to stop opening her door. She crossed her arms at her chest.

August came out of the kitchen carrying a half gallon of milk and drinking from the jug. "Next time, buy whole milk."

He plopped down on the sofa and put his dirty shoes on the coffee table.

"Was there popcorn?" Scout asked.

"I didn't see any, but Mike found cookies," August replied.

Scout raised his voice and called over his shoulder. "Come one, dude. Share the cookies."

"I found something better than cookies," Mike called back.

"What's better?"

"Ice Cream!" Mike appeared holding a half gallon of chocolate swirl and a serving spoon.

"Get out!" Lyn yelled over the chaos. "I didn't invite you. I don't want you here. Get out. Get out. Get out!"

Killian crossed his arms. "No," he replied calmly.

Lyn felt the anxiety in her chest start to rumble. She turned and thrust a finger in Killian's chest. "I. Said. Get. Out!" She slashed the extended finger in the direction of the door.

Killian smiled. "No." He maintained eye contact and smirked.

Lyn heard a drumbeat. Light at first, but fast. Gathering both volume and tempo. Lyn's pulse synced up and the rumble in her chest grew. She bared her teeth and growled.

Killian bared his own, sharper teeth, and growled back.

The growl echoed around the room.

Lyn felt a tremor in her spine, but she didn't want to run. She wanted to fight.

Lyn swung to rake her nails over Killian's face, but he caught her hand.

Lyn heard a thud from upstairs, her mother's room. She snapped.

The tremor resonated with the drumbeat and Lyn's back legs quaked and gave out. She screamed at the agony.

Her breath skipped and she fought for the next one.

"Killian?" Her anger was replaced by fear.

"Don't fight it."

The next breath brought more pain. She bucked against it and folded around her stomach. Killian guided her to the floor.

Sweat beaded up from Lyn's skin. Her clothes felt too tight. The room too small. It moved without her.

A third wave of pain and nausea washed over her.

Lyn heard the low growl of a wolf near her ears. The sound grew until she realized it was her own.

Her knees snapped. The pain shot through her legs and up her spine.

Lyn's mind fled from the pain. Darkness closed around her.

CHAPTER FORTY-FIVE

"Did she pass out?" Steve asked from the banister. Archie stood at his shoulder.

All eyes were on the snow white wolf panting on the floor behind the couch. Strings of a ruined shirt and shorts clung to her fur covered body.

"Yeah," Killian said and put his hand on the wolf's neck. She was more gorgeous than he imagined.

"She lasted longer than you," Archie teased Steve with an elbow to the rib.

Steve punched Archie in the arm and they both came down the stairs. "I was seven. You passed out too, I bet."

"Did you two break something up there?" Scout asked.

"No. We heard her growl, thought we'd help out. Steve jumped. He shook the whole room." He laughed and looked at Scout. "Nothing broke." He lifted his hands in surrender.

"Everyone clean up your messes," Scout demanded. "We are not going to leave Lyn's house trashed."

The team grumbled but did as he asked.

Killian stayed down by the wolf. He watched the in and out of her breath. He imagined the glint of moonlight on her fur after a long run.

"Scout, can you cut the rest of this off her?" Killian moved to allow access.

Scout reached in his pocket for a knife and carefully slid it between Lyn and the cotton clinging to her new form.

When he was done, Scout sat back and leaned on the stair rails. "She'll need help coming back."

"So, we'll stay," Killian said. "Everyone else can go home."

They watched the rapid rise and fall of the wolf's chest. Lyn's human lungs would have been hyperventilating at that speed.

Scout stood a few moments later and directed the crew in their tasks. Killian knew that the house would be left better than they had found it. There were many reasons Scout lived up to his name.

The clean up was done in no time. When six people worked on one task, it got done fast, especially when Scout was in charge of it. His second was worthy of his position.

Killian sat with his back to the banister and a hand on Lyn's pelt. The speed of her breath was still too quick.

When the team finished, Killian stood and faced his pack, minus the newest member. "She's one of us."

"Pack." The team announced their agreement.

Killian nodded. "She'll be vulnerable until she's trained."

The team murmured.

"Scout and I will wait here until she wakes up. She'll be more comfortable and change back more easily without a crowd. Go home."

August reached into his pocket and pulled something out.

"Don't you dare leave her a dog treat," Flynn said and slapped him on the back of the head.

"But she'll be hungry."

"Steak not kibble, August." Mike punched August in the arm.

"They're pretty tasty." August bit the end of the small bone.

"Ugh," several voices said.

The team pushed him out the front door.

Scout closed and locked it behind them. "When do you think she'll wake up?"

"Her breathing is slowing, but it's still fast." Killian sat on the ground by her head, his back up against the railing and stroked the space between her eyes with one finger.

"Good call with the music," Scout said.

"Thanks for coming through with the playlist on such sort notice," Killian returned.

"Albino?" Scout sat at Lyn's tail and stroked her coat.

"Maybe, but we won't know until she opens her eyes."

Scout leaned his head back on the wall. "We finished folding a load of her laundry. She must have been in the middle of it when we got here."

"Of course you did." Killian chuckled. "Did anyone take a souvenir?"

"Someone tried, but I stopped them."

"Who?"

"I'll tell you if it becomes an issue."

Killian nodded.

Lyn's ear flicked back and forward. Her eyes blinked open.

"Shhh," Killian cooed. "You're okay." He pet her neck and upper back. He slid down the wall until his face was within inches of hers. He looked into the wolf's eyes. "They are not red. They're actually two different colors. What's that called?"

"Heterochromia," Scout answered. "It's not usually hereditary. More likely caused by trauma. She didn't have it in her human form. Right?" He paused. "What colors?"

"No, I would remember two different eye colors. When she stared me down they were green, hazel maybe? Now, one is amber, the other one is silver." Killian looked around at the lighting. Nothing in the room would be causing the difference.

Lyn trembled. Scout stood up and grabbed the blanket off the back on the couch and placed it over Lyn's wolf form and walked out of the room.

Lyn's two different colored eyes were glued to Killian's brown ones. Their heads resting on the cool floor. Her pupils were too big for her to be focused on anything. Her long pink tongue still hung from her opened jaws, panting.

Killian spoke to Lyn's wolf as if she were a small child. Watching her dilated pupils slowly settle back to normal size. "Stay calm and slow your breathing. Your pulse will follow."

Scout hung a yellow dress over the banister and sat back on the ground next to Lyn's prone body. He pressed a few buttons on his phone.

A classical piano, matched with the sad sound of a cello drifted in the air.

Killian felt the wolf's breathing begin to slow. "Your musical range astounds me," Killian said as he sat up and placed his back to the railing. "Is there anything you don't listen to?"

The cello died out and the piano played out the end of the song. The piano part in the next sound was more playful.

"No," Scout answered. "This playlist is calming and great for test taking. As long as you can stay awake."

Two more classical songs started and ended.

"Who is it?" Killian leaned his head back and put his hands in his lap. He let his eyes close.

"This is Luke Faulkner. The first was Rachmaninoff. You've..." Scout looked at Killian, "...never heard of him. Schumann? Chopin? Bach."

"Metallica did a concert with an orchestra." Killian fixed his posture and peered at Scout. He placed his hand back on top of the figure wrapped in blanket. He felt a slight shudder,

Scout laughed. "Not the same thing at all."

"The San Francisco Symphony," Lyn said, her voice hoarse. She shook under Killian's hand.

"Welcome back." Scout looked at his watch. "Faster than I expected. Maybe we're on to something with the music. I wonder if it would work for anyone other than Lyn."

"My head…" Lyn said through gritted teeth.

Scout stood up and left the room, leaving his phone on the floor.

Killian lifted Lyn's head and slid over to cradle it on his leg. "It'll feel like the flu. Your body will have trouble regulating your temperature between forms at first. Wolves run warmer. Sore muscles and bones go with the territory." Killian felt her shiver again.

Lyn tried to sit up as Scout returned with a glass of water and a small brown pill. "For soreness." He pulled up the yellow fabric from the banister. "I also have some clothes when you're ready."

"Umiko's."

"That explains the sunshine and salty air smell."

"Can you sit up?" Killian looked down at the white haired girl in his lap. Her irises were swirling with colors. "What color are your eyes supposed to be?"

Lyn tried to sit up, but it took more energy than she had and she leaned on Killian for support while Scout helped shift her legs. He sat on her other side. Her weight between them.

"It hurts." She closed her eyes and whimpered.

"I know," Killian and Scout said together.

Killian stroked her hair and continued on his own. "Sounds will be too loud, smells too strong."

"You'll feel confined in clothing. Compelled to run, when you can walk," Scout said and held up the dress. "You'll eat more meat," He chuffed.

"Hot."

"Yes. That too."

Scout and Killian worked together to get Lyn's arms over

her head and into the straps of the dress. She was barely able to help.

Once they had it settled around her shoulder, they unwrapped her from the blanket and pulled it down around her hips. She leaned her weight on Scout, unable to hold herself up.

"You'll sleep for a couple of days." He propped her up and lifted her hand to place the pill in it.

She managed to move it to her lips. She shook her head when he offered her the water, content to swallow the small pill dry. She grabbed her head.

"School." Lyn fluttered her eyes opened.

"Skip it," Scout said.

"Can't." She took a breath. "I promised."

"I can tell Umiko you are't feeling well," Scout offered.

Lyn shook her head and a tear fell from her eye.

Killian got up from the ground and with Scout's help, lifted Lyn to carry her.

"We'll fight in the morning. You're about to pass back out."

Killian carried Lyn up the stairs while Scout stayed down. She was dead weight by the time he reached the top of the stairs.

Killian laid Lyn in her bed and pulled the covers over her shoulders.

Her eyes fluttered open and closed again. "I hate you."

"You'll hate me more when the training starts," Killian said and backed out of the room.

CHAPTER FORTY-SIX

The next morning, Lyn woke up when the sun did. Her sore muscles ached.

She did a few stretches in her bed, trying to loosen the tight muscles before she put weight on her legs. Her knees screamed nonetheless.

Lyn hobbled to a warm shower. Her skin was clammy and she hoped the warmth would loosen her muscles further.

Afterwards, Lyn brushed her long white hair in less than two minutes. Braided a small section on the side of her face and secured it with a clear rubber hair band.

She picked a white fitted T-shirt with a screen print flower on one shoulder from her mother's closet and paired it with jeans that fit better than her own. She skipped the make-up, as usual, besides, any shade that her mother owned would be all wrong for Lyn's milky skin.

Lyn took a moment to admire herself in the tall mirror in her mother's room. Her hair was white as fresh snow. Her skin was pale and blemish free. Her eyes were the same green as her mother's. The same they'd always been.

She'd have to get used to the girl in the mirror, but Lyn had to admit, she was pretty, in a creature type way.

When she was dressed and ready, she walked downstairs, her muscles threatening to quit with each step. The smell of coffee propelled her forward.

"Good morning."

Lyn nearly fell down the last three steps. Instead she sat. Her arms drawn up to her chest trying to blend in and away from the voice.

"You're a little nervous." Killian stood from the couch and walked to the stairs. He held out a cup of coffee. "Show me your teeth."

"What the hell, Killian?" She reached for the coffee.

"No sign of shifting." He nodded and walked toward the kitchen. "Bacon and eggs for breakfast?"

Lyn stayed glued to the stairs. She breathed in the fresh nutty scent of the coffee and took a sip. She listened to the sound of bacon popping, and a fork hitting glass.

"There's orange juice on the table. It's good for the bruising," Killian called from the kitchen. "Pain meds, too, if you need them."

Lyn used the railing to stand. She shuffled to the kitchen and sat at the breakfast table. "Why are you here?"

"Are you really planning to go to school today, even after waking up feeling like you were run over by a car?"

"How do you know I feel like …?" she ended her question and met his eyes.

He knew.

"Yes. I made a promise to my mom before she died. It's non-negotiable." She took a sip of coffee and realized her eyes weren't leaking.

"Then I'll forgo the fight." Killian looked her up and down. "You're just as stubborn as I am."

Lyn cocked her head and stared at him over her coffee cup and though the sweet aroma of caffeine.

Killian plated a few strips of bacon and a healthy pile of scrambled eggs. He walked over to the table and sat in the chair beside her. "If this isn't enough, I can make more." He handed her a fork.

She accepted.

"Until we teach you to control it, you'll be monitored. You need to make sure to have your earphones and a slow playlist on you at all times. Scout made you one. It starts with some guy named Rockmanov. He'll give it to you this morning when he sees you." Killian took a bite of eggs from the shared plate and picked up a piece of bacon. "And he will see you. You'll be seen a lot. You're not to avoid the pack. And hiding in the girl's bathroom won't stop us, so don't try."

Lyn set her cup down and started to speak.

Killian cut her off. "It's for your own good," he paused and looked straight into her eyes "and the safety of others."

"So I'll be stalked through the halls? Like all of last year?" she finally spoke. "You and your team can just back off." Lyn pushed the chair away from the table to storm off, but lost her balance.

Killian caught her before her knees hit the tile floor. "Yes. Exactly. My goal from day one was to break you." Killian helped Lyn stand. "To get you to realize you were hiding your true self. You were locked up inside yourself so far that the only thing the pack could do was needle away at your defenses until you finally broke free of your bonds."

Lyn got quiet and she stared past Killian as her mind hurried to catch up. "Bond." Her mind raced back through what Ms. Evans had said, and what Umiko had told her later. "It was camouflage."

"What was?" He helped Lyn into her chair.

"She bound up my creature self and when I stopped taking the herbs, it started coming back." She took a bite of bacon.

"Who?"

"Ms. Evans." She took a sip of orange juice. "Clark was

right. Umiko too." She focused of Killian's face. "You too, I suppose."

"Thanks," Killian said. "I guess," he added and bit into another slice of bacon.

Lyn shared the plate of eggs with Killian and they sat in silence. Her trying to think through the last 48 hours and 16 years before that.

She always tried to please everyone, her entire life. Her mom first. If she couldn't please them, she tried to stay out of their way. Like with Killian and the pack.

When her mom died, the camouflage, already weakening, went haywire and tried to attach itself to Umiko, the only other person Lyn spent considerable time with.

"Can you smell what else I am?"

Killian pushed the last bit of eggs to her side of the table. "Are you still hungry?"

"Ravenous." She forked the last bite and stuck it in her mouth.

"You smell like wolf to me. The confinement odor is gone. You smell like a long run and there's a hint of rainstorm. I can only compare your scent to other things I've smelled. Scout could do better."

"So, you can confirm I am not a vampire?" Lyn lifted her cup of orange juice.

"With 100% accuracy. You lack that special eau du death that Sasha has." Killian smiled at her from the kitchen stove.

He cracked open another egg and let it sizzle in the pan. "Is over easy good?"

CHAPTER FORTY-SEVEN

Umiko's arm was still wrapped in gauze when they met later that morning to walk to school.

"That was weird. Killian helping yesterday. He was helping, right?" Umiko asked as she stepped at Lyn's pace.

"Yeah, it was weird," Lyn agreed. She didn't mention that he apparently slept over and made her breakfast this morning.

"Do you think he's changed?"

Lyn almost laughed.

She had changed a lot in the last three days, but she didn't think now was the time to get into it. She looked at the hair falling over her shoulders and shrugged. "Weirder things have happened."

She and Umiko walked quietly for a few moments.

"So," Umiko said and with a laugh she started to run from her friend. "I guess you're not a vampire," she called behind her.

"No. I have it on good authority that I'm not," Lyn called. "But I can run faster than you." Lyn didn't increase her pace.

Umiko stopped running and waited for Lyn to catch up.

"Are you happy about being part shifter?" She asked when Lyn was close enough to be discreet.

Lyn stopped in her tracks. "What?"

Umiko reached into her purse. "August wanted me to give you this." She handed over a paper gift bag. A glimmer of mischief in her eyes.

Lyn unfolded the top and looked inside. "Dog bones?"

Umiko laughed. "He was so proud of himself. I thought he was joking, some sort of bully prank idea, but I couldn't figure out the angle."

Lyn looked sheepishly at her friend.

"Until just now," Umiko said. "So, how do you feel?"

"Sore." Lyn caught up to her friend. "I have a long story to tell you, but it will have to wait until after school."

Umiko nodded. "I wonder what else you are?"

Lyn punched her friend in the arm. "Not that again. Is half-human not good enough for you?"

Umiko rolled her eyes. "Ms. Evans made a deal with your 'real mother.' She did some sort of binding thing. I'm not quite sure what she meant by that. She was mentally unstable by that point, but whatever." Umiko shook her head. "Why bind shifter genes? You could have been taught to control them. Don't you want to know why your real parents went to all that trouble?"

Umiko and Lyn spotted Greg on the corner a block from the school.

"No." Lyn lied. "I'm half shifter, half human. The end."

"I doubt that." Umiko mumbled.

Greg walked across the street to meet them. "Mind if I walk with you?"

Umiko looked at Lyn.

"Please," Lyn said.

The three walked the last block to the high school in an awkward silence. Lyn and Umiko next to each other, Greg two steps behind.

Umiko looked at Lyn. "Your hair looks nice. I like it like this," Umiko called over her shoulder. "What about you Greg? Do you like Lyn's hair?"

"I do."

Lyn rolled her eyes and increased her pace. She heard the bell ring. "We should hurry inside, the bell just rang."

"I didn't hear anything?" Umiko said increasing her pace to keep up with Lyn.

"My hearing is better than yours, too."

"It must be. Why don't we meet at Lyn's house after school?" Umiko said as they neared the group of kids waiting outside the cafeteria for their chance to push and shove their way inside the building. "I'll go invite Clark." She didn't wait for an answer. Instead, she filtered into the mass of students on their way through the cafeteria and on to first period classes.

"You have the papers to give the CPS woman, right?" Greg asked.

"Yeah. I called her. She's meeting me at home right after school."

"Good." When the mass of students had thinned out, Greg opened the door. "See you later, then." Greg held the door for her and she was pulled into the stream of students.

～

*L*yn's day was strange. Several times she caught pack members being nice to her.

Michael walked beside her though the morning rush, holding back the crush of students and told her to have a nice day.

She saw Killian twice in the eight hours she was in school. The first time he and a few other members of the football team were surrounded by cheerleaders. The girl standing nearest him glared at her and stepped between Lyn and

Killian. Lyn was glad there was a hallway separating them. The girl looked ready to rip her throat out. The second time, it was just him and the cheerleader and she looked upset at him this time.

Both times he saw her, but didn't do anything except acknowledge her presence. No bullying, no snide remarks, no taunting, jeering, or making fun of her.

Scout met her at her locker and twisted the shiny new combination lock. "Do me a favor? If you decide to pull the petals off, start with 'He likes me.'" He smiled and walked off after he cracked open the locker.

Lyn opened her locker and found a vase of daisies. She smiled and sniffed. The light scent of the fresh flowers drifted out to her, along with cedar and something she couldn't name.

A moment later she got an airdrop notification. She looked down at her phone and accepted the playlist.

She looked around and saw Scout at the end of the hallway, leaning against the wall, his phone in his hand typing something.

A text message vibrated her phone. She looked down at the screen.

"I'm looking forward to getting to know you better. -S"

When Lyn looked back, Scout was gone.

At lunch, Steve waved her and Umiko over to get in line ahead of him.

"Wow." Umiko said as he handed her and Lyn a tray each.

Lyn agreed.

If it held, this was going to be a much better year of school. There were perks to becoming a shifter.

ACKNOWLEDGMENTS

Special thanks first and foremost to all my readers. Whether you got this far either in the dead of night when you should be sleeping, or in the light of day when you could be doing something else. I'm very happy you are here.

Thank you to my family, whom I neglected in favor of writing them a story. Specifically, to my oldest for pushing me to turn a completed story into one worthy of extra credit in her english class. To my youngest, thanks for not dying while I was toiling away. Thanks to my husband who was always ready to listen even when he had no idea what I was talking about, which was often.

Thank you to Chuck C. for falling into the plot holes so my fans wouldn't have to, to my editor, Betsie E., for helping make sure this was the best version out of all the versions, and to Callie R. at Literary Designs for the cover design.

www.literarydesigns.com

Thank you also to all the friends and family that made me who I am today, gave me stories to tell, and pushed me to tell them.

ABOUT THE AUTHOR

Jennifer L. Moore grew up in central Mississippi and moved to central Texas. She dreams of one day living in a place that has four seasons and magic, whether or not it's central to anything

For more books and updates check out:
www.jenniferlmoorewriter.com

www.ingramcontent.com/pod-product-compliance
Lightning Source LLC
Chambersburg PA
CBHW051647180726
48284CB00006B/1895